Airside

By Christopher Priest:

Airside

Christopher Priest

First published in Great Britain in 2023 by Gollancz
an imprint of The Orion Publishing Group Ltd
Carmelite House, 50 Victoria Embankment
London EC4Y 0DZ

This edition first published in Great Britain by Gollancz in 2024

An Hachette UK Company

1 3 5 7 9 10 8 6 4 2

A CIP catalogue record for this book is
available from the British Library.

ISBN (MMP) 978 1 399 60885 5
ISBN (eBook) 978 1 399 60886 2
ISBN (audio) 978 1 399 60887 9

Typeset by Input Data Services Ltd, Somerset

Printed in Great Britain by Elcograf S.p.A.

MIX
Paper from
responsible sources
FSC® C104740

www.gollancz.co.uk

An earlier version of Chapter 9 first appeared in *Cinema Futura*, edited by Mark
Morris, 2010. Copyright © 2010, Christopher Priest

An earlier version of Chapter 15 first appeared in *Kong Unbound*, edited by Karen
Haber, 2005. Copyright © 2005, Christopher Priest

Dedicated to the memory of Mae Clarke, the original
victim of the grapefruit, and to Rosalind Knight,
who was not

I

On April 13th 1949 a woman travelling under the name V M Kalutz caught the overnight flight from Los Angeles to New York City. After landing at LaGuardia Airport, and with the help of a member of the airport staff, she deposited most of her baggage, three large suitcases and four smaller ones, in the left luggage office. She departed the airport without attracting any attention.

She stayed the night in a hotel close to LaGuardia, then returned to the airport the next morning. Here she had a reservation on a Pan American Douglas DC4 headed for London. Her transit through New York had been belatedly discovered by the press, and as she arrived back at the airport she was surrounded by a small crowd of reporters and photographers. She spoke to the reporters, answering a flurry of questions about the reason for her flight, her future filming plans and the state of her relationships.

She evidently saw the questions as intrusive and at first she would not talk about the upcoming lawsuit brought against her by her ex-husband. She finally gave way under persistent questioning. She dealt with the questions politely if vaguely.

She said that nothing could be said about the lawsuit until after the court hearing. When asked about the name of the male companion who had been with her at the recent preliminary court hearing, she said she never commented on gossip. Some of the reporters guessed a few names, but she declined to confirm or deny. She posed willingly for photographs, the recurrent flashing of bulbs drawing the attention of other passengers and staff passing through the airport building. Many paused to try and take a look at her.

She was known to the public as Jeanette Marchand. She was a film star, under long-term contract to Warner Bros but recently lent out to other studios for single projects. After two decades she was still one of the most famous women in American cinema, with around fifty films to her name, in many of which she had taken leading roles.

The photographs published in the newspapers the next day were carefully selected by the picture editors to emphasize her beauty and glamour, and to confirm her status as a major star. Two days later, when they learned what happened to her when she arrived in London, a few reporters remarked privately that although she had put on a brave front for the cameras, she had looked tired and seemed fraught and nervous. The lawsuit being brought against her by her ex-husband Stan McPherson, star pitcher with the Los Angeles Dodgers, was likely to cause a sensation when the case opened. They revealed that she had been noticeably upset by the judge at the preliminary hearing, who had made several financial and restraining orders against her.

While she was still being interviewed at the airport one of the reporters asked her about her travel plans. She was going to England, she said, to take a short vacation and to explore the possibility of making some films over there. American actors were in demand in the British studios, but few were working there because post-war conditions of austerity were said to be uncomfortable. Jeanette Marchand said this made no difference to her – she came from a working family in Pittsburgh and had grown up without privileges. She would not confirm that Warner Bros had released her from her contract. Asked about her relationship with Dirk Halliday, she said no other films with him were being planned at present. She denied the rumours about Halliday, and said that she had always found him a serious and professional co-star, for whom she had the highest regard. She would not reveal where she would be staying in London, but said she would return to California in about a month's time.

A Pan Am representative appeared and politely interceded, then led Jeanette Marchand through to the VIP lounge. From there she was conducted to her seat in the first class section of the plane, where she asked for a champagne cocktail. The aircraft took off about half an hour later.

This was to be her final journey. Jeanette Marchand did in fact arrive in London, but she never returned to the USA.

Many years later, the film critic and essayist Justin Farmer gave a wide-ranging interview to the UK film magazine *Sight and Sound*. Amongst many other things he was asked about his beginnings, what it was that had originally sparked his interest in cinema.

He replied immediately, 'Seeing two of Jeanette Marchand's early films when I was seven years old.'

He explained. He was born towards the end of the second

world war, a period when Marchand's career was starting to fade. He was only five years old at the time she flew from New York to London, so of course was completely unaware of everything that happened then. He noticed her after his family bought one of the first television sets to be made available to the general public in the UK. This was in the early 1950s, a time when there was only one channel, a limited service provided by the BBC. The television signal was restricted at first to the London area, then soon to parts of the Midlands and the North, so there was not yet a mass audience. Live programmes were few and far between, and the signal was prone to break down because of technical problems.

The BBC had access to a tiny library of films, all of which they broadcast in turn several times. Two of Jeanette's films were among them, and as a pre-teen child he had watched them repeatedly, learning her name from the credits, but not at the time registering the titles. He had fallen innocently in love with her beautiful face and was amused by the clever way she delivered her lines. This had stirred emotions in him he did not understand. The interest she created led eventually to his lifetime involvement with cinema.

He went on that as an adult, when he had access to reference works, he had worked out which of her films they must have been. They were both from the pre-Code era of Hollywood: one was *The Dashing Young Man* from 1932, and the other was *Frozen Hearts* from 1933. As a filmographer he said he was intrigued by this. Many of the films made at that time had been subsequently withdrawn by the studios because of the Hays Code and were rarely seen, let alone shown on television. How they had reached the BBC was

4

something he had not been able to find out, but was still interested to try.

Justin Farmer added that he learned about Jeanette Marchand's mysterious end while he was still at university, and that he had made a special visit to London Airport, not with the thought of trying to solve what had become a notorious mystery, but simply to have a look at where it was thought to have had happened.

Jeanette Marchand was born Verity Mae Kalutz, in Pittsburgh, Pennsylvania. She was an only child. Her mother was a pool typist, her father managed a small grocery store. She studied acting and dance while still at school, and moved to New York City in 1928 when she was sixteen years old. She worked as a dancer in vaudeville and as a hostess in night clubs. She roomed with a friend called Ruby Stevens, whom she met while they were dancers in a burlesque show. Ruby, who was slightly older, also had ambitions to act in films.

In 1929 the two young women travelled overland to Los Angeles, where they managed to scrape up occasional paid work as uncredited extras and walk-ons in a handful of Hollywood musicals and gangster movies. They were part of a whole generation of young women and men who dreamt of becoming film stars.

They both changed their names. Verity became Jeanette Marchand, and Ruby called herself Barbara Stanwyck – as Stanwyck she was the first of the two friends to find a breakthrough role, in a romantic drama called *Ladies of Leisure*, directed in 1930 by Frank Capra.

Jeanette followed a few months later. She made a brief but memorable appearance in a Chicago-set crime thriller called *The Public Enemy*. In this she was in the uncredited role of

Kitty, the unhappy girlfriend of a mobster played by James Cagney. She had only one scene with the star and just two short lines to speak. She sat with him at breakfast while he vented his anger at her. Suddenly, he stood up, seized the half-grapefruit she had been eating and thrust it violently into her face. It was not in the script and to all appearances the attack took the young woman by surprise. In the following few seconds of the film Jeanette Marchand can clearly be seen in distress. She was humiliated by it and afterwards left the studio in tears, but when the film was released a few months later the brief scene hit the headlines. She went straight into working on another film, this time with a role in *The Headline Story*. Her rise to fame began there.

Throughout the 1930s Jeanette worked regularly, becoming one of the highest paid actors in Hollywood. She made around forty features before much of the studio activity was reduced by the start of the second world war. Jeanette starred in many of her films, but towards the end of the decade the quality of the films she made, the standing of the other actors she worked with, and the roles she was given to play, steadily declined.

She was soon mostly appearing in derivative and hurriedly made B-features. Just before the Japanese attack on Pearl Harbor Jeanette was playing the abandoned wife in a romantic comedy for Warner Bros, and for the rest of the war years she played similar secondary characters. In 1946 she returned to making main features, but a new generation of young actors were competing for the starring roles and she was usually cast as a teacher, an older relative, a nurse. She had been married twice, and had a young daughter.

*

The plane Jeanette boarded took off from LaGuardia on time. There were two planned intermediate stops for refuelling, in Newfoundland and west Ireland. There was only one other passenger in the first class section of the aircraft: a man travelling alone. He sat apart from Jeanette in the seat to which he had been allocated. According to the cabin crew she spent much of the first part of the journey sleeping. She woke up from time to time to eat a meal and take several glasses of wine.

During the stopover at Gander Airport, then known as Newfoundland Airport, all the passengers transferred to the terminal building while the aircraft was being refuelled. The crew did not know what passed between Jeanette and the other passenger while on the ground, although they were together in the airline's VIP lounge. When they reboarded the man took the seat beside hers, and remained there for the whole of the next part of the journey, the long non-stop flight across the Atlantic to Ireland. Jeanette sometimes seemed tearful, and for extended periods stayed silent, her shoulder turned against the man. At one point a female member of the crew approached Jeanette to check that all was well, which she said it was.

When the plane landed at Shannon the man left the plane and did not reboard. Jeanette was alone in the first class compartment for the final leg of the flight.

After the aircraft landed safely in London, Jeanette was allowed to disembark before the other passengers. She first spoke warmly to the cabin crew who had served her during the long flight, and autographed the menu cards for them. The captain, second pilot and flight engineer left the cockpit to speak briefly to her. She then walked down the mobile steps alone. One of the cabin crew watched her as she crossed the tarmac towards the ex-military marquee that served as an office for customs officials, airline staff and where travellers could retrieve their baggage. Two other similar tents stood beside it. The other passengers were only allowed to start disembarking from the plane once Jeanette reached the entrance to the marquee.

The flight stewardess who had observed Jeanette crossing the tarmac later told a reporter that Miss Marchand seemed well as she walked from the plane. She confirmed that they had served her with several glasses of wine during the flight, but these were evenly spaced over a long duration. She did not appear to be under the influence.

The captain of the aircraft, who returned to the cockpit after briefly meeting her, also watched from his window as she walked away from the plane. He said that she appeared normal, but added that many passengers were visibly tired after long transatlantic flights, and if Miss Marchand had seemed a little unsteady on her feet then it would have been nothing unusual.

When she entered the tent he turned away from the window. He was the last person to see Jeanette Marchand alive. What happened to her after she entered the marquee, or where she went next, no one knows.

She was a famous celebrity, suffused with the aura of stardom, and her appearance stood out almost everywhere she went, but once she was inside the marquee she was not seen by anyone who could recall her. Her passport was not checked. Customs officials had no recollection of her passing through. No one was at the airport to meet her. It turned out that she had not ordered a car and driver to be at the airport to collect her. No one approached the small information office to enquire about her.

Her baggage was unloaded from the aircraft but it remained unclaimed.

The cab drivers who regularly served the airport were later interviewed, but none of them had taken a fare from her, nor had even seen her around the taxi rank. They all said they would instantly have recognized her if she had been there.

She never arrived at Claridge's, the hotel in the Mayfair area of London where she had reserved a suite of rooms.

It was not realized for some time that she had gone missing. It was only the next day that staff at Claridge's made telephone enquiries with the airline and the airport management. At this point the airport passenger area was searched, but there was no sign of her. Later, when the police were called in, all the airport marquees and other temporary buildings were searched again, this time more thoroughly.

Jeanette Marchand had no family in Britain, and as far as anyone knew she had no British friends or other personal contacts. Her American parents were both deceased, as was her first husband, an actor from the silent era, who died in 1933. She was divorced from her second husband, Stan McPherson – when he was contacted by Los Angeles Police, McPherson stated that he was convinced she was still alive and was in hiding somewhere. He claimed she owed him large sums of money, which was why she had tried to disappear. He could provide no more information than that, but he pointed out that all her property, contacts and business interests were in the USA.

Her talent agency said that they had heard nothing from her and did not know where she was, but that there was the possibility of an offer of a part from Warner Bros. A representative from the Warner studio said she was still under contract to them, but she had been granted two months' leave of absence.

The two largest film studios close to London had not had any contact with her, and were in fact surprised to hear that she was intending to work in the country. They said they would make enquiries, but they never came up with anything.

For a week Jeanette's disappearance was widely reported in the popular newspapers. Photos of her familiar face were on the front pages of most of them. Some speculated that she had been kidnapped or even murdered, but no body was ever found and there were no demands for a ransom. There was a brief rash of alleged sightings of her: on the beach promenade in Bournemouth, at a race meeting in Leeds, in an exclusive store in London's Bond Street. All of these turned out to be mistaken. The story soon slipped from the headlines and eventually was no longer of interest. The police file was closed.

2

At the age of twenty Justin Farmer still knew nothing about Jeanette Marchand's disappearance. He had in fact barely thought about her for several years – the memory of those old films had largely faded away into the muddles of childhood experience.

He had been born and brought up in Field Green, a Cheshire village on the outside southern edge of Manchester, but the family moved to the London area in 1960.

Justin was about to go to university at the time and he had already been selected for a BA course in Media Studies, part of which was a Film Theory module, at Reading University. Reading was in the Thames valley to the west of London and was sufficiently far from his parents' new home on the other side of the city to feel like he was making a break, but it was also close enough to the centre of London for frequent visits to the wide range of first-run cinemas. He sometimes travelled in with a group of other students from his course, or more often he went alone. Film had become his passion.

One of the screens he visited most frequently was at the National Film Theatre, on the South Bank. As a child his film-going had been largely governed by the choices of his parents and sister, so he had grown up with comedies, musicals and a few WW2 pictures. Now living a semi-independent life Justin was restless to catch up with what he realized he had been missing. He was relishing his belated discovery of European, Asian and independent American movies. The French nouvelle vague had forged a radical new approach to film, and German and Japanese cinema was emerging from post-war trauma. In Sweden, Ingmar Bergman was at his peak.

As for films of the past: many of the revivals were shown in repertory at the NFT, some because of their art house qualities, others to illustrate the careers of certain directors, actors, cinematographers, and so on.

In 1964 one of the NFT's retrospective seasons focused on the career of the British film director James Whale, who had had a long career in Hollywood, and who was probably best known for his film adaptation in 1931 of *Frankenstein*. While catching up with contemporary cinema Justin had not yet given much thought to the past. Curious to find out about Whale's work Justin went to see a few of his films. One in particular, also made in Hollywood in 1931, gave him a start of surprise and recognition. The film was called *Westminster Bridge*.

It was set in London during the 1914-18 war, and dealt with the brief relationship between an American soldier on furlough from the war and a streetwalker. Made before the strict censorship of the Hays Code clamped down on perceived immorality, the film contained what with hindsight was considered to be inappropriate material. Although innocuous by the much freer standards of the 1960s the original version was almost never shown after its first release, but the NFT had managed to obtain an uncut print. As it began, Justin was astonished to discover that the female lead, the prostitute, was played by Jeanette Marchand.

He had lost touch with his childish infatuation with her, but he had never forgotten her beautiful appearance and her dry, witty way of delivering dialogue. As he watched *Westminster Bridge* he knew it was not a film he had seen before, so it was not one of those shown by the BBC back then. But to see Jeanette Marchand again through more grown-up eyes was a revelation to him. She was just as attractive to him as he remembered. In *Westminster Bridge* she looked as if she was the same age as he was now. It saddened him to think of the many years that had passed in the meantime.

She was no longer famous. That he was sure of. The NFT's mimeographed information sheet about the film, available in the foyer, said more about Whale's work than that of his actors. Justin picked up a copy after the end of the film and read it straight away, eager to learn more. It did mention Bette Davis, who was then at the beginning of her career. She played a small part in the film, the third she had been in. In the notes, Jeanette Marchand was referred to only in passing, even though she and her male counterpart were described in the credits as the leading actors. The sheet mentioned that she had appeared in a minor role in Whale's extraordinary adaptation of *Frankenstein*.

He went to the NFT's bookstall and browsed through their well-sourced stock of film books, in particular the biographical and encyclopaedic works they had on sale. Jeanette was listed in them all, with several of her films described in detail. Most of them were not. It was while he was looking through the books that Justin began the process of elimination from which he eventually worked out the titles of the films he had seen her in years before on television.

The next day he went to the cinema section of the university library, gradually finding out what more he could learn of Jeanette Marchand's career. The information in the books he had browsed at the NFT was confirmed: she made no more films after 1949. Two of the reference books described her as having died in that year. Another referred obliquely to the fact that she appeared to have retired from the film industry and was living in obscurity, while yet another, published by a popular newspaper, speculated that she had run away with the actor Dirk Halliday. The entry for Halliday himself interestingly made no mention of Jeanette Marchand, other than that he had starred in two features with her. He was said to have retired from acting and now lived with his Canadian-born wife on a ranch in Southern California.

In a biographical encyclopaedia Justin found a full and appreciative entry for Jeanette Marchand. It described her as an unjustly neglected actor, as talented and versatile as her contemporaries Barbara Stanwyck, Joan Crawford, Myrna Loy and Bette Davis, but overlooked in the present day because of the premature and tragic end to her career. It noted her family background, it named both her husbands, and listed and evaluated many of her films. It also mentioned the mystery of her flight to Britain and her disappearance at London Airport, as well as the fact that no trace of her had ever been found. She had been declared legally dead in 1955.

Now intrigued, Justin went into London to research the British Museum's newspaper archive, hoping there were extra facts to be found. He was by this time interested not so much in the story itself but in the way it had been told to the public by the press. He spent a long day in the archive, discovering how repetitive and shallow the reporting had been. He saw that much of it was obviously intended to remind the public of the glamour of Hollywood during post-war austerity.

Justin came away having learned only one element of the story that the biographies omitted. Treating it as a minor irrelevance, the *News Chronicle* and the *Daily Mirror* both remarked that a man travelling on the same plane, in the first class section, had sat beside her for at least a part of the long flight.

Justin wondered about the real significance of this. Did Jeanette Marchand know the man before this flight? Or was he an intrusive stranger? Why did he leave the aircraft before it landed in London? The newspapers called him the 'mystery man', but the reporters had not uncovered who he might have been.

One Saturday morning a couple of weeks later Justin left his student accommodation in Reading, travelled by train to London, then took the tube to Hounslow West at the extremity of the Piccadilly Line. Here he caught a bus to the airport. It was still identified as London Airport and was the main hub for London, but there were official plans to change the name to Heathrow in the near future.

Certain experiences with aircraft in his childhood had given Justin a particular and nervous interest in passenger flights. Now he never flew and at that time had no plans to do so. As an impoverished student the thought was for him anyway academic. But the discovery that Jeanette Marchand had disappeared at an airport induced an intangible feeling of identification with her.

He walked around the central area of the airport, with its constant noise and movement of cars, taxicabs and service vehicles, as they drove slowly along the maze of roads and one-way traffic lanes. The noise of jet engines intermittently rose up from beyond the terminal buildings, adding to the sense of urgency. A smell of kerosene drifted everywhere. He tried to filter all that away, imagining how the airport might have looked a decade and a half earlier in the era of propellers, at night, in the dark.

Until the late 1940s Heathrow was a mere aerodrome, sometimes used as a wartime overflow from the RAF base at Northolt, or taking the occasional civilian flight diverted from Croydon. For several years Croydon was the main airport for London. With the opening of transatlantic flights, the grass runways at Heathrow were replaced with concrete and made longer and more durable. The airlines switched from Croydon, which was incapable of expansion because of the surrounding density of houses and other buildings.

Development of the service areas at Heathrow had been going on for many years since Jeanette Marchand flew in from New York. Building work on new terminals, multi-storey car parks and administration offices was visibly in progress, and there was practically no remaining trace of the former RAF temporary buildings, some which had still been in use in 1949.

After walking around for a while Justin noticed a couple of derelict shacks on the edge of one of the car parks. He found a way to walk to them, having to cross the crowded road system a couple of times. They were clearly disused and were contained behind a closed wire security fence. He tried to imagine what Jeanette Marchand might have experienced after she left the aircraft, walking away from the plane across the tarmac in the cool air, heading for the unheated tent where incoming passengers were received. No welcoming staff in neat costumes with ready smiles and calming words, but maybe officials of some kind or a couple of police officers.

The huts that remained were common sights across Britain in the immediate post-war years. At Heathrow in 1949 they were repurposed as administrative buildings: passports and tickets were examined there, and luggage might be searched. Bare light bulbs, old furniture, evidence of austerity and shabbiness everywhere. That day from beyond the wire Justin took only a brief look at the old structures which served as the terminal back then.

He returned to the main part of the concourse and walked towards the nearer of the two large modern passenger buildings. The traffic congestion and constant noise around him was increasingly unpleasant. He headed for the door area with the overhead sign: *Departures*.

As he raised a hand to push against the swing door Justin experienced a strong and momentarily disturbing sensation: not fear, not dread, nothing as identifiable as those, but a general apprehension, a feeling of dislike, a ghost memory, a bad association from the past. It was almost as if he had been here before when something disagreeable occurred.

He paused, reacting to the vague feeling. This was the first time he had been to London Airport, the first time in fact that he had ever entered a large international airport. Other people were close behind him, hurrying to get into the building. One man, struggling with two heavy pieces of luggage, pushed past to step around him but one of his unwieldy suitcases knocked against Justin's leg. Justin instinctively moved to one side to make way, then followed the man, suppressing the uncomfortable feeling of unfocused dread.

The interior of the building was high and spacious, with daylight falling in through many windows high up. A huge throng of people filled the floor, all appearing to be moving in different directions. Music was playing in the background, and although it was frequently interrupted by announcements there was no sense of urgency or warning.

On the contrary: the announcer's voice sounded calm and reassuring, mentioning flights now waiting to be boarded, reminders to have tickets and passports ready, and so on. The airport was a place of transit, of temporary occupation. It was a hall of individuals who were all in different ways heading away, part of a multitude and subsumed temporarily into it but not of a collective single mind. They were travelling alone, or with one other, or with a few others, all with different motives and intentions, none of which involved joining the crowd or being in the airport longer than necessary.

A mechanical departures board clacked around, listing current destinations: Rome, Lisbon, Alicante, West Berlin, Nice. Every time the board was activated, the flight at the top of the list disappeared and a new one appeared at the bottom. Nothing was permanent, secure. To one side a row of desks served queues of travellers, who moved forward slowly to have their paperwork checked or approved, dragging or shuffling their luggage with their feet, or reaching down to scrape it a few more inches forward. These people eventually drifted away to find their aircraft, to be replaced by new arrivals – they were in a sort of human synchronization with the mechanical board.

Justin wandered about the concourse looking around at everything. The music was loud enough not to be in the background, and partly because of it the terminal was a noisy place. Voices were often raised over the music. Some people were silent while they waited, but others sounded petulant, annoyed with each other. Men travelling alone looked impatient, as if they did not feel they should be made to wait. Couples stood apart, not communicating with each other. Some of the children looked sullen or restless. But many of these people were dressed lightly, almost frivolously, ready for the Mediterranean sunshine and warmth to which they were heading.

The paradox was that the terminal was a zone of imposed reassurance and bland prospects. The light music seemed intended to induce a feeling of familiarity and relaxation in the passengers. The brightly lit display advertisements for expensive drinks, cosmetics and hotels suggested career success and worldly sophistication. The ever-changing departures board promised exotic foreign places and glamorous vacations that were now within reach.

All the staff were wearing smart uniforms of one kind or another and smiled calmly whenever they had to speak to passengers.

Other places of work – offices, railway stations, schools, factories – did not deliberately try to foster a sense of safety. In this airport tension was undeniably if intangibly in the air. Did the enforced blandness actually make things worse? Justin sensed it all around him, even though he was not one of the passengers. Was it a reaction to fear of flying, known to be suffered by many air travellers? Flying was safe, and the statistics made that overwhelmingly clear – a passenger was more likely to be injured or killed on the journey to the airport than in hundreds of thousands of miles of flight. Many people still worried about being involved in a crash. Justin's own earlier experiences of flying had not been good. Was this apprehension shared by everyone, or was it only in him?

The airport would certainly have looked different on the day, the late evening, when Jeanette Marchand flew in from the USA: those were the austerity years after the end of the second world war. In 1949 many buildings across London were still unrepaired after the Blitz, and large fenced-off areas existed where the rubble had been cleared away but nothing had been put up to replace it. Much of the infrastructure of roads, water mains and gas and electricity supplies had been patched up. Only since the mid-1950s had there been the public funds available to begin the concerted effort to rebuild the cities and replace the damaged infrastructure. An airport, already with functioning huts, would be low on the list of priorities for modernization.

There were hardly any intercontinental flights: there was a regular route to and from North America, long-haul services to South Africa and Australasia, plus destinations in post-war Europe. At the time of Jeanette Marchand's flight, a round-the-clock military airlift of essential supplies of food and fuel into West Berlin was still going on.

The era of inexpensive air travel did not begin in the UK until the end of the 1950s, when the resorts of southern Spain, France and Greece were made affordable by chartered flights.

That kind of traffic was increasing every year, as shown by the crowds milling about in the terminal building, and the leisure clothes they were wearing.

Ringway, the main airport for the city of Manchester, and one Justin knew well from his childhood, used to have similar RAF temporary buildings, a hangover from wartime. As a teenager he had sometimes cycled down to Ringway and wandered around. It was open to the public, an operational RAF station but with an increasing number of civil flights going in and out.

Ringway intrigued him for reasons he did not try to understand. It was a mile or so from the house where he had grown up. That was immediately beneath the flight path, so incoming planes were constantly going over. No one complained about the noise or the risk, probably because the adults at least were hardened by the drab years of air raids and fighter patrols. Planes fascinated Justin, though, and he always looked up to watch the aircraft come in. When he went to Ringway people probably thought he was a plane spotter; several boys of his age were often there with their notebooks and binoculars. Justin did try spotting for half a day, but he found it boring and he never went back to it. The allure of airports he experienced was something more subtle, nothing he could put into words or even thoughts.

The officials and the customs officers should have been aware of Jeanette Marchand the moment she landed. She was famous and knew how to make herself look her best. Her physical appearance was impressive and startling. That was presumably still true on that day, even after her long flight. She would certainly have been seen, noticed, recognized. The people who were there would have recollected her afterwards, even a few days later when her disappearance was known about and being investigated. But after she left the aircraft and arrived at the entrance to the passenger marquee, Jeanette was not seen by anyone. In all the newspaper accounts Justin had read there were no reports of interviews with airport officials, or none where anyone remembered her. Had those people been questioned properly about her?

It was a decade and a half ago. Everything had changed, and not just the physical aspect of the airport. People leave their jobs, new people take over. They work shifts. They take leave. They don't remember everything.

Justin saw a place where refreshments were being sold, so he paid for a cup of tea and took it to one of the bright-red formica-topped tables. He focused on Jeanette's mystery.

He thought through what he knew. There must be a rational explanation for what had happened to her. Abduction, kidnapping, murder – all these had been suspected, investigated and in different ways eliminated as explanations. Or there was a mistake of some kind: she had not flown all the way to London as everyone thought, but had disembarked at one of the refuelling stops.

The 'mystery man' was said to have left the aircraft at Shannon – did Jeanette go with him? And who was he? He seemed to have known her, or at least had become known to her during the long flight. Maybe she even changed her mind at the last moment, had not taken the London plane at all, remained in the USA to try to work out the personal dilemmas clearly haunting her? But how then to explain the statements of the plane's crew? They knew who she was.

The last possibility was that on landing in London she had slipped away somewhere, and somehow, of her own volition. She was tired of the limelight, exhausted by interviews and photocalls wherever she went, was ground down by the publicity machine of Hollywood, where the private lives of celebrities were tested and interrogated daily, by gossip columnists, by film reviewers, by newshounds, by the admiring public whose gaze had created her in first place. Enough was enough. She fled into obscurity.

None of these possible explanations was plausible. How had she not gone through the airport routine checks: passport, customs, and so on? And assuming that somehow she did, and without anyone noticing her and remembering her, where did she go and how did she travel away from the airport?

Even at this age, still an undergraduate feeling his way, Justin was aware of a trait in himself: he felt an urge to get details right, to try to understand shapes and forms. He was already compiling his indexed notes on the films he saw, the notebooks which after many years of consistently maintaining the entries were to provide him in adulthood with his encyclopaedic knowledge of cinema. He later became legendary amongst other film critics. He saw it as a sense of tidiness, not obsessive completeness, but sometimes he did wonder where the difference might lie.

The missing clue in Jeanette Marchand's unexplained disappearance snagged at his sense of an unfinished story: it was apparent to him that the identity of the man on the plane was the key to what might have happened. It also seemed impossible so many years later to establish the truth. The only references to the other passenger were in the newspaper stories, and those treated the incident as a sensation. But it was a minor sensation which quickly died down.

One day not long after his fruitless visit to London Airport Justin had an idea. On his next trip to London to see a film he took a slightly earlier train than usual and went first to the British Museum's newspaper library. He had realized there was a strong American interest in the lives and doings of film stars, one he had ignored before.

He requested access to whatever American newspapers there might be in the archive, published in the days following Jeanette's flight. The only titles held by the museum were the *New York Times,* the *Wall Street Journal* and the *Washington Post.* In the latter two there was no mention of Jeanette or her flight, but the *New York Times* had put the story on the front page the day after it happened – it said little more than the reports in the London papers. A week later, though, when the flight staff returned to the US, the paper ran a background story about the experiences and feelings of the crew who had been on the aircraft with her.

The two stewardesses who worked in first class were named: Bea Harrington, born in Chicago, and Annette Wilson, who came from Ohio.

Justin wrote a letter to the Pan American head office in New York City, asking if either of these two women still worked for the airline, and if so would they tell him anything they remembered about the incident and the identity of the man who had spoken to Jeanette.

Three weeks passed. Then, on Pan Am notepaper, a typewritten letter:

Dear Mr Farmer:

Thank you very much for your letter. It is always a pleasure to hear from our friends in England. Pan American Airways is the #1 carrier across the Atlantic.

You asked us for the name of one of the passengers on our Flight No. PAA 6, New York City (LaGuardia) to London, England, April 14 1949.

This information is found on the manifest, or passenger list. We would love to help you with this, but normally we release passenger lists only when obliged to by a District Attorney's office. We feel that we have a duty to respect passengers' rights to privacy. We hope you understand that passenger confidence is crucial to our successful operation as a major carrier. We are proud of the special service we offer our passengers.

For the same reasons we cannot release personal information about our crew members. Here too we are, as employers, under obligation not to supply names to third parties.

However, we understand that you have a special interest in this particular flight, where certain names are already in the public domain through the press coverage following what happened on arrival in London.

I can therefore confirm that Flight Stewardess Annette Wilson was appointed to first class duties on that flight, but Miss Wilson has since left the employment of Pan American Airways. Flight Stewardess Bea Harrington was the senior crew member in first class on that flight. That is myself and I remember the flight well.

Because of the interest that arose, Miss Wilson and I discussed in detail what we knew shortly after our return to New York.

There were only two passengers in first class on that flight.

25

One was the person you name in your letter, who as you know was ticketed as Mrs Verity Mae Kalutz.

The other passenger I cannot name for the reasons I have just given. I can however inform you that the man in question was carrying a British passport. We remembered him not only because he seemed to know Mrs Kalutz, but because he spoke excellent English with a slight but distinct foreign accent. Both Miss Wilson and I thought at first it was British, but as the flight went on we became sure it was European: Dutch or German, perhaps? Knowing Mrs Kalutz was in the film world we also wondered if he was someone else we should have been able to recognize. We did not. I confirm that he left the flight at Shannon Airport although he was ticketed through to London.

I regret I may furnish no further details about the flight than this, but should you require any more information of a general nature I will be pleased to respond. We will also be delighted to welcome you at some future date on one of our deluxe services between London and New York City.

Yours sincerely,

Beatrice Harrington

Vice-president, Customer Relations, Pan American Airways

3

Justin Farmer was six years old when he was first sent to primary school. The building was a traditional Victorian-era schoolhouse on the edge of Field Green, with its own areas surrounding it for play and exercise. He attended the school for two years. This early experience unexpectedly created his interest in aviation and the psychological impact of flight, a direct influence, if not one that developed straight away.

Justin's family background was conventional. He had one sister, four years older than him. Her name was Amanda. Her friends called her Mandy, but Justin and his parents invariably called her Amanda. His father's name was Mortimer, and his mother was Nicole. Their names for each other were Mort and Nicky.

Mort commuted daily to a studio in the centre of Manchester, where he worked on the design and layout of several magazines. Before Justin was born Mort had been working as an engineering draughtsman, a job which had given him a reserved occupation during the second world war, but he disliked almost everything about it and as soon as the war was over he retrained as a commercial artist and moved on.

Now the magazine chain gave him a great degree of creative freedom. During most of the war years Nicky had stayed at home to bring up the children, but after that, around the same time that Justin started school, she began work as a receptionist at the doctors' surgery in the village. Both his parents seemed happy with their lives.

Justin grew up with a rational love of film and cinema, but also with an irrational fascination for aircraft, airports and their effect on ordinary people.

The primary school he went to was on a suburban road, with a few houses close by and farm pastures at the back. The road, originally a country lane which had been widened when houses and the school were built along it, had developed into a principal access route to Ringway Airport. The main entrance was about half a mile to the west of the school. The constant overflying into the airfield of American-built transports and newly introduced RAF jet fighters was in contrast to the old-fashioned decor and facilities of the school.

To Nicky and Mort the physical shortcomings of the building were less important than the fact that a certain teacher, Mrs Humber, had a reputation for getting children into the direct grant grammar school in the next village. This turned out to be true, but day-to-day life in the primary school was another matter. The washrooms and toilets were primitive, there was only a small library of mostly pre-war children's books and there were few other educational aids. The classrooms were high ceilinged under the arch of the roof, which made the teacher's voice difficult to hear if you were not near the front. Traffic noise from outside was more or less continuous, and the closeness to the airport led to frequent intrusive aircraft engine roars. The children were seated at long tables, the surface too high for most of them, and the stools on which they had to sit were wooden and unyielding and had shiny seats. Kids often slid off them, sometimes deliberately.

Almost from the first day Justin became fascinated with the proximity of the aircraft. Coming in to land they flew much lower and more slowly than when they passed above his house. The main runway had been built right out to the edge of the school property, so that the end, where incoming aircraft aimed to touch down, was less than fifty yards away. Any aircraft coming in for a landing passed low over the roof of the school, so close that if you were in the playground and looked up, as Justin invariably did, you were for a second or two directly beneath the belly and the wings – there was a brief glimpse of the mechanical workings of the wheel assemblies, the silver body, the huge engines and propellers, even a fleeting sight of the nuts and rivets that held everything together. The noise of the engines was awe-inspiring – it deeply thrilled Justin. Other children were often scared and would lower their heads or slap their hands over their ears, but Justin soaked up the sensation.

He spent most of the break periods pressing himself against the school fence, staring out at the runway, learning a lifelong lesson as he did so, that preoccupation could be an effective defence against the brutalities of the outside world. A slum-clearance estate had been thrown up close to the school in the immediate post-war period, and many of the boys who came to the school from there were physical and aggressive. Justin already wore vision-correcting spectacles and behaved quietly, both of which made him a natural target for bullies, but his apparently vague manner meant they soon tired of trying to bait him.

On the far side of the airport the RAF maintained an operational squadron. The hangars and a control tower were distant, but in clear view of the school. There were many of the older, propeller-driven aircraft, but much more interesting were the jet fighters which took off and landed every day. At this age, Justin was just starting to pick things up from the conversations between Mort and Nicky and their friends, talking about what they had experienced during the war, still not long over. Most of the aircraft they had seen in those days, or learned the names of, were already out of use in peacetime and were being replaced by jets. The fighters were now de Havilland Vampires and Venoms instead of the Spitfires and Hurricanes remembered well by everyone who had lived through the war, and the two-engined Gloster Meteors, which were designed as fighter-bombers. All these aircraft types were being flown at RAF Ringway, and every day they passed low over the school. Sometimes the teacher looked annoyed at the intrusion, but Justin felt differently.

His time at the primary school came to an end: the gentle cramming applied by Mrs Humber had the hoped-for effect and when he was eight he passed the entry exam into the junior level of the grammar school. Three years later he graduated to the senior level. The ancient days of tall stools, chalk dust and social abrasion, and the close passage of the low-flying silver bellies of jet aircraft, were behind him.

When Justin was twelve, and on the last weekend of the summer school holiday, Mort and Nicky took their children for a family outing. They drove to the seaside resort of Southport on the Lancashire coast, which they had been to several times in the past. Before they reached there, Mort turned the car off the main road to the coast at Ainsdale, the town next to Southport, famous for its golf course. This was the only fact about Ainsdale known to Mort, who then said he had no interest in golf. Justin and Amanda had heard him say this many times. Ainsdale and Southport were on the southern bank of the estuary of the River Ribble, and the low tide exposed a vast flat beach made up of firm sand. Cars were able to drive on the sands, where traffic laws did not apply.

Mort bumped the car off the paved road, across the rough shoreline grasses and down through a wide gap in the dunes to the sands. He immediately started driving in a way Justin had never seen before: he accelerated hard, swung the steering wheel from side to side, and swerved sharply to right and left while the car tipped over alarmingly and the road wheels threw up torrents of sand. The engine made a roaring sound that inside the cramped passenger compartment briefly almost reminded Justin of the jets. Around them other cars were being driven in the same madcap way. Most were, like their own car, small and sedate family saloons. Two sports cars with their roofs down were racing in a sort of acrobatic competition: young men were driving uproariously, their girlfriends next to them with their heads covered by scarves. Mort was laughing and shouting to Nicky over the noise of the engine – she was reaching forward with both hands to steady herself with the dashboard, but appeared to be enjoying herself.

Justin and Amanda sat together in the back seat, trying to see what was going on. They kept being thrown against each other – Amanda crossly pushed him away from her. Justin held on, terrified but enthralled by the dangerous swerves and skids.

After a few minutes of this Mort seemed to have had enough and he slowed the car and drove calmly across to where there was a kiosk selling ice creams. They all jumped out. Mort treated them to something described as a 'Coronation Treat': red, white and blue, a double vanilla-and-strawberry cornet with bright blue syrup squeezed across the top. He leaned back on the cowling of the engine, staring across at the distant sea. Nicky went to stand next to him, facing him, smiling and teasingly mimicking his movements as he slurped and sucked at the slowly melting ice cream. They both had sticky streams dribbling down their chins. Justin tackled his more scientifically, turning the cornet around in a systematic way to lick the next side before it began dripping. He tried unsuccessfully to identify the flavour of the blue stuff.

Returning to the car they went back to the road, then drove the short distance to Southport. Here too vehicles were allowed on the beach, but it was more organized and controlled. Cars were permitted to park only in a certain area, and visitors had to pay sixpence to the council for the privilege. Mort grumbled but paid up. The sun had come out after they left Ainsdale Beach and now the vast stretch of golden sand was inviting.

The sky was a brilliant pastel blue, the sea a calm and silvery mirror. Nicky fussed around with sunhats, and she pulled the children's beach stuff out of the back of the car. She suggested walking along the beach a short distance, to where it looked less crowded.

Justin was barely aware of any of this. He had spotted a

single-engined plane flying low over the sea, banking and diving, rolling from side to side. He watched it in fascination, absorbed in the sight. The plane suddenly climbed much higher in the air, executed a daring turn at the top of the climb, then banked steeply and after a brief and thrilling dive headed straight back towards the beach. It looked as if it was flying directly at the people walking or sitting on the sands. After it crossed the breaking waves the plane turned again and headed along the beach. As it flew lower Justin could hear the engine throttle back, popping and coughing, and the plane visibly slowed. Its wings waggled slightly as it came down to ground level. The wheels touched the firm sandy floor, bounced once, then the aircraft gently settled. It ran a short way along the beach, the engine spluttering. It came to a rest with the propeller still turning. A faint smoke drifted around the engine housing, dispersed by the flow of air.

Justin pointed with excitement.

'Did you see that, Daddy?' he shouted. 'The plane landed on the beach!'

'They're here most weekends. They'll take us up for five bob, half a crown for children.'

'Then can we go up, Daddy? *Please!*'

Amanda turned away, not interested.

'Just me?' Justin said.

While they were talking a youth in a peaked cap had moved forward and opened a hatch in the side of the plane, above the lower wing. Three people climbed out of the plane and shuffled down to the sand, sliding on their backsides across part of the wing. Four others from a small group who had been waiting walked forward to take their places. Justin watched them enviously. He could see the pilot in the open cockpit: a head was showing above the rim, with a leather helmet and flying goggles. The sun glinted off the shiny paint on the wings and fuselage.

There was a delay while these new passengers clambered through the hatch, obviously having to squeeze awkwardly into the compartment inside. Justin stared at the aircraft, trying to work out what type it was. He had an aircraft recognition chart on the wall of his bedroom, which he knew in every detail, but this one did not seem to fit any of the familiar profiles. It was a single-engined biplane with an open cockpit halfway along the fuselage. It looked like a Tiger Moth, a popular aircraft used for private and club flying, but this was larger and heavier than a Tiger Moth, with the passenger cabin inside the fuselage, just behind the engine and in front of the pilot. Because Justin was used to seeing jets and bigger commercial aircraft, it looked to him like a veteran machine, an outdated model. But it flew. It was real.

Justin pulled at Mort's hand. 'Daddy, can we?'

Mort looked around at Nicky, who shook her head. Amanda was already walking away.

So it was just the two of them. Mort paid for his and Justin's tickets and then they stood with a small crowd of others, waiting their turn. They watched the next three take-offs, turning their faces away from the stinging cloud of fine sand thrown up by the propeller. Justin was thrilled – he was closer to an aircraft than he had ever been before, even closer than to those descending jets and transports that years before had skimmed over the roof of his primary school.

The ride always took the same course. The plane taxied

slowly away along the beach, gouging a trail in the sand with its main undercarriage and the tiny wheel beneath the tail-plane. It turned, faced into the light sea wind and the engine gunned to full power. After a short run the aircraft lifted easily away. It turned, headed out to sea. Almost as soon as it was above the waves the plane banked, the wings on the right-hand side looking as if they were perilously close to the water, but then it levelled off and climbed towards the sun. Justin shaded his eyes, avidly watching everything it did. A series of turns and dives followed, interesting to observe, but he wanted to experience them for himself, not just see from the ground. He had already seen too many aircraft from the ground.

At last it was going to be their turn. The plane descended, making a bumpy landing on the beach. The lower wing tipped to the side, almost scraping the sand, but it came to a safe halt. When the people inside had disembarked Mort and Justin and the young couple also waiting hurried across to take their seats. The lad in the cap helped them up across the wing, telling them where not to put their feet on the tight canvas surface.

The inside of the compartment was much more cramped than Justin expected. There were two bench seats facing each other, so close that they had to press knees with the person opposite. Mort, a tall man, settled and wriggled, trying to find a way of being seated on the hard, uncushioned board so that he was not pushing against the legs of the young woman now in front of him. The four of them were still trying to get comfortable when the youth in the cap slammed the hatch closed and the plane's engine revved up.

The flight was nothing at all like what Justin had

anticipated. The bleak and cramped compartment was close against the engine housing, immediately next to where he and his father were sitting. The thin partition did nothing to reduce the deafening noise, and everything was vibrating so violently that his teeth chattered together. There was an overwhelming, almost suffocating smell of petrol, oil, sweat, smoke, something else. The engine sounded loud and grating, as if there was some kind of mechanical fault. And although there were windows on both sides of the cabin they had become grazed and scratched with time so that visibility through them was strictly limited. Whenever the side of the plane briefly turned towards the sun white-orange light glared brilliantly and blindingly. The windows could not be opened from inside.

As the plane taxied noisily along the beach Justin felt panic rising in him, a claustrophobic feeling of being helplessly trapped, unable to breathe or hear properly, or even see where he was. He tried to calm himself.

The plane turned, the engine roared and the aircraft moved swiftly back the way it had just come. It took to the air within a few seconds, and almost at once the compartment was less awful to sit in – the noise from the engine was the same or worse, but the vibration had ceased and the painful bumping from the uneven beach was absent.

Justin turned to the window, desperate to see out. Much of the view to the outside was blocked by the lower wing, but he glimpsed part of the beach where people were walking. Then the plane tilted and all he could see was the sky. When the plane tilted back again he was looking straight down at the sea.

His stomach lurched as the plane seemed to falter in

the air, the engine momentarily missing a beat – another glimpse of the sky, a swooping sensation down, a tipping to one side. He fell against his father's body. The legs of the man opposite him bashed against Justin's knees. His stomach felt again as if it was being purged and his ears made an internal popping sound. The aircraft flew straight and level again for a few seconds, then carried out several steep turns and climbs. The flight was never smooth – the plane kept knocking and bumping like a car being driven too fast along an unmade road. Finally, another unexpected dive, making his heart seem to leap towards his mouth, then a dizzying turn with a quick and blurry view of the shallow waves as they broke against the beach, a loud roar from the engine, a coughing sound of backfiring, and relative peace as the engine was throttled back.

There was a thump up from the bench seat through his back, a scraping sound from below, a snaking motion from side to side, and through the window Justin briefly saw some of the people waiting their turn for the next joyride. When the plane came to a halt there was a wait of a few seconds before the hatch was opened from outside. The young man in the cap helped them all to the ground. Justin felt unsteady.

Mort said, 'Did you enjoy that, Justin?'

'Yes, Daddy. Thank you.' He was by habit always polite after a treat, but he felt his knees shaking.

The experience overall had been so complex and full of unexpected sensations that the word 'enjoy' barely covered it. He was thankful to be back on the ground: the familiar sounds of the beach, the breeze blowing along the sands, the plane's engine clattering away behind him. The sun blazed down. The next four people were already clambering across the lower wing, crouching and squeezing through the hatch.

Mainly he felt a sense of relief at having survived a frightening situation. He and his father, and the other two people, had been in every way trapped inside the cabin. Had anything gone wrong they would not have been able to escape. At the same time he was inspired and thrilled by the brief glimpses that had been possible from the sky, the sense of space and height and speed, and a dizzying new perspective.

He turned back to watch the aircraft start its next flight. He lacked a camera, so he made a conscious decision to memorize the plane's appearance as accurately as possible. It was white-painted, although there were patches on the fuselage where it had been repaired, and close to the engine housing there were windswept streaks of oil. Overall it looked grimy. A horizontal red line had been painted along the side, interrupted by the large letters of the registration code: G-ACCB. The wing struts were also painted red.

Back at school on the Monday following the day at the beach, Justin went straight afterwards to the bookshop in the village and searched for books that might help him identify the plane accurately. He found what he wanted more or less straight away: the aircraft was a de Havilland 83 Fox Moth, described as a light transport and passenger plane, no longer in production. It was based on the Tiger Moth, but the original design had been enlarged, making space for the passenger cabin or for carrying cargo. The book was an expensive production on glossy art paper, way beyond his pocket money, so he returned it to the shelf and left the shop.

Later that week, Justin went to the reference section of the local library. With the help of one of the staff he looked through a registry of current commercial airplanes and quickly located the entry for G-ACCB.

This provided him with what he immediately felt was interesting extra information. The plane had a serial number as well as a registration. He noted it down because he liked that sort of detail. The aircraft had been manufactured at a factory in England in 1933. The company who operated it was based in Southport, and owned two other aircraft, both also Fox Moths. Those were used for postal deliveries around the Merseyside and Fylde towns, from Birkenhead in the south to Fleetwood in the north. The nominated 'Use Type' of the aircraft he had been on was described as Taxi/Charter, operating Non-Scheduled Revenue Flights. The plane was crewed by one person and the maximum number of permitted passengers was three, not four.

On the way home Justin bought a notebook and that evening transferred all this information to the first page. His intention from now on was to record every flight he took, or any other matter of flying interest. He planned there would be one entry per page, with room below for annotations.

He loved making records of what he saw and did in his life. He already had similar notebooks where he wrote down the titles of records he heard played on the radio, and another where he painstakingly kept notes about the films he saw.

As things turned out, and in an unexpected way, a short time later he had to make an annotation to that first flight.

During the last weekend in September, G-ACCB, a Fox Moth passenger plane on a non-scheduled pleasure flight from Southport Beach, crashed shortly after take-off. The plane suddenly lost height when a lull in the wind coincided with a temporary loss of engine power. The plane was banking to climb out over the sea. A stall immediately followed and the aircraft plummeted straight down into the waves.

Although the pilot and all four passengers survived, they suffered multiple injuries, and prolonged immersion in the cold water before they could be pulled to safety. All were treated in hospital; none was critical. The wreck of the aircraft was recovered from the sea a day or two later, but it was written off as being beyond repair.

Justin wrote this secondary data on the first page of the notebook, trying to maintain an objective view of the crash, but as he read the details in the newspapers and saw the reports on television he was filled with a sense of horror. He could imagine only too well what it must have been like to be jammed into that noisy, cramped compartment as the engine failed, the wings fluttering in a deadly stall, followed by a steep fall and a sudden violent immersion in the sea. All four of the passengers would still have been trapped behind a hatch that could only be opened from the outside.

After this, Justin never went anywhere without a camera. His father had a compact Comet 'S' he did not use any more. Justin borrowed it and carried it with him for several years. Even when he went to school he carried it in a small special compartment in his saddle bag.

4

The notebook where he wrote down aircraft data was slow to fill, because Justin wanted to collect information only about planes he actually saw close up, or went inside, or travelled in, or which had some other kind of personal meaning to him. As an early teen, still at school, his opportunities for most of these were few. He did not want to become a sort of superior plane spotter, listing numbers for the sake of listing them. After the Southport incident there were no more joyrides at the seaside, and winter set in. The rest of the notebook remained untouched, but ready. Just in case.

Similarly, he began to feel foolish for writing down a list of the pop records he heard. What was the point of that? His interest dwindled, then failed.

The remaining notebook was an altogether different matter – it was to change and to a certain extent define his life. Here he listed films.

When he was eight years old his parents had taken him and Amanda to see a film in one of the cinemas close to where they lived. It made a vivid impression on him.

It was the story of a circus travelling around America, a

major business and organizational enterprise, with several troupes of wild animals like lions and elephants, as well as speciality human acts: jugglers, acrobats, tightrope walkers, a squad of clowns, also dancers, musicians, roustabouts and so on. Justin had never seen anything like it in his life, and he was enthralled from start to finish by the skills, the dangers, the tensions, the sheer scale of the operation. Various stories emerged: one involved the mystery of a clown who never removed his make-up. There was a struggle for power involving the manager and the owners of the circus. One of the trapeze artists took a heavy fall during a performance. Towards the end there was a terrifying train crash.

Justin left the cinema enthralled and dazzled. He realized the film was drama, that the people were actors, but even so the sheer scale of the film made him believe in it. On the way out through the lobby he saw a poster advertising the film and he finally took note of the title. It was *The Greatest Show on Earth*. To him, the title was true. As soon as he was home he wrote it down, and a few days later, after he brought back a notebook from school, he copied the title in large letters on the first page. He wanted to write more, but knew nothing else about the film.

Then he remembered that this was not his first visit to a cinema: he had seen a film earlier about Snow White, a totally different type of story. He had laughed at it and sometimes had to clamp his eyes closed in terror, but at the end he had cheered. His mother told him the full title: *Snow White and the Seven Dwarfs*. He had not been inspired to keep a record of it then, however long ago, but now he was. He wrote that title in big letters on the second page.

Amanda reminded him that the previous Christmas they

had all gone to see a film called *The Wizard of Oz*. Justin remembered the images from it, but the actual trip to the cinema was forgotten. He wrote the title on the third page.

These were the childish beginnings of the detailed database that Justin was to maintain and build all his life. As he went through his teen years every time he went to the cinema he scribbled notes in the dark, later transferring them to his notebook. It was a way of externalizing his memories – not the stuff he liked, the images and stories and characters, which stayed alive anyway, but the practical annotations like release dates and running times, otherwise soon forgotten.

He also watched the increasing number of old films being broadcast on television. At this time the films of Jeanette Marchand, which had so impressed him as a small child, were no longer being broadcast. He remembered her, but not the actual films, or at least not enough about them to be able to note them down. Details became discoverable years later, in adulthood. The memories of a child are powerful but disorganized. Children do not at first make connections or recognize sequences, or even the wider context in which something happens.

Soon after he started his notes he decided to award each film a personal rating. He started of course with *The Greatest Show on Earth*, awarding it an immediate 10/10. On the other hand, *Easter Parade*, to which his parents had dragged him for a matinee, and which bored and annoyed him, received an equally indisputable 0/10. Other ratings wavered between these two extremes.

Later, more sophisticated and with a better knowledge of the history of cinema, and a deeper understanding of the complex process of making a film, Justin revised some of these scores. *Greatest Show* went down to a more arguable 6/10. *Easter Parade*, which he continued to dislike, was promoted to 4/10.

He continued awarding ratings to films until he was about eighteen, when he packed it in. He realized that a numerical system was too blunt a critical weapon. A poorly acted or directed film could be redeemed by a stunning musical score, or beautiful photography. There were no absolutes.

The first notebook soon became unusable and untidy, because of his constant crossings out and insertions. A serious complication was that it was impossible to see films, and therefore catalogue them, in chronological order. He was always watching old films, or recent ones that happened along. Films shown on television were invariably from the past. Later, when he was in London and regularly attending the NFT, any attempt to maintain a list of films in year order, or even by period, was a hopeless task. He was developing a sense of cinema's evolving state, its trends and periods, its genres, its past.

He bought his first book about film-making when he was fourteen: this was a book about filming *The Dam Busters*, which had been released in 1955. After that, he made regular visits to secondhand bookstores and jumble sales, steadily adding titles to what became a serious collection of film information. He quickly discovered the diversity of the subject. He collected not only books about particular titles, but biographies of directors, stars, camera operators, screenwriters, and so on, as well as technical information about cameras, film formats and censorship.

After leaving university Justin obtained his first job: he became an assistant-cum-trainee in a small photographic

44

studio in the West End of London. It was relatively well paid but the work was uninspiring. The firm's largest customer was a mail-order catalogue retailer, and they required an endless supply of pictures of the goods they sold. Justin spent most days in an airless studio photographing cooking utensils, transistor radios, garden implements, pairs of shoes, and so on.

He had been there a few weeks when he realized that the card index system on which the studio admin staff stored details of the negatives and prints could be adapted to his own purposes. After he had taken home a few of the blank index cards, and experimented with a transfer of his film data from his notebook, Justin bought his own card system. For the next few weeks and months he spent his evenings and weekends copying his records across. He also bought a secondhand typewriter, which he taught himself to use.

Towards the end of the 1980s, by which time he was recognized as a film critic, and his first book, a history of British-made war films of the 1950s, had been published in London and New York, he employed an assistant to transfer the data across to a computer, and after that to maintain the entering of new film information that he was accruing every week. By the end of the twentieth century Justin Farmer's film database was a unique and valuable research tool. Only he or his assistant could edit or expand it, while a growing online audience subscribed to a slightly stripped-down version. It became a full-time occupation, correcting errors or omissions, but also keeping up with the torrent of new films appearing from countries all over the world, all the various versions, reissues in foreign languages, remakes and sequels, and so on. He gradually built up a data studio, with several people working on the database.

The other notebook remained as it was, representing a similarly growing interest, mostly independent of his fascination with film, except in the rare instances where film and aviation coincided – *The Dam Busters* was the first example of this. He maintained an old exercise book bought cheaply from a newsagent's shop, handwritten throughout on the crudely lined pages, a record of air life and activity, planes and journeys and airports, and his experience of them all. No one but he ever saw this information. It had a different purpose.

5

On the second page of Justin's aviation notebook he summarized the following:

In the late morning of Thursday March 14th 1957, a Vickers Viscount four-engined turboprop airliner operated by BEA, British European Airways, took off from Schiphol Airport in the Netherlands. Its registration was G-ALWE, and the destination was Manchester Ringway Airport. After an uneventful flight the aircraft was approaching a landing in the early afternoon. The weather was calm, with medium cloud cover. The descending plane broke through the clouds and the pilot reported to the control tower that he had sight of the runway directly ahead. When the aircraft was a few hundred yards from the runway it suddenly entered a steep right-hand diving turn, sharply descending. Witnesses said that the plane banked so extremely that the wings were almost perpendicular to the ground. It fell rapidly, exploding and consumed by fire as it crashed. Its momentum catapulted it across the ground and it collided catastrophically with a row of terraced houses.

Everyone on the plane was killed on impact. Two people

in the worst damaged house, a mother and her baby, also died. There were no other casualties on the ground.

Justin heard about this tragic accident as he was leaving school. He was thirteen. Instead of bicycling home as normal he rode across the village to the far side, where he guessed the crash site was likely to be. Naturally, he remembered the area well. His compact camera, as usual, was locked away inside the saddle bag.

As he drew near to the airport the road was blocked with many ambulances, fire appliances and police cars, so Justin left his bike and continued on foot. He took his camera with him. No one challenged him as he neared the scene of devastation, and he was able to walk right up to and across some of the wreckage. Most of the fires had already been dealt with, but the emergency services were still searching through the torn remains of the aircraft for bodies and the passengers' belongings. Justin had braced himself against the sight of the wreckage, but he was horrified to see the tangle of possessions strewn everywhere: clothes, shoes, papers, children's toys. There was a disgusting smell drifting with the oily smoke and the steam that still rose from parts of the debris.

Most of the aircraft had disintegrated on impact, but a short section of the rear part of the fuselage was intact. It was lying at an angle, upside down, blackened by fire. The registration g-alwe was still visible on the fin.

Trying to stay calm he took several photographs of the scene but was soon coming to the end of his roll of film. He moved away from the centre of the rescue activity. He was acutely aware of not having a legitimate reason for being there. He was probably in the way, but no one appeared to notice him. Teams of men were trying to pull metal parts away from where they were embedded in the ruins of the houses. Stepping over bricks and charred remains of upholstery, as well as hundreds of sharp metal fragments, Justin passed through a broken fence into the garden of the house next to the crash, and went on from there to the main road.

Away from the smoke and confusion he could see across to his former primary school. He stared at the old building, struck by the familiarity of the sight. Where it stood, next to the scene of horrific chaos, it was a symbolic reassurance of normality. His hands were shaking and the stench he had inhaled made him feel sick. Just beyond the school building was a row of airport landing lights on a huge skeletal metal structure.

Justin looked back at the scene of the crash. The plane would have been flying directly towards the school before it swerved to the side. Only that catastrophic turn had saved the school.

With the last remaining shot in the camera he took a photo from that position – a clear view of the edge of the field of wreckage, the airport landing array and the runway immediately beyond. When he lowered the camera he noticed that the lights inside the school building were still on.

The next day many of the newspapers printed photographs similar to the ones he had taken himself, alongside graphic accounts from witnesses of what they had seen as the aircraft fell to the ground. Everyone remarked on the school's miraculous escape from a disaster – the crash had occurred at about a quarter to two in the afternoon. The building was full of children aged six to ten.

The school was closed the following day, and by the middle

of the following week all the children had been transferred to different primary schools in the district. The original building at the end of the airport runway remained empty, but at the end of the year it was demolished and the site was cleared. A larger array of landing lights was later set up in what had once been the playground.

6

The March 1995 edition of *Sight and Sound*, published monthly by the British Film Institute, carried an in-depth interview with Justin Farmer.

It was part of a series of items in the magazine questioning and challenging the role of the film critic. Justin at this time had four books in print, covering various aspects of the history of film. The most recent, a collection of his essays on films set in the American West, had just been published in the UK and France, with an American paperback edition to come later in the year.

Justin himself had felt slightly bemused by the fact that he was to be made the subject of an interview. He saw *Sight and Sound* as a vehicle for film criticism, analysis and discussion, and that the proper subjects for attention were the makers and originators of film – the writers, directors, actors, photographers, technicians and so on. For him, *Sight and Sound* was where the hunters rode, where the hares were pursued. It struck him as unusual that he should be thought of as a hare, even for one issue, but he cooperated with the two affable young people who interviewed him and he believed when it was published that the interview fairly represented his views.

In any event it appeared not to excite much reaction. None of his journalist colleagues, whom he saw every week at the screenings of new films, mentioned it. No one wrote to him, congratulating or condemning him. He had said what he believed and put into practice every time: that the work of a critic was in proper terms reactive only, that it was not a performance art, an expression of the reviewer's personality, or a medium for controversy. His criticism of films was sometimes at odds with many other reviews, and he never shrank from going against the grain. He loved film, had spent his life staring at cinema screens, treated film as an art form that relied on the expert application of craft, and said so. Those had always been his critical baseline.

The next issue of the magazine appeared a month later. The critical debate moved on to other people. No one commented on what Justin had said. He had not expected otherwise. It was a debate, not an argument. But print magazines have a long lead time, and it was only later, in the May issue, that someone wrote in and had a letter published on the correspondence page at the back of the magazine:

Dear Sir, I was intrigued and pleased by the comment made by your reviewer Justin Farmer that he was a fan of Jeanette Marchand. She is rarely mentioned these days, her career overshadowed not only by her more luminous contemporaries – Davis, Harlow, Garbo, and so on – but also by her own choice of films. In the space of a few years she went from being a headliner in major films to being the queen of the B movie and the weekly Republic serials. Her famous beauty endured.

All seems now forgotten after her untimely death nearly half a century ago. Not forgotten by Farmer, though, and apparently not in Germany either. While I was in Germany a few months ago I saw an interview on TV with a man named Engel. In the 1930s he worked as a camera assistant and film editor with Leni Riefenstahl on Olympia. *An intriguing background. Herr Engel has retired and now lives somewhere in England, but he happened to mention during the interview that like Justin Farmer he had been deeply impressed by Marchand as a young man. Her pre-Code performances especially had influenced his decision to go into film. These movies obviously had something. I for one would love to see them. What are the chances of them being revived?*

F D Robeson, Richmond, North Yorks

Through his contacts at the BFI, Justin obtained the correspondent's address and made contact. He wrote a brief but polite note to F D Robeson about his own continuing interest in Jeanette Marchand and reported what he knew from film restoration specialists working with the BFI: that it was unlikely that any viewable prints remained of most of her early films. Then he asked if the German TV interview had contained any other grains of information about the man called Engel.

F D Robeson turned out to be a woman: Florence Robeson. She replied a few days later, thanking him for his information about the loss of prints of Marchand's films. On the other matter, her memory of the German television interview was vague but she recalled that after Engel moved to England he worked for British TV in the 1960s and 1970s, directing several episodes of a couple of TV series (she couldn't remember which). One of these had recently been shown on German TV. Elstree and Bray Studios were both mentioned as places where he worked. During the interview Engel had been asked about Leni Riefenstahl but he had not said anything Florence Robeson could now remember. He spoke passionately about Jeanette Marchand. And she believed his first name was August, or possibly Albert. She added that he had looked old and frail in the interview.

Justin wrote back, said thank you. Florence Robeson did not reply.

He looked up Engel: there was an August Engel who had directed some crime series episodes for Yorkshire TV. He could not locate a contact address or agency listing for him.

7

Her name was Kathleen Ann Stringer and she was twenty-three, a little under a year older than Justin. She was his first real girlfriend, but after a good start things had suddenly become uncertain. She had returned with him to his bed-sitting room after dinner and a couple of glasses of wine in an inexpensive restaurant, but it was all going wrong. She was holding one of his notebooks, which she had picked up to read the first two pages. It suddenly became clear to him which one she was looking at.

'Why have you done this?' she said loudly, tears forming. 'You humiliated me.'

'Did you read it all?'

'Enough of it.'

'I didn't mean anything by it, Kathy. No one else would ever see it.'

'And you do this to every girl you meet?'

'No. You're the only one.'

'I'm being given special treatment.'

'You're the only girl I've ever been with.'

'So you always say.'

'It's true – I mean it. There's never been anyone else.'

'You're acting like a creep.'

He knew from her anger he was in danger of losing her and it was entirely his fault. He stood up, went to her and tried to put his arms around her. She pushed him off, wriggling away from him, ducking her head. He reeled back, furious with himself, not able to look at her because she had turned her face away from him.

'Can I explain?' he said.

'What's the point?' She threw the offending notebook on the chair where he had been sitting. She stalked towards the door and in a harsh moment of clarity Justin realized he was about to lose her, had already lost her. It was a heated flash of understanding, immediately over. But at the door she paused and turned back.

'Just tell me why,' she said.

'Because it's what I do, the way I work. I thought it was harmless. I realize now, you've made me realize, what a mistake that was. A terrible mistake. I shouldn't have – I can't say how sorry I am.'

Justin had known Kathy for slightly less than a year, and they had been dating for the last few weeks. It was still early days, but she meant more to him that he felt he could ever adequately express to her.

They met through their jobs. She worked then as a bike messenger for the agency that arranged the commissions from the catalogue printers, and came into the studio where he worked in Frith Street every two or three days. As one of the most junior members of staff Justin normally had to break off from whatever he was doing and attend to callers in the reception area. Mostly this meant signing for packages that were being delivered, or handing over job lots that were for collection. Kathy did both.

At first she came into the office wearing her full motorbike gear, including the crash helmet. Justin had no idea what she looked like or how old she was – even, for the first couple of times he met her, what gender she was behind the dark face shield. It was winter and her body was wrapped up in bulky bike leathers. They hardly said anything, because there was hardly anything to say, so he didn't hear her voice. On her fourth or fifth visit she pulled off the helmet while he was signing the paperwork, and when he looked up he saw her face for the first time. The next time she came in without the helmet, and she smiled as he walked out to greet her. Later, when the weather was warmer, most of the leathers disappeared.

Hardly daring to believe she would be interested in him, Justin spent every day at work with half his attention listening for the faintly audible sound of the elevator, the footsteps on the bare boards of the hallway, the studio entrance door being pushed open. It wasn't her every time, of course, but his heart lifted anyway.

One day she leaned over to peer as he wrote his signature, which he always scribbled as *J Fmmmmr*.

'John?' she said. 'Jim?'

'It's Justin,' he said.

'I'm Kathleen. Kathy.'

'Nice to meet you at last.'

It went on like that for a few weeks, her visits to the studio becoming progressively longer, with him trying to think of ways of delaying her for a few more moments before she had to pull on the helmet again and disappear. She said her boss was always on her case, and so she could never stay as long as he would have liked. He had flirted with a few girls in the past, but never with much hope or interest, and always felt he must seem gauche and unattractive to Kathy. Finally, he plucked up courage to ask her if she'd like to meet him for a drink after work.

Things developed from there. She lived in Kilburn, a tiny shared flat with two other girls. Her messenger job was a temporary one, she said. It had started as standing in for a friend, but the guy had gone off to France, where after becoming engaged he still was, and so she carried on. She was on the lookout for something better. She didn't like the risk of riding the motorbike in London. She had a degree in journalism, but apart from a short spell on an evening paper in Norwich the previous year she hadn't yet found anything she wanted to do.

Justin was slightly in awe of her at first because she seemed so focused. His indecision about his own future was something Kathy said she was sympathetic to, but did not share. She had already travelled to the Far East and Australia, she was learning Russian, she was taking judo classes, and had numerous friends. She made him feel like a closeted nerd, which in truth he was, or at least at risk of becoming one with his hours of note-keeping and sorting. Kathy entering his life had started saving him from that, he thought.

She was applying for a job to several magazines and a tabloid newspaper. One of the weeklies had already interviewed her and she was waiting to hear from the others. A month after she and Justin started dating regularly she was given a job as a junior editor on a women's magazine.

Then came the first weekend when he suggested tentatively,

nervously, they could go back to his place after the film they were intending to see. Kathy had accepted with a pleasing sense of it being nothing exceptional – anything might happen, anything at all.

But that was when the row, their first ever, blew up. Kathy had left the room to use the bathroom across the hall, and while she was there Justin went to his notebook to scribble down some details of the film they had just seen. As usual, he would type it out on one of the index cards later. He put it aside hurriedly when she came back into the room, but she noticed the movement and asked him what he was doing.

'Just taking notes on the film.'

'I've seen you do that before.'

'I like to keep a record of what I've seen.'

So he described to her how he was building up a database: thoughts he sometimes scribbled in the dark while the film was actually showing, more detailed notes made later with a brief synopsis, then once a week he would transfer everything to his card index.

Kathy said she liked the sound of that – they reviewed films in the magazine she was working for. She loved movies and always read reviews. When they first came back to his room he had shown her his shelf crammed with books about films, and she had seemed interested. Now she reached over to where he had put the notebook, and took hold of it. She looked at it for a moment, but then her expression changed.

Justin did not immediately pick up on her reaction. He was thinking fond thoughts of her: the way she was standing by the desk, holding the notebook, her light-brown hair falling about her face, made him remember his early impressions of her. Back then, until he became used to her, she had sometimes reminded him of the way Jeanette Marchand looked. Both had light hair, wide pale-blue eyes, good but not prominent cheekbones, a face that some people would describe as heart-shaped, but in fact was regular in a special way. It was already many years since Justin, as a child, had become infatuated with the film star, but Kathy brought those feelings back once more, reminding him. They had been together long enough that by now Kathy looked only like Kathy, but occasionally he glimpsed the memory.

The memory died. She turned towards him, the notebook open in her hand.

'What is this? What have you been saying about me?'

'Nothing!' But he realized then that one of his other notebooks had been sitting beside his typewriter. His film notes were still there where he normally left them. He stepped quickly towards her but she turned her back on him, leaning protectively over the pages in her hand.

'Are you a weirdo? You never told me about this!'

'I can explain. Please, let me have that back. Kathy, *please*!'

'No – I want to read it all.'

He managed to take her wrist in his hand, trying to force her to release the book. She was strong, and pulled away from him. Her discovering what he had been writing about her was the worst thing he could imagine happening. It was unexplainable, even though he urged to pour excuses out at her.

'I thought you liked me.'

'I do! I love you, Kathy!' But it was the wrong thing to say and the wrong way and the wrong time. She glared at him, then threw the notebook at him. Pages fluttered in the air, and the book landed on the chair where until a few moments before he had been sitting. She did not open the door, or try to leave. He did not try to keep her there. He was deeply embarrassed and feeling contrite.

Kathleen always interested him, excited him. He had never known such feelings before. Love and affection were new experiences. His emotions stirred when he was with her, or when he was about to see her. It began that memorable day, not the first time she came to the studio but the time she took off her crash helmet. She had stood beside him while he did the paperwork, and then he looked up to see her face. He was so stricken with her that afterwards he wanted to record her, capture the essence of her.

He had no idea, when that first glimpse of her was allowed, that he would ever see her again. He fervently hoped so. He bought another notebook on his way home from work, and that evening he wrote down what he had seen of her: the brief sight of her face, her eyes, her hair. A quick smile, slightly knowing. Not much to go on. Then she was away again, her face hidden inside the helmet's dark dome. He described what he had seen, not what he had felt. After the next meeting he did the same. Week after week he wrote little notes about her. He knew it was wrong, that he was acting obsessively, but he saw no harm in it. It was private, innocent.

He kept the notes going after they started dating, even though he knew it was a further invasion of her privacy. He described the clothes she wore, reported what she said, what she told him of her past life, her excitement about her new job. Every now and again he added a note of how much he liked and admired her.

Was he wrong to do this? He did not think or frame the

word 'love', although he knew what it meant, or what it impended. It was all new to him. He never intended her to see any of it.

But then who was it for? She was here for real, often around him and with him, with no need at all to externalize his opinions on paper. He shouldn't have done it, he shouldn't even have started it.

'What on earth were you thinking?' she said. 'Is it some kind of weird fantasy that I'm part of? Without me knowing?'

'No,' he said miserably.

Eventually she sat down on the side of his bed, and there was a long silence between them. Justin was relieved that at least she was no longer threatening to walk out on him, but he was embarrassed, feeling guilty and defensive. While she was still glowering silently, staring away from him and down at the worn old carpet he had inherited when he moved in, he took the offending notebook and tore out all the pages he had written about her. That made her look up at him.

'Are you going to tear me up now?' she said.

'No – but you can.' He offered her the pages but she shrugged and turned from him. He put them back on the table where he kept his typewriter.

'You said you wanted to explain.'

It was slowly becoming calmer between them at last.

'I don't want you to think I'm making excuses,' he said, but feared that anything he said would sound like that. 'I'm really sorry. You're right to be angry. I'll never do anything like it again.'

'OK. But why did you start? How did it happen?'

He began by telling her about the index of films, how as

a child he had learned about the significant creative roles people played in the actual making of a film. Writing them down, the details gradually becoming more complex. Without understanding why he wanted to capture and keep this information. He liked comparing his notes with some of what was published in the collection of books he owned. He began to see connections: certain directors often worked with a particular photographer or editor, for instance.

'I discovered I liked making a record,' he said. 'It started a long time ago, and the longer I do it the more I feel I'm learning about films. Then you came along and I wanted to write about how you seemed to me, how you looked. It probably proves I'm mentally abnormal or something, and you've made me realize that. I know it sounds obsessive, and I suppose it is, but it helps me understand and appreciate new films if I keep a record of the past. I think I was trying to do the same with you.'

'Just old films, then? I'm the same as an old movie?'

'All films are old once you've seen them. You're not like that. I love new films, and I keep up with as many of the current movies as I can. We both do.' Impulsively, he then did something that until this evening he thought he never would. He leapt up from where he was sitting and pulled out the wooden drawer where most of his file cards were kept. He thrust it towards her. She rested it on her lap. 'Have a look,' he said. 'Pull one out and read it.'

She used her thumb to tip back the tops of the cards so she could read them. The title was always on the top line. 'You've seen all these films?'

'Most of them.'

She lifted out a card.

It was for *Le Beau Serge*, a film made by the director Claude Chabrol, date 1958/1963/1964, principal actors Gérard Blain, Jean-Claude Brialy, Michèle Méritz and Bernadette Lafont, released in France in 1958 but only shown in London in 1963. Justin had seen it three years earlier at the film club, while still at university. It was Chabrol's first film, it was one of the earliest nouvelle vague films from France, and it had won awards.

Standing beside her he pointed out the difference between the three dates.

Kathy said, 'There's a review here. Did you write it?'

'It's not really a review. It's just what I thought of it.'

'Same thing, isn't it?'

'It's a way of reminding myself.'

She replaced the card and took out another. Then a few more, which she riffled through. She was still in the Bs. She said, '*Blow Up*! We saw that together . . . last week, or the week before. You wrote it up then?' She read his note on the card. 'It says here you liked it. That isn't what you said at the time. I thought we agreed we hadn't enjoyed it.'

'We did. But I thought about it afterwards, when I was typing up the card. I still agreed with what you said. It's pretentious and the plot doesn't hang together. But I wasn't sure any more, and I need to see it again. Maybe I missed something.'

'I thought that too. That's why I didn't like it much.'

'But you know – Antonioni is a great film-maker. I often think maybe a film should be about more than the plot. *Blow Up* seems to be all about the plot, that's what is so fascinating. You think it's going somewhere but in the end nothing comes of it. That was annoying. But it was intriguing, so

I was wondering what the film was getting at. And I liked the scene where David Hemmings was enlarging the photographs. We could go back and see it again, if you like. It's still showing at the Pavilion, isn't it?'

They talked about the film a while longer, gradually retreating from the sudden and bitter argument. He went over to sit beside her on the bed. They cuddled briefly. The torn out pages were lying on his table next to the typewriter. They were like a rebuke.

It was getting late. Earlier in the day, Justin had been thinking ahead to the prospect of Kathy being here in his room at night. Who knew where that might have led? But the argument had spoiled the evening. After eleven he travelled back on the tube with her to her flat, they kissed outside, then he walked home chastely through the warm and mildly petrol-fumed London air.

Once he was back in his room he tore up the pages. What had he been thinking? Never again, never. He was still kicking himself for the damage and hurt he had caused Kathy, and the disaster of losing her, somehow averted.

Two weeks later Kathy told Rick Deptford about her friend who was obsessed with film and wrote a review of everything he saw. Rick was an editor on the magazine where Kathy worked, and had been trying to find someone to take on regular film reviewing. He contacted Justin and asked to see a few samples of what he had done.

Justin's first three reviews were published at the end of the month, and for the next four years he wrote the film column in the magazine. It was his first professional job and the beginning of his career.

8

Once the shock of his close-up look at the wreckage of the crashed Viscount began to fade, Justin felt a persisting interest in the event. He was still in his early teens, but he was taking what seemed to him to be a grown-up approach to his own experiences. After reading several newspaper articles about the accident, he shared the sense of disbelief expressed by many journalists and commentators that the layout of the airport and its runways could have been so perilously close to populated areas. In particular, to the primary school.

Why had no one ever seen the danger? No one would think of building a school on the end of an existing airport runway, so presumably the runway had been extended towards the building, without any serious thought given to the potential for disaster. It had been a local school since the previous century. How was the runway extension allowed to happen? Did no one think the school would be at risk? He had been there, and his six-year-old self stood in the playground and looked up at aircraft descending just above him. But could that possibly be true? Had his memory betrayed him, building up his fears after his visit to the scene of the crash and supplanting his real experiences?

Justin sometimes detoured on his way home from the grammar school, riding his bike across to the vicinity of the airport. The position of the school, now abandoned, was still exactly as he remembered it.

His visits therefore enabled him to witness the slow, deliberate efforts by the authorities to repair the damage caused by the accident, clear away all signs of what had happened, rebuild the houses, replant trees. The work took several months, with the damaged houses rebuilt last of all. They could not help but look more recently construct-ed than the otherwise identical ones around them. They remained vacant: Justin never saw signs of new occupiers moving in.

He carried his camera on most visits, but he took only one or two more shots of the accident zone. There was nothing much of interest to see, except in the context of knowing what had happened. The rolls of film were expensive, as was the cost of processing and printing. Ingeniously, the Comet camera had been designed to allow twice the number of exposures on a 127 film, but even so the expense was usu-ally beyond his pocket. In years to come he would learn the economies of darkroom skills, but not then.

Planes coming in to land continued to fly low over the zone, the engines roaring, the bulky undercarriage assem-blies seeming to skim the roofs of the houses slightly further away. Sometimes, fancifully, Justin would stare up along their descending flight path and imagine them as ground-attack aircraft, a slow but sustained offensive against those who stayed on the surface. However, the real military aircraft, the RAF jets, were no longer operating from Ringway. All flights now were civil: passenger or cargo.

As a veneer of normality around the streets was quickly restored, and the reconstruction became a work site, Justin took a greater interest in what was happening further down the road, at the airport itself.

At this time, in the mid and late 1950s, security measures against the threat of terrorism were more or less non-existent. Almost every part of the Ringway airport complex was open to casual visitors. One could wander around the whole area. There was an inexpensive self-service café that local people liked to visit, sitting by the picture windows with slices of cake and a cup of tea. They would watch the aircraft land and take off, or see them as they taxied across the apron to disgorge or take on board the passengers. Some said you would occasionally see film stars or famous football-ers arriving on the planes from London and Europe. There was also an extensive aircraft viewing platform on one of the roofs: this allowed people a close view of all activities, sometimes only a few yards from the aircraft as they refuelled or loaded.

It was during this period Justin first started feeling the almost indefinable sense of transience, dread and excitement in an airport terminal. It was nothing he could positively identify, because consciously he liked and felt at home in the place. It thrilled him to think of travel, flying away from the humdrum existence of schooldays and living at home with his parents. Ringway offered him this temporary illusion of escape. He liked the sleek appearance of the aircraft, built for speed and lift and distance, and when he saw one of the bigger passenger aircraft accelerating down the runway and taking off he felt a tremor of jealousy, a wish that he too could be on board.

But whenever he left the airport, pedalling home on his bicycle, he almost invariably experienced a sense of relief, a returning of certainty, a solidity and assuredness.

The airport itself was constantly in a state of shifting stasis, always being changed or expanded or replaced while remaining the same. The differences were mostly superficial, and unexplained. Signage was often amended: areas where passengers were allowed to go, or more often not to go, places where cars were not permitted to drive or park, doors marked No Entry while others were permanently open. Temporary partitions were in use everywhere.

Everyone who worked there seemed to operate from day to day, minute to minute. There was no sense of memory or continuity. No one had any idea of how the airport would be in the future – sometimes Justin would notice building work going on, and the one time he asked what was happening he could not get a reply.

Whenever he looked around the public areas he gained the impression that there had been changes since his last visit, that when he returned next time there would be more changes. One day, the place where he normally propped up his bike while he was walking around was fenced off, and he had to pay to leave it in a special rack instead.

On one of his later visits the friendly café overlooking the arrivals apron was closed and boarded up. The next time Justin went a chain restaurant had opened in its place. It was now selling snacks and fast food in plastic packs. There were no windows overlooking the tarmac any more, merely large panels with brightly lighted advertisements.

The shabby-looking former huts and hangars from the wartime days were still in use to some extent, but they were no longer central to the operation of the airport. Newer ones, built of concrete and glass, were being thrown up. Around the time Justin and his family moved to the London area some of the old buildings were demolished to make spaces where people could park their cars. Large areas of ground around the perimeter were cleared of trees, replaced by wire fences. And the main runway was extended, this time at the far end, away from the site of the school.

It was as if the airport had an inner sense of life, a need to grow. That life was restless, stretching and spreading out across what had been the green Cheshire countryside.

During the early months of 1958 there was a long spell of wintry weather all over Europe, and every day after school Justin rode straight home on his bike to get out of the cold. He had no direct experience of what was to occur at the beginning of February, although like thousands of people in the Manchester area he felt indirectly involved.

On February 6th 1958, G-ALZU, a British European Airways twin-engined Airspeed Ambassador, returning to Manchester Ringway Airport from Belgrade, stopped in Munich for refuelling. When the plane attempted to take off again in a heavy snowstorm an accumulation of slush on the runway prevented it from reaching flying speed. It crashed in rough ground at the end of the runway and burst into flames. On board was the whole of the Manchester United football team, as well as staff members, officials and several journalists. Twenty-three people died in the accident, including eight of the leading players. Two of the surviving footballers were injured so seriously that they were never able to play again.

It was a national tragedy – most of the players were young and widely recognized as rising stars in the game. In Manchester there was a particular wave of shock and sadness, not only because of loyalty to the team but because many of the footballers were local lads.

A few weeks after the accident a commemoration service was announced. It would be held at Ringway Airport. Justin at first resolved to be there, but as the day came closer he was less sure. He was not especially interested in soccer, but that was not the main reason.

The nature of the disaster was appalling in human terms, but the destination of the flight seemed to Justin to be a matter that connected the crash to him. How was the airport involved? He spent much time brooding on this, remained uncertain about how he related to it, but when the day came he decided to stay away.

Later, with the same sort of misgivings, he recorded the accident in his aviation notebook, just the facts as he knew them.

9

La Jetée in Retrospect
by Justin Farmer

The screen is black. The first sound you hear is the whine of jet turbine engines, a plane taxiing at an airport. The opening visual image appears: this is la jetée itself, the long public viewing platform on the roof of one of the terminal piers at Orly Airport, outside Paris. The picture is a still photograph, a crisp monochrome. The sound of the engines gradually mixes with soaring liturgical music. The image zooms out to reveal the full length of the pier and the film credits briefly appear.

Jet airliners are waiting by the terminal to disgorge arriving passengers, or to take on new ones. Above them, the viewing platform is almost deserted. A few people stand in isolated groups of two or three in different parts of the long expanse. Depersonalized by distance and immobilized by the capture of the still photograph they are reminiscent of the guests in the grounds of the hotel in Alain Resnais's *L'Année derniere à Marienbad*.

This is the opening of a remarkable film by the French director Chris Marker. The title is *La Jetée*, and it was made in 1962. We had to wait three years for it to be shown in the UK for the first time. Its running time is just under half an hour, so presumably no exhibitor felt it worthy of a solo appearance. It therefore came to Britain as the support feature to Jean-Luc Godard's *Alphaville*, briefly screened in London and a few other cities at the end of 1965. It has also been shown at film festivals. It is no longer being screened anywhere. *La Jetée* is without question one of the most hauntingly beautiful, original and memorable films ever made, but its short duration ensures its audience is at least for now a restricted one.

The time is the present, or more accurately the period described in the film as 'some time before the outbreak of World War 3'. A contemporary audience will of course be aware that this image must be a few years in the past, in *our* past, when the photograph was taken, but there are few signs of datedness. Most of the aircraft we can see are the same sort of commercial passenger jets in use now. The pier and the terminal are part of a modern-looking construction, presumably still there today in the real Orly Airport. The viewing platform is not crowded. There is a glimpse of a parking lot, not full. The slip road leading to the front of the terminal is not a crush of cars and taxis. The pier stands as an icon of a generic airport, recent but timeless.

All this is seen in the opening image of the film. Nothing can move in the stationary ambience of the photograph. Even the usual scenes of activity around waiting aircraft are missing: there is no sign of passenger movement, baggage handlers, ground staff, fuel bowsers. A quality of timelessness permeates the whole film. Every scene in the film, bar one short fragment, was photographed as a still black-and-white

73

image, a tableau vivant, a moment glimpsed and fixed into immobility.

On that quiet pre-WW3 day, 'lit by a frozen sun', a boy visiting the viewing area of the airport with his parents notices a young woman (played by Hélène Chatelain) standing alone at the far end of the pier. We assume she and the boy's family are among those unmoving distant figures we saw in the opening scene. The boy sees her face and stares transfixed by her beauty.

They are beneath the flight path of a jet aircraft – we gain a glimpse of it as it flies low overhead with a roar of engines. The woman gestures with horror or fear, and a man's body crumples to the concrete floor of the pier. Later, the boy realizes he has seen a man die. The incident will haunt him forever, linked inviolably to his memory of the young woman's face.

Memory is not a narrative. It is not linear or chronological in form. Memories from five or ten or twenty years earlier will present themselves in a seemingly random sequence not created by the calendar, but sorted by the unconscious. What priority does the unconscious mind work with? Why do we remember some events with such clarity, often the most trivial, while omitting others, sometimes crucial, leaving the rest in a disorganized generality?

Some years after the incident on the pier at Orly the third world war breaks out. After nuclear exchanges Paris is in ruins and radioactive fallout poisons the ground. Most of the population of the world has perished. In Paris, a handful of survivors take to the underground ruins in the tunnels and galleries beneath the Palais de Chaillot. One of them is the boy from Orly Airport – he has grown into a man (played by Davos Hanich). The conditions are grim: it has become an empire of deprivation and rats.

Strict rules are enforced by a small group of technocrats who have assumed control. Many of the ordinary survivors feel like prisoners. A crude scientific project is under way, a desperate attempt to contact the world of the future, seeking help. Most of the experiments fail: disappointment and madness almost invariably follow. The tunnels are haunted by the wasted men and women who have already been trialled in the risky project. Their faces are thin and gaunt, their eye sockets dark.

One day the experimenters come for Hanich, and although he fears the head of the team the man turns out to be reasonable in manner. He explains the project to Hanich in calm but daunting words. The human race is doomed, he says. The only hope for mankind lies in Time: the past or the future. Hanich has been selected because of the strength of his obsessive memory of the past: the shocking and violent incident at Orly Airport, the unforgettable beauty of the young woman.

The efforts to make Hanich travel in time begin. After many painful, terrifying and unsuccessful attempts he begins to see glimpses of a remembered pre-war world: a field where horses are grazing, a dozing cat, a sunlit bedroom, pigeons flapping away in a town square. Finally he sees the pier at Orly. He visits it again and again. One day he sees a woman on the pier he thinks might be Chatelain, but he passes her by. Later she smiles at him from inside a car.

Certain now that he recognizes her, Hanich makes repeated contacts with her, his confidence growing with each encounter. They live in a continuing present, having neither past nor future, lacking memories of each other, free of plans. She says she thinks of him as a ghost, who comes and goes. They are in pre-WW3 Paris. He knows the terrible truth about her, that she is certain to die in the nuclear holocaust ahead, but cannot tell her. They conduct an innocent love affair, meeting in sun-filled parks, in crowded streets, among the cases of the Natural History Museum.

One day she sleeps while Hanich watches over her. As she stirs, her eyelids move open lightly. It is an intense and poignant moment, the only use of a motion camera at any point in the film. Those few seconds are full of understated, undeclared meaning. She properly sees Hanich at last.

He becomes embedded in her consciousness, in her sense of the present time. Now he is less of a ghost, he may stay longer with her. Love is growing between them.

Hanich does not know, Chatelain cannot know, that the experiment is about to change. His ventures into the past were only the first stage to establish his suitability for the main experiment. The second stage now follows: he must travel to the future to negotiate with the people there. They too have mastered time travel. He is charged with bringing back from them some lesson or device which will help mankind survive the present crisis. He penetrates their society, and because they are waiting for him he succeeds.

Hanich's reward is that he is told he has been accepted as a member of that future society and may stay there permanently in safety. He has an alternative request, though. Against the wishes of the technocrats he asks to be returned to the time of his childhood, to the pier at Orly Airport, where he knows the young woman will be waiting for him.

His destiny on the pier at Orly is to become a fragment

of tragic embedded memory, for the woman who waits for him and for the child who observes him. The circle is closed.

La Jetée is a rare example of high cinema meeting serious speculative fiction. The images from this short but sublime film seep inextricably into the memory. It is impossible to see the film and not be moved.

Neither of the two actors, Hanich and Chatelain, have appeared in any other film since their memorable work in *La Jetée*. Their faces are forever fresh, their frozen gestures and gentle affection becoming visual metaphors for the fleeting joy and ultimate tragedy of a passing love. A third world war remains a constant threat in this real world of ours. Orly Airport remains. Passenger jets fly to distant places, airport terminals are packed with strangers. All this will somehow preserve *La Jetée*'s purity, leaving it ageless, immutable, unfading.

[Film retrospective feature, The *Guardian*, July 17th, 1967]

IO

Justin was approaching his twenty-fifth birthday, and had been sharing flats with friends, or living alone, or for a few weeks the previous year had been in a small flat with Kathy. That relationship had gone wrong. Since then, and for now, he was living alone. His present girlfriend was called Penelope, but she obviously did not want to spend so much time in cinemas, and he was growing interested in a young Spanish woman called Isabella, who worked for his agent. His relationship with Mort and Nicky had become distant. Not because of any disagreement or anything like it, but he and they all had busy lives and they were in different parts of the London area. He had returned to live in Fulham while his parents still lived in the big house in Chigwell, the one they had bought at the time the family moved south. It was relatively easy to get out to the Essex suburbs but in practice his casual or regular visits to see them were increasingly rare.

His career as a freelance film reviewer and commentator was quickly developing, and absorbed most of his time and nearly all his interest. He dutifully phoned home every couple of weeks or so – sometimes they called him.

His sister Amanda was also away from what they both still thought of as home. She was in a long-term relationship with a guy called Phil. Their apartment was in Walthamstow in north-east London. She and Justin hardly ever saw each other, but they also spoke on the phone occasionally.

The four of them were still a family, still like-minded in certain ways, but they were all adults and they lived apart.

The only time the family came together was for a couple of days each Christmas, and one other occasion two years before on his parents' wedding anniversary, but Justin felt restless whenever he was away from his usual work and the routine he had established around the advance press screenings. His wish to leave always became obvious, at least to Nicky. Afterwards, when he was back in his flat, he invariably felt guilty and inconsiderate.

One day, towards the end of the year, Nicky phoned him with the news that his father was being offered early retirement from his job. He would be receiving a large sum of money in compensation. She said he wanted to treat the family to a holiday abroad. It took a few seconds for that to sink in.

'What – all of us together? Amanda and me included?'

'Of course.'

'Not of course, Ma. I've a lot on.'

'You always say that – couldn't you, just once, give us some of your time? It would mean everything to Mort and me.'

'Well, when would it be?'

'We're thinking of April or May. I've always wanted to go to Paris, and that's the best time of year.'

'Paris?'

Justin started to think of grumbling excuses: that was the period when there was usually a rush of new cinema releases, where would they stay?, how much would it cost?, and so on. He aired none of them because he always tried to please Nicky, and he hadn't been prepared for the suggestion. Then he thought of Paris, the way the nouvelle vague movies inhabited the city in intriguing and memorable ways, considered the chance to see some films in French and in Parisian cinemas, perhaps to visit the Palais de Chaillot. Perhaps to explore Orly Airport.

Mort came on the line and said they could take the car over to France, stay in Paris for several days, then afterwards drive south, or into Switzerland, or up to the Brittany coast. He said there was now a way of flying across the English Channel, taking the car.

'I don't want to fly,' Justin said, without thinking about it. 'Couldn't we use the cross-channel ships like everyone else? I don't like flying.'

'You've been up before.'

'That was the joyride on the beach. Years ago. It doesn't count. Anyway, the plane crashed afterwards.'

'Is that the main reason?'

'No.' But he couldn't think of another reason straight away. He added, 'I don't like being in big airports.'

'You'll be all right, then,' Mort said. 'The company that runs the flights operates from small airfields at both ends of the journey.'

At this stage in his life flying was for Justin a complex subject, full of negative associations. He did not normally dwell on it. He had no need to fly anywhere because all his work was in London. He never had to go abroad, and in fact did not have a passport. Flying was either too expensive or, if affordable, it involved cut-price chartered package flights to the sort of mass-appeal holiday destinations he did not want to go to.

He still had memories of the one aircraft he had flown in. What had happened to the Fox Moth not long afterwards had induced contradictory feelings in him. One was relief that it had not crashed while he was on board, but the other, much stronger, was his recollection of being confined in the tiny cabin, the uncomfortable seats, the restricted view, the noise and shaking and vibration, the doors which could only be opened from the outside. The thought of being trapped inside as it plunged into the sea had featured in several dreams since – not nightmares as such, but vivid and all too personal dreams. Then later, his close-up look at the shattered wreckage of the crashed Viscount near his old school had at the time been more interesting than traumatizing, but it nonetheless left a lasting impression.

'I don't have a passport, Pa.'

'You've several weeks to send off and get one,' said Mort.

'I know.'

Something else. By April or May he would be twenty-six. He had been living independently, and it felt decidedly weird to go back and take a holiday with his parents and sister. He wondered if Nicky and Mort had already spoken to Amanda, and what she thought about it. Perhaps she would want to bring Phil along with her? If so, what about his own possible new girlfriend, Isabella? Or if it didn't work out with her, someone else? Was there room in the car for six people?

Nothing was decided during that phone call, but the following week he did send in a postal application for a passport. He also spoke to Amanda. She felt, as he did, that a family vacation was low on the list of things she wanted to do, but she told Justin she had been talking recently to Nicky. She and Mort were both slightly uncomfortable with the idea of a trip with their parents now they were in their twenties, but something Nicky said had given Amanda an insight.

'I think Pa might be worried about his health,' she said. 'I know his asthma has been getting worse, and there have been some X-rays. I thought it was odd the firm would give him early retirement, and that might be connected.'

'OK,' said Justin, now doubly ill at ease with the whole idea.

But in the end the plans went ahead, and towards the end of May he travelled across London to his parents' house. Mort and Nicky were to cover all expenses of the trip. They would travel and stay in the same hotels together, but he and Amanda would be free to go off on their own. He slept that night on the bed in the spare room, the one that had been his own bedroom before he moved out to go to university. It had been redecorated and refurnished, but even so.

The next day the four of them drove in Mort's car to Southend on Sea, where there was a small airfield, a former RAF station. What Mort had said was true: there was only one hardened runway, and the terminal building, such as it was, looked from the outside like an old RAF hangar and barracks. The airfield had been converted to civil use after the end of the second world war. A small number of short-haul passenger flights operated out of Southend, mainly serving airports in France and northern Europe. One of these operators was called British United Air Ferries, flying

82

twin-engined Bristol 170 Superfreighter aircraft to fields in the Channel Islands and France.

Justin had previously read up on the background of both the airline and the aircraft, and although BUAF had a good safety record the aircraft type had been involved in numerous accidents. Developed during the war to carry troops and materiel it was an antiquated design, remodelled in recent years for use as a car ferry by widening its fuselage and putting access doors in the bulbous nose.

Justin kept his misgivings to himself. He sat with Amanda in their habitual childhood places in the back seat of the car, not saying much. The glimpse they had of the cumbersome looking aircraft they were about to fly in was less than reassuring. Justin tried to close his mind to it.

Mort parked the car in the area designated for BUAF passengers, leaving their luggage in the car. They walked into the terminal building. Prepared to be critical of it from its outward appearance, Justin was mildly impressed by the way in which the shabby old building had been modernized inside. The BUAF operation was smartly run, with obvious efforts to ensure a smooth transit to the aircraft. The small café served complimentary home-made snacks, and there was adequate space in which to sit around in comfort and wait for the flight.

They watched through one of the large windows as the ground crew drove their car up the front-loading ramp into the plane's cargo bay. Three other cars went in too. When Justin and the other passengers walked out to board, the flight crew greeted them as they reached the aircraft. Justin, still an inveterate note-taker, automatically memorized the registration, G-AMWA, and when he could he jotted it down.

The air of careful modernity changed abruptly as soon as they were on board. The passenger cabin took Justin back to his memories of the flight on the beach at Southport, a decade and a half earlier. The seats were made of looped canvas buckets, sagging like deckchairs after years of use, and were crammed close against each other. The seat belts were non-adjustable, and lay loosely across their laps. There were several small windows. That was about it as far as passenger comfort was concerned. There was an inescapable impression of having climbed into a WW2-era military transport.

It was a short flight, less than an hour from Southend to Calais. It felt longer than that: the take-off from Southend seemed to require the whole length of the runway, the aircraft rolling forward with painful and bumpy sloth along the concrete before at last lifting away at a shallow angle, engines roaring, then circling around slowly until it was over the sea. The noise of the engines inside the passenger compartment was shattering, and the entire craft shook and vibrated. Where Justin was sitting he could look up through one of the windows towards the starboard engine, a chunky piston motor, the casing and nacelle looking battered and streaked with oil.

As they lost altitude to land at Calais Justin had a view of the ground on Cap Gris Nez, and he stared down at it with a feeling that once again he had been pushed back in time. The whole area was pockmarked with craters, presumably left over from bombing or shelling operations during the war. This was the spring of 1970 – the second world war had been over for a quarter of a century. Why was the land still churned up by the military activities of so long before? He

84

barely had time to think about this: the aircraft was close to the ground, and soon, after a bone-jarring bump against the runway, it landed.

Relieved to be back on the ground he said none of this to his parents and sister as they disembarked, went along with them quietly. Not long afterwards they were back in the car, driving south towards Paris. He stared out at the French farmland, which looked reassuringly normal in the sunlight. The nerve-racking flight was behind them and soon forgotten.

They stayed in a Paris hotel for five days, which turned out to be not long enough for Justin, who had prepared in advance a checklist of twelve new films he wanted to see, mostly French or American. He managed to catch eight of them before they left the city.

On one day he travelled out of the city to Orly Airport.

He discovered that the viewing platform photographed by Chris Marker for *La Jetée* was now closed to the public, and that since the film had been made a decade earlier part of the terminal building had been enlarged. It was difficult to work out where the film might have been shot. No jets overflew the airport while he was there. The still and alienating sense of isolation depicted by Marker was replaced by modern bustle. The only engines he could hear were from the apron, on the far side of the building he did not want to enter. He went back to the centre of Paris, disappointed.

When they left Paris Amanda stayed behind, having run into an old schoolfriend who was now living there. Mort drove Justin and Nicky across northern France, ending up in St-Malo, a quiet port and seaside town on the north coast of Brittany. It was an attractive place but Justin felt he was wasting his time there. The cinemas in the town were both good, though, and he was able to catch up with two of the films he had missed in Paris, and another, a regional Breton broad comedy, which was by a French director he had never heard of and featured amateur actors. They returned eventually to Calais, where they joined up with Amanda again. The next day they flew home to Southend: the plane was the same one, G-AMWA.

As the plane climbed laboriously out of Calais Airport towards the sea Justin stared down at the ground, wanting another glimpse of the scars of war. Mysteriously, perhaps because of the angle of the sun, there was now almost no trace of the craters he had seen before. One or two large ones remained, but they were indistinct and might have been natural features. The mass of smaller ones were no longer visible.

Two weeks after they returned to England, Bristol Superfreighter G-AMWA was taking off from the airport at Le Touquet Paris-Plage, heading for Southend. It veered off the runway as it was accelerating before take-off, ran chaotically across ground made soft by recent rain, tore off half its undercarriage and crashed at speed into an adjacent field. It was carrying three cars, fifteen passengers and a crew of three.

All the passengers survived, although some were trapped in the wreckage when the plane caught fire. They were quickly rescued, but suffered cuts and burns. All three crew survived. The cars in the cargo bay were destroyed. The plane was written off. The enquiry later established that one of the tyres on the plane's main wheels had suffered catastrophic deflation, causing the sudden swerve away from the runway.

Justin found his old notebook and recorded the details of the incident. He had now flown twice, and both aircraft had subsequently crashed.

Justin was not superstitious. He was used to working with data and records and written evidence. In his own quiet way he was a rationalist. When he told friends and acquaintances what happened to aircraft after he flew in them, he made light of it. One friend from university said that bad luck always comes in threes: on the contrary, Justin said, his luck if that was the word for it was good.

His interest in maintaining the aircraft notebook was declining, but from time to time he would add a note here and there if something unusual occurred: a big crash, a hi-jacking, a discovery of a plane's design fault.

Not long after his flights to and from Calais, Justin was commissioned by a weekly magazine to interview and write a profile of the German director Werner Herzog. This would involve a trip to the city of Frankfurt – his first flight on a passenger jet. He ordered the Lufthansa tickets without a qualm, and on the day of the flight he boarded the aircraft feeling more interested than nervous. Nothing happened, nothing went wrong, he arrived safely. The next day he flew back to London, already starting to experience the two real but commonplace difficulties of flying: the amount of time having to wait around beforehand, and the general discomfort and tedium of flying as a passenger, even on a short flight.

After the journey to Frankfurt Justin was involved in an increasing number of long flights abroad, and soon thought little of it. But he never grew used to the routines of passing through a terminal.

II

On the train down from London to Eastbourne Justin read the file of newspaper clippings that he had picked up the previous week. He had glanced briefly at them then, long enough to learn what the press had said about Teddy Smythe, the actor he was going to interview. He knew her name, of course, and had seen her in several films, but until this he had not taken a special interest in her or her work.

The file was lying around his flat all weekend and he kept putting off taking the time to brief himself properly. There was a mini-festival of recent German films on in London over the weekend, where he had agreed to take part in a Q&A, and as he was unfamiliar with two of the films being shown he had had to spend the best part of the weekend preparing.

Now it was early Monday morning and the after-effects of the strenuous weekend lay on him. The train arrived in Victoria filled with commuters and he boarded it after they dispersed. It still had an airless, lived-in feel. He sat mutely for the first few minutes of the journey south towards the coast, slowly coming to a state of normality. He had already written and published other celebrity interviews, but it was not his usual sort of work. This one was a chance to place an article in a major Sunday newspaper, which might lead to other work in future. Someone called Rosalind Day had phoned him the week before.

'Would you be available to write a profile early next week?' she said. 'It's a woman actor who appears in the new Spencer Horvath film. That opens next Thursday, so the magazine would like to print it in the Sunday edition.'

'Magazine?' Justin had said. 'Which one?'

'The colour supplement.'

'So you'd need it by when?'

'Wednesday at the latest. Is that possible?' She mentioned a fee, substantially larger than anything he would normally be paid for a review. For a freelance it was of course instantly possible. 'Bring it in to the *Observer* office before midday. Ros Day, in the Media & Arts section.'

'OK,' Justin said.

'The name of the actor is Teddy Smythe. She was in a lot of British pictures, and was a regular in *Coastal* on television. They might revive that soon.'

'Oh yes. I know of her.'

'She lives in Seaford, near Eastbourne. Her address will be in the file. I'm told there's a train from Victoria every half-hour. She doesn't normally like being interviewed, so go gently. But the Horvath people made an interview part of their contract with her. The magazine wants to run it as an exclusive.'

Teddy Smythe was a well-established British character actor who had been active in films made during the 1950s and 1960s, but she had been away from the screen for some time.

Justin had seen a preview of the new film from the American A-list director Spencer Horvath, *The Silent Genius*. It was big box office in the USA and was likely to top the charts in the UK too. Justin liked the film and had written a review of it, scheduled to appear in a film magazine in the next couple of weeks. But he did not remember Teddy Smythe among the personnel. There was a huge cast of named characters – presumably she was in a small or minor role which had scrolled past without him noticing.

He still had the distributors' hand-out from the preview. When he looked more closely at the production notes he saw a line which before he had skipped over: 'The role of Lois is memorably performed by the British actor Teddy Smythe.' He did not remember any character called Lois in the film.

Justin read the clippings file, noting down possible subjects for questions.

He was already broadly familiar with Teddy Smythe's work. During her most active years she had become a familiar but largely unsung stalwart of British cinema. One of the newspaper articles carried an old photograph of her, and Justin at once recognized her. She was a character actor, the sort whose face most people in the audiences would usually remember straight away from other films, without being able to put a name to her. She had appeared in around fifty films throughout her career, almost always in small parts: a headmistress, a cook, a driver, a policewoman, a spymaster, a hospital matron. She reliably played both broad comedy and drama, and had appeared in two of Hammer Films' horror movies. She also worked on television and had taken several roles on the West End stage. She suffered a mild stroke in 1969, following which she went into retirement.

Earlier this year, in 1977, she had made an unexpected appearance in *The Silent Genius*. Spencer Horvath had lured her out of retirement in some way that Justin hoped to discover while interviewing her. A new Horvath film was always something of an event. As she was the only British actor in the otherwise all-American cast, she was suddenly of interest to British audiences.

Her modest career meant that her background was only sketchily known outside the film world, and from the evidence of several of the cuttings past writers and journalists had made guesses about it. She was born Theodora Smythe, on a date unknown but possibly in 1910 or thereabouts. Nothing was known about her parents, or if she had siblings. She was born in the small market town of Leighton Buzzard, in Bedfordshire. Where she went to school was unknown, but it was presumably in the locality. Nowhere was there any mention of her having been to drama school. Spouse and children? No mention.

She started acting professionally relatively late in life, having previously worked in some other job that was unrelated to cinema. The cuttings file gave no idea of what this work might have been. In this sense she appeared from nowhere. Her first credited film role was in *Chalkdust and Cheese*, a farcical comedy for Ealing Films, in 1951.

Over the years that followed she built a professional reputation amongst other cast members and technical crews. She was mentioned as a popular and amusing colleague in published memoirs by several eminent actors: Michael Redgrave, John Gielgud, Ralph Richardson and so on. The file Rosalind Day had assembled included photocopies of extracts from their autobiographies.

Teddy Smythe now lived alone in Seaford, a small town close to Eastbourne on the south coast. When Ros Day arranged the interview with her, Teddy Smythe had apparently warned that she was a cat lover and had several of them in her house – whoever the magazine sent, she said, should therefore meet her in a restaurant or a pub if they were allergic. That was not a problem to Justin. Wherever possible he preferred to meet the subjects of celebrity profiles where they lived or worked. Anyway, he liked cats.

After a change of trains in Eastbourne, Justin walked from Seaford station to Teddy's house. It was in a narrow street two roads back from the sea front, a tiny detached villa, white-painted with the woodwork picked out in dark red. The small garden had a strip of lawn that was overgrown, and one huge bed of flowers that needed strenuous weeding and tidying up.

Teddy Smythe answered the front door to him, and the instant Justin saw her he experienced the uncanny sense of recognition that strikes when you meet someone from film or TV you have not met in person. It made him smile spontaneously.

She was obviously now older than the photos that were in the clippings file, but she looked much younger than he had been anticipating. He had lazily imagined she would have become a retired old lady, but Teddy was vigorous in her movements, and her voice was clear. She had a good head of grey hair, slightly untamed, and remarkable blue eyes. Her smile was slightly aslant, a downturned corner, but he assumed this was a result of the stroke a few years earlier.

He followed her into the house. Inside there was a smell of cats, but not strong and not unpleasant. A tortoiseshell ran into the hallway as he walked in, and scampered out of sight towards the back of the house. Teddy led him into a compact but comfortable living room: there was a television, a video player and a stack of tapes with handwritten labels, a table partly covered by magazines, two small sofas facing each other across the fireplace, three shelves of books. More books were piled up on the floor. A large tabby cat was sprawled on one of the sofas – he or she did not stir the whole time Justin was there.

Ornaments cluttered a glass-fronted corner cupboard. A silver goblet, long in need of polishing, was on the top of the cabinet. There were several small paintings on the walls, and some framed black-and-white photographs.

Justin put down his bag. While Teddy was out of the room preparing a cup of coffee for him and a pot of tea for herself he looked closely at the photos.

One was obviously of herself, a few years younger, at some kind of awards ceremony. She was on a stage. The actor Richard Attenborough was next to her with his arm lightly around her shoulders. He was in a dinner jacket and she was in an evening gown. She was holding a silver goblet, the one now displayed on the cabinet. It was glittering in the beam of spotlights. She wore a broad and unforced smile. Attenborough's free arm was waving to an unseen audience. There was a lectern off to one side, some frilled curtains behind and a large plaster replica of the goblet coated in shiny gold paint.

Justin squinted up at the engraving on the actual goblet:

The other framed photo was a studio portrait of a young, round-faced and good-looking man, hair greased back flatly across his head. It was an old photo, rather showing its age. It looked like a publicity shot of a Hollywood matinée idol from a former era, but Justin did not recognize him. Some retouching appeared to have been carried out, because his features were seamless, unlined, almost waxy. An autograph and what looked like a dedication, indecipherable and fading, was scrawled diagonally across the bottom right-hand corner. The words gave no clue as to who was in the photo.

Justin was immediately intrigued. He loved film memorabilia. He wanted to look more closely but then Teddy returned to the room.

'May I ask who this is, Ms Smythe? Was it someone you knew? Or might have worked with?'

She put down the tray and moved to sit on the sofa with the tabby cat, lowering herself gently beside it. The cat did not react.

'Please – call me Teddy. Everyone does. That's an old photo. Isn't he lovely?'

'Is he someone I should recognize? An actor?'

'I don't know. I've never found out who it is. Someone sent it to me, saying he was a sort of symbol of the old Hollywood. Maybe you or someone you work with could find out who he was. You're a film expert, aren't you?'

'Not exactly.'

Her expression briefly revealed that this questioning had gone on long enough.

'The time when actors had to pose for photos like that is long in the past,' she said. 'All the big studios did it back then. Now, here's your coffee.'

She put the cup with his coffee on the end of the low table next to the other sofa. Justin noticed the slant of her mouth had deepened. It made her look irritated. He decided to retreat from the subject, and sat down opposite her.

'I'm pleased to meet you,' he said in a formal way. 'I've always admired your work and I've seen several of your films. When I heard Rosalind Day had obtained this interview for the *Observer*, I volunteered for it immediately.' The white lies slipped out glibly.

'I liked Ros.'

'I haven't actually met her. We spoke on the phone.'

'So – you work in the film business?'

'Not in the same way as you. I'm just a writer, a journalist. A film reviewer.' He reached into his bag and pulled out his tape deck. He set the microphone on the table between them, and put on his headphones. 'I need to check a voice level.'

When the tape was running, but before he could put a question to her, she said, 'You surely haven't seen all the films I was in? Most of those old ones have disappeared. I don't think they were much good.'

'I don't agree. All films are interesting in some way. I've seen a few, but I know of the rest. You're mentioned in most reference books on British films.' He nodded back to the silver goblet on the cabinet behind him. 'And the award. The Film Writers' Association?'

She looked surprised that he would know this. 'That was a film I made about ten years ago. Kenny More was the star of that, one of his comedies. But I didn't get to know him, not during the filming. I was only in a support role. I saw him at the wrap party, but I didn't have a chance to speak to him.'

'And that photo up there. Do you know Richard Attenborough?'

'Dickie? Everyone in the business knows Dickie, but I couldn't claim him as a friend. I was in two of his early films, before he was a big star.'

'Those were the war films, I think?'

'He was a sailor in one of them. I can't remember the other too well. I was doing a lot of film work at the time. I played a Wren.'

'Petty Officer Sarah Wilson, I think she was called.'

Teddy Smythe nodded her approval. 'You've done your homework, Mr Farmer. I didn't share any scenes with Dickie, but in a couple of them I could be seen in the background.'

'Sarah Wilson was the signals officer whose son was killed?'

'Maybe. Yes, you're right.'

Justin had read through his own data files the previous evening. 'And I think the other film with Mr Attenborough was set on an RAF station during the second world war. A bomber squadron. He played a Flight Officer.'

'I think so. You've been looking things up, haven't you? I always admire people who do that. Some of it's a bit of a blur to me now. You are given these jobs and you have to turn up at the studio day after day, but actors at my level are mostly paid to sit around and wait. Making a film is not as exciting as most people seem to think. It's a job. And if you are in a supporting part, the sort of role I was usually given, you almost never meet the leading actors unless you have a scene with them.'

She went on to talk about some of the other films she had made.

In the last two or three years Justin had profiled or interviewed a few film actors, some of them famous, some of them, like Teddy, working character actors. At first he had been surprised how many of them liked to chat or gossip about their work before getting down to the interview proper, even if there was an agency PR person sitting restlessly by, anxious to move the interview on so that the next one could begin. There was sometimes another journalist waiting outside. Justin was glad today to be spared that time pressure.

He had discovered that letting his subjects reminisce informally for a few minutes was an easy way of breaking the ice. He was still kicking himself for having pressed Teddy about the photo on the wall – not the best way to start. Was it something she was sensitive about? He wondered again who the young man was. The journalist in him remained intrigued. But she seemed pleasant, was now opening up. He was happy just to let it run.

She was interrupted by a Siamese cat walking into the room. It glared at Justin, then went to sit on Teddy's lap. The sleeping tabby did not respond.

Rosalind's brief to Justin was principally to ask Teddy Smythe about working on Horvath's new film, but he wanted to get as full a picture of her past as possible, approach it in his own way. He took advantage of the pause.

'I'm interested in the work you've done with Spencer Horvath, but before we get on to that the magazine suggested I might ask you about *Coastal*. Just a couple of questions.'

Her mouth went more aslant again. 'That old thing. No one's interested in that any more.'

'The *Observer* has been told that BBC-TV are thinking of reviving it.'

'They'll have to revive it without me. Wild horses, etc.'

'But Mr Horvath persuaded you out of retirement.'

'Spencer Horvath is Spencer Horvath. An afternoon soap on the BBC is not. Now, please excuse me for a moment.'

She stood up, steadied herself with a hand against the mantelpiece, then squeezed past him and went out of the room. He put the recorder on pause. He heard her walking down the hall and then climbing the stairs slowly, perhaps one step at a time. Justin sat and waited, listening to her footsteps overhead.

Another faux pas? Ros Day had in fact only mentioned *Coastal* in passing. That wasn't what the magazine was interested in. He should have skipped it.

The tabby slumbered on, while the Siamese, displaced when Teddy stood up, was beneath the table, washing energetically. Looking around the room he glanced once more at the photograph of the matinée idol. The mystery of who it was again snagged at him, and on an impulse, while Teddy was still out of the room, he decided to make a copy of it.

He took his compact camera from his bag, attached the shoe of the electronic flash to the mount, and waited while the battery warmed up the gadget. As soon as the guide light went green he snatched a close shot of the photo. Then, because the picture was framed behind glass, he took a second shot from a different angle in case of reflected flash. His camera and flash unit were back in his bag before Teddy returned.

She came in with a plate of biscuits and a bottle of red wine already opened.

'Peace offering,' she said, putting the bottle down on the table and placing two clean glasses beside it. 'I normally steer clear of talking about *Coastal*, but since you've mentioned it – a lot of people do remember it fondly. I've never known why. Finish your coffee first, if you wish.'

'Thank you. You say you wouldn't go back to *Coastal*?'

'Wouldn't and couldn't,' she said, filling both glasses. 'I'm too old for it now. And why won't they let it go? It was never any good. The scripts were repetitive and it was almost impossible to put life into the characters. I spent the last six months trying to persuade them to get rid of Mrs Galbraith. Did you know that if they kill off a character in a soap they sometimes pay the actor a bonus? I'd have accepted that. It would have made up for a lot.'

Teddy had played Mrs Galbraith for more than two years. She was the matriarchal housekeeper at a large seaside hotel, dealing with the irrational demands of guests and trying to keep the younger hotel staff members reined in. It sounded promising, but it was one of those soap operas where the occasional spoofs of it on comedy shows para-doxically made it look more interesting than it was. No one seemed to miss it when it was taken off the air, and Teddy had returned to working in cinema. She made two more films, both comedies, before the stroke caused a long hia-tus in her career. She had faded from public view until the Horvath job.

'So, no more Majestic Hotel?' Justin said.

'Frankly, I'd rather you didn't even mention it.'

'I wish I hadn't. Let's move on. Probably your most famous

role was in 1956,' he said. 'You played Madame Charpentier in an adaptation—'

'Yes, another job I did back then. The French book, the one that got me into so much trouble.' This time she did not look irritated.

'Not trouble, surely?' Justin said. 'It was a challenging role, probably the best you ever did. Can you tell me how you felt about it when it was made, and what you think of it now?'

The story of Madame Charpentier was a true one, an actual incident in the nineteenth century in rural France. It concerned a particularly grisly triple murder. The crimes had been the basis for a novel written in the 1930s, which was widely condemned by French clerics as a salacious and lurid work. Of course that guaranteed *Mort en Auvergne* immediate status as a bestseller in France, followed by a translation published in Britain and the USA. The author, Jean-Pierre Jovin, died during the second world war, and all his books, including *Death in the Auvergne*, fell out of print. It had been reissued after the end of the war, and that led to a small production company in London acquiring the rights for a low-budget film version. The script was adapted by an established British screenwriter, and the film, directed by Hugo Marshal Turnbull, was shot at Shepperton Studios near London.

The story was set in France and the characters had French names, but the cast was entirely British and the dialogue was mostly in English, sometimes with intermittent French-sounding accents and occasional Gallic exclamations.

The story was of three brothers, two of whom are farm workers while the youngest is training as a wheelwright. Their lives are monotonous. They talk about vague plans to move away from the poverty of the countryside and seek their fortune elsewhere. They are rivals over girlfriends, they drink too much wine and they sometimes commit minor crimes. One of the brothers is a talented singer who talks about moving to Paris, the oldest boy is a bully, and the young wheelwright is a dreamer who secretly reads books and keeps a diary. They go regularly to church, but mainly because it gives them an excuse afterwards to chase around with the local girls. They mock the village priest, Father Francis.

Throughout most of the film their mother, Madame Charpentier, played by Teddy, is a distant and shadowy figure, always there but not there. She has no husband – he disappeared before the story begins and is not mentioned. Perhaps she was never married – the young men know nothing about their father, not even his name. She is a figure of darkness, ignored by her sons and only barely seen or glimpsed by the film's audience. She prepares simple meals, cleans the house, weaves at a loom, goes to market once a week, works in the farmyard, rarely speaks. She often has her back to the camera, blending into the dark and ill-defined background. Sometimes she is seen quietly weeping, for no apparent reason.

In the final reel Madame Charpentier has an unexpected meeting with Father Francis. He corners her by the wall of the church. She is clearly guilty of something in her past, and the priest makes use of it to manipulate her. Father Francis warns her of divine retribution. She escapes him and wanders in distress through the countryside. The sun is setting. Suddenly, and for the first time, the bright low angle of the sun allows the audience to see her face clearly and in close-up. She is exposed, revealed. It is a genuine shock: her features are rigid with anger. Her eyes seem to glitter. Her hair is blown wild by the wind. There are traces of scar tissue on her cheeks. She has become haunted, possessed. She reaches home and marches inside. Her sons are there. Without warning she attacks them with an axe, violently and unrelentingly. Soon all three young men are dead, or in the process of dying. Her twisted face reveals no regret. She is spattered with blood. The film ends when she walks through the night to Father Francis's house, goes inside and closes the door.

Death in the Auvergne was a minor film made quickly, intended as a support feature. The director, Hugo Turnbull, was not well known to the public. The film ran for just over an hour and lacked a real plot. Because most of it had been shot in the studio, including many of the country scenes, it had an implausible and artificial look. But in the context of a British film made in the conservative mid-1950s it was a shocking and unusually savage film. What everyone remembered was the disturbing moment when the camera moved in for a close look, a frighteningly close look, at Madame Charpentier's mad and distorted face, revealed and shadowed by the setting sun.

Film fans loved the scene, critics wrote about it, major directors cited it as influential, photographers tried to emulate it, film theorists analysed it. It was pure classic cinema. Even today, few people knew or recognized the name of the woman who portrayed Madame Charpentier, and when told who it was most ordinary filmgoers had never heard of her.

Teddy Smythe returned to her unsung but regular work as a supporting character actor.

Justin said, 'Before the film came out had you any idea what sort of reaction there was going to be?'

'No one gave it a thought. I certainly didn't. I went on

to make two other films immediately afterwards. *Auvergne* wasn't released for about a year.'

'But playing an axe murderer must have been a different kind of role for you.'

Teddy smiled. 'That's the life of a jobbing actor. You take the work that comes along. While we were shooting it the scene didn't seem in any way exceptional. When you're actually involved, when you're on the set with all the equipment and lights and the technical crew, you don't have much idea of what it's going to look like on the screen. There's a lot of waiting around. Everything is shot in short sequences, sometimes a day or two apart, often even in reverse order. Most people never seem to realize this. And when the film is edited, and sound effects and music are added, everything looks bigger, more exaggerated. But it's all make-believe.'

'Did you see the rushes?'

'I never stayed around for the dailies. Some actors do, but many of them often don't. I was one of them.' She leant towards him and briefly held the wine bottle up against the light from the window. 'How is your glass? I have more.'

'Excellent, thank you.' Justin held his glass towards her. 'This leads me to ask you about working with Spencer Horvath. That's impressive. Did Mr Horvath contact you himself about the role in his new film?'

'No. The job came about in the usual way – my agent called me and said a casting director had asked to see me. The only unusual thing about it was that it took them some time to discover who my agent was. I've been retired a long time. Even the agent didn't have my current phone number.'

'I wondered if Horvath might have chosen you himself.'

'Not that I was aware of.'

'I'll tell you what I'm thinking. About three years ago he gave an interview to *Rolling Stone*, and in that he revealed that he was an admirer of low-budget British films of the 1950s. He said there was no equivalent in the USA. He mentioned a few films by title, and *Death in the Auvergne* was one of them. He said he particularly liked the many ingenious thrillers that were made in Britain then, and that he learned a lot about film from all of them.'

Teddy said nothing, but smiled again. She was leaning over the Siamese cat, who was back on her lap, purring. She was fondling his head and ears.

The way she was petting the cat reminded Justin of a scene in Horvath's new film. He should have connected before. Suddenly, it was obvious. The ironically named silent genius of the title is a well-meaning academic who discovers that he can kill merely by staring. It was a role tailor-made for the actor, a Hollywood personality at the top of his form. The story is about the man's efforts to free himself of what he sees as a curse. In one scene he is being chased and takes refuge in the house of a colleague, an elderly woman who in earlier scenes has always been glimpsed in the background, invariably wearing dark glasses. She is leaning over a plate of food, just as at that moment Teddy was leaning over her purring cat. In the scene she looks up at him as he bursts into the room, removes her dark glasses and their gaze meets. She is unmasked, exposed. The camera zooms in on her face, a shock reveal. He has briefly met his match: he recoils, collapses, manages to crawl away. The story goes on.

Of course, that was Lois, that was Teddy Smythe.

'So when you were working with him, did Horvath say anything about *Auvergne*?'

'You see what I mean? You've obviously done your research, Mr Farmer. Did Spencer Horvath say anything to me? Oh – just a little. Not much.'

'Go on?'

'He had an office at the back of the studio, and on the second day he called me in before we started work that morning. He said he was a great admirer of my career, and was proud to be working with me – but, you know, people in the movie business say that all the time. I'm sure he meant it, though. He was a nice man and I liked him, although a lot of people in the industry think he's weird. He is pretty eccentric. But I think his new film is very good, and I'm pleased to be in it.'

'He went out of his way to say that? Is that all? Did he ask you about any of the films you had made in the past?'

'Well, not really.'

'What about *Auvergne*?'

'Yes, but I'll tell you what he actually said. Everything. He complimented me on how well I was looking, and more or less said I shouldn't have retired, I should have returned to work as soon as I was back on my feet. He asked if I felt better now, and I said I did. In fact, the stroke left me more or less as I had always been. Then he said, "I spend every day of my waking life learning about film. I am obsessed with film, a committed student of cinema, an intensive researcher. Your scene in *Auvergne* haunted me until I understood why. I know who you are, Teddy." So I replied with something complimentary about him. And then Spencer Horvath said, "No – I am who I am, and you are who you are. You know exactly what I mean. I'm proud as all hell you have agreed to work with me. I have dreamed of this for many years." And that was all.'

'How did you feel about that?'

'I was pleased and happy. He's one of the greatest directors now working.'

'Well, he did call you out of retirement. Anything else?'

'After that I only saw him while we were shooting.'

'He never explained what he meant?'

'No. Have you seen the film?'

'I saw a preview of it last week,' Justin said. 'There's one more thing I wanted to ask you. A lot of people have pointed out that you are the only British actor in the film. But part of the film was shot in the UK, in Dorset. You play an American, and the lines you speak were done in a really convincing American accent.'

'They sure were. Kinda goes with the territory. It's an American film about Americans. They shot those scenes here because they needed the location, that big house close to the sea. The accent was no problem – I can do accents. It's one of the things actors learn how to do.'

'So you don't think Mr Horvath wanted you in the film because of *Death in the Auvergne*?'

'Maybe he did, maybe he didn't. You'd have to ask him.' She had slipped back into her English voice, immediately sounding less confident of herself.

Justin glanced down at the tape counter. There were still several minutes left to fill, and the whole of the flip side of the cassette. He mentally reviewed the subjects he had wanted to ask her about.

'I think that's about all I need,' he said to her. 'Thank you.'

He switched off the recorder and leaned back in his seat. Teddy immediately picked up the wine and topped up their glasses. 'Do you have to get back to London, straight away?' she said. 'Or shall we kill this bottle together?'

Justin raised his glass.

He sat with her for another hour or so, sipping at the wine and chatting comfortably about old films, ones they liked and ones they didn't, her films and other people's.

She had plenty of gossip, mostly about some of the actors she had worked with. He always enjoyed listening to film people talking about each other. She said she had not kept up with other actors after retiring, and already some of those she befriended had passed on. None of this must go into the published interview, she said. Justin promised, but did keep his mind open. Teddy said that Rosalind Day had warned her the previous week that the editorial policy of the *Observer* magazine wouldn't let her have prior approval of the interview. She accepted that, but Justin promised Teddy that if she said anything now off the record he thought should go in he would call her before he submitted the text.

In particular, he was hoping that while she was in a more relaxed mood she might have something to say about the early days: what attracted her to the film world, how she actually made a start, what contacts she had, and so on. They quickly finished the bottle of wine. She said nothing about the old days, though.

He asked her a direct question about the job she was doing when she was younger, before she became an actor – she merely shook her head. That part of her background remained undescribed.

Soon he had finished and he walked to the train station. A couple of hours later he was back in his apartment in

London. The following day Justin transcribed the recording, and while he was doing this he remembered that a few years earlier he had purchased a book about the career of Hugo Marshal Turnbull. He had only skimmed through it at the time, and since then it had been on his shelf unread. Turnbull was not widely known outside the film world in the UK, but recognized by many in the business as a professional and workmanlike director, a safe pair of hands. *Death in the Auvergne* was one of several short films he made at the time. It occupied a whole chapter.

As soon as he was home Justin took the book from the shelf and gave it a proper reading. It was well written and engaging in tone. It helped him with a few factual details about the making of the film, and contained a detailed description of Teddy's role in it. He was able to work everything into an affectionate profile of her.

In his profile he not only reported the questions and answers, he tried to convey an impression of what she was like to meet, how she lived. He mentioned her tiny house, the treasured goblet, the peaceful cats. He wrote at length about the French-set thriller of the past, mentioning that Spencer Horvath had told her he recognized her and knew exactly who she was. He had obtained a brilliant performance from her.

Ros at the *Observer* accepted the article, and it appeared in the magazine supplement the following weekend, two days after *The Silent Genius* opened in London. The film was well reviewed – Teddy was mentioned approvingly several times.

Justin and Ros went out on a couple of dates together, but it didn't last.

★

It was only several weeks later that he finished the cassette of film in his camera, and another three weeks before he set aside an evening for darkroom work. When he saw the negatives he remembered the minor mystery of the studio portrait hanging on the wall of Teddy's living room. He made an enlargement of the better of the two snaps he had taken, and carried it around with him in his shoulder bag.

One day, visiting the British Film Institute's library, Justin thought he would try and see if he could identify the actor. After a lot of browsing and searching through old books and film magazines he found the picture in an old 'stars of the silent screen' book – in fact, it was identical to the photograph Teddy Smythe had on her wall.

The actor's name turned out to be Roy Tallis. It meant nothing to Justin, and a search of several reference books turned up no more about him than the fact that he had made several silent films in the 1920s. He transferred successfully to sound pictures, but made only two more films in 1931 and 1932. He died in 1933. One reference said it was of an unknown cause, but another said emphatically that it was suicide following years of alcohol abuse.

Those early years of cinema were a period to which Justin had never paid as much attention as he knew he should, and apart from his interest in Jeanette Marchand and a few other major stars of the era he was hazy on many of the film titles. He knew few of the names of other personalities. Justin made a mental note of what he had discovered about the photograph, and later dropped a line to Teddy Smythe to let her know.

A couple of months later he came across a reference to Roy Tallis in an American encyclopaedia of pre-WW2 films.

Tallis's real name was Boris Mikhailovich Morozov. He was the son of Russian immigrants, born in Chicago in 1901. He moved to California in search of stardom and changed his name. As Roy Tallis he made half a dozen silent films as a supporting actor but his first leading role was in 1926, just as sound recording was being introduced. He made several more films afterwards, but none of them as a star. He was a contract artist with RKO Radio Pictures.

Most of Tallis's sound films were made in the era known to film historians as pre-Code, the relatively short period in Hollywood between the advent of sound and 1934, when the strict censorship of the Motion Picture Production Code was imposed. After 1934 the studios had to work within the Code's tightly defined moral framework.

As well as restricting what could be shown in new films, it had a retroactive effect. Many of the films which had been made pre-Code were latterly withdrawn by the studios. Under the so-called Hays Code they were belatedly seen with hindsight as immoral or risqué, or controversial in some other way. The Hays Code made everyone in Hollywood acutely sensitive not only to sexual content, but gambling, religion, narcotics and alcohol abuse, racial stereotyping, homosexuality – only romance, gangster movies and musicals were seen as safe subjects. In several cases the negatives and prints of pre-Code films were destroyed by the studios, or deliberately mislaid. Many films of the era were irretrievably lost. No copies of Roy Tallis's films existed.

At the end of Tallis's entry there was a note about his off-screen life. He was the first husband of Jeanette Marchand, from 1928 until his suicide in 1933. They had one child, a girl called Natasha.

12

Romance and Reality – Casablanca revisited

Justin Farmer, Arts Correspondent

This year marks the fortieth anniversary of the release of *Casablanca*, widely regarded as one of the greatest and most influential films ever to come out of Hollywood. It is certainly one of the most popular, having not only packed cinemas all around the world for four decades but contributed many phrases, images and feelings to the culture. The roles played by Humphrey Bogart, Ingrid Bergman and Claude Rains have become iconic.

Although the film is so familiar, here is a partial synopsis. The setting is the town of Casablanca in French Morocco, in the period of the second world war when it was controlled from France by the Vichy puppet regime. An expatriate American, Richard Blaine, or Rick (played by Bogart), has opened a nightclub-cum-casino in the narrow streets close to the airport. A former mercenary and gun-runner, Rick Blaine is embittered by a traumatically broken love affair, two years earlier in Paris. He has buried his feelings behind a façade of non-committal disinterest. His lucrative business, called *Rick's Café Américain*, is based on the transit of refugees passing through Casablanca, who are hoping to escape to a neutral country, or to the USA.

Trafficking and exploitation of the refugees is a major source of Rick's income, but the shady business also fuels the black economy throughout the town. Rick is no better or worse than other racketeers, but beneath his cynical exterior he retains a level of gritty integrity and human compassion. This moral duality is taken advantage of by another prime mover in the town: the corrupt chief of the local gendarmerie, Captain Louis Renard (played by Rains). Rick refuses to commit to any political cause, claiming he is simply a saloon keeper.

Rick's life is disturbed and his emotions thrown into confusion when his former lover from Paris, Ilsa Lund (played by Bergman), walks unexpectedly into his café one evening with an inspirational resistance fighter called Victor Lazlo (played by Paul Henreid). Although Rick and Ilsa are still passionately in love with each other, and desperately trying to suppress it, Ilsa reveals not only that Lazlo is her husband, but that she was married to him when she and Rick had their affair in Paris. She believed then that Lazlo was dead. Rick happens to have possession of official documents that would enable Lazlo and Ilsa to fly out to neutral Lisbon, but to hand them over would mean he would never see Ilsa again.

The film culminates in a final meeting at the airport, after Rick has promised Ilsa that he and she will fly away together. At the very last minute Rick abandons his habitual attitude of selfish non-involvement, commits to Lazlo's resistance cause and hands over the documents. Lazlo and Ilsa take the plane to Lisbon and fly to freedom.

Images of impermanence and lost lives haunt this beautiful

film. Everyone is in transit, either running away from the past, avoiding the dangers of the present, or seeking a better life elsewhere. Disappearance is desired, and frequently achieved. Some people manage to flee, others are rounded up by the police and never seen again.

Rick's café is the focus, the terminal post, where everyone goes. It is so close to the airport that it is directly beneath the flight-path of incoming planes – the low-flying aircraft represent both potential freedom and danger. One of the first images in the film is of a passenger plane skimming perilously low over the entrance to Rick's. A searchlight mounted high on an airport tower looms over the town, and every night its beam plays over the streets, flashing against the windows of the café.

The airport is the only way in to or out of Casablanca: Victor Lazlo and Ilsa Lund arrive by air, as does the Nazi major (played by Conrad Veidt) sent to capture Lazlo. Much of Captain Renard's corruption is based on the granting of expensive exit visas, with sexual exploitation of young women usually built into the deal. These visas can only be used at the airport, and are anyway of debatable worth. They grant departure, not a safe arrival somewhere else. The documents Rick holds are different: they are said to guarantee free passage in the Allied world.

This intrigue is played out in a microcosm of political and emotional tension. We rarely glimpse anything of the ordinary people who live in Casablanca, just as modern air passengers in an airport terminal are in a sort of limbo, cut off from the habits and freedoms of normal life from the moment they enter the building. Everyone is forced to wait.

Casablanca is a film based on fantasy. Even as filming was under way in Hollywood, in the real world the Allied forces were invading North Africa from the Atlantic coast, over-running Casablanca and the rest of Morocco and driving the occupying Germans eastward to Algeria and Tunisia. Such was the success of the military action that by mid-January 1943, around the time the film went on general release, a summit conference was being held in Casablanca. Churchill and Roosevelt were there, together with de Gaulle – the remainder of the war was being planned and strategized.

So although fiction is fiction, as we expect, there never was anything but a shred of wish-fulfilment about the reality behind *Casablanca*'s story. Needless to say that does not matter in the least. We remember great fantasy for the dreams it fulfils, the hope it inspires, the love we feel for the characters depicted.

No one who sees *Casablanca*, even today when the events are so far behind us, can fail to be moved by the moral and emotional struggle so brilliantly underplayed by Humphrey Bogart, or the devotion and warmth of Ingrid Bergman in her greatest role, defining her skill at embodying romantic passion, evident throughout her later career.

There were other realities about the filming, although they were not necessarily obvious to the cinema audience.

The film depicts a gathering of people of different national-ities, waiting to pass through Casablanca to freedom. We hear about those who cannot move on just yet, they have to 'wait in Casablanca, and wait, and wait, and wait . . .' This was a reflection of real life in Hollywood at the time: of the more than seventy actors who appeared in the film, only three were 'real' Americans: Humphrey Bogart, Dooley Wilson (who played Sam, the pianist) and Joy Page (playing Annina Bran-del, a Bulgarian refugee). The rest of the actors were recent immigrants, many of them refugees from Hitler's Germany. A large number of them were Jewish, including a few who acted the part of the Nazis. Some of the players of small parts had been major stars before having to flee their home countries.

Although of course everything in the film is fabricated, this blurring of the lives of actors with the parts they were playing adds a definite frisson of earned reality. Unforgettably, the scene in which everyone in the café defiantly sings *La Marseillaise,* one of the most memorable and stirring scenes in all cinema, closes on the tear-stained face of the French film star Madeleine Lebeau, herself a refugee from Paris. '*Vive la France!*' she cries.

And what of the casting of Humphrey Bogart as Rick? There have always been rumours that other actors might have been chosen in preference to Bogart. Two names that frequently come up on this subject are the current US President, Ronald Reagan, and an actor well known for gangster films, George Raft. It is impossible now to imagine *Casablanca* having the same emotional impact if either of these men had taken the primary role. In fact, Bogart was decided for the part of Rick from the start, so there was never any truth to the rumours, but there was one actor who had an intriguing influence behind the scenes, and who also was briefly considered for the part of Rick. This was the pre-Code film star Leslie Howard.

Howard was British, and seemed to embody a certain attractive British diffidence and charm. He had risen swiftly in Hollywood and made several successful films. Between 1930 and 1933 Leslie Howard had co-starred with such famous pre-Code leading ladies as Norma Shearer, Marion Davies, Ann Harding, Jeanette Marchand, Conchita Montenegro and Mary Pickford. More recently he had starred as Ashley Wilkes in *Gone With the Wind.*

The idea of him playing Rick Blaine as compellingly as Bogart is not easy to imagine, and in fact the likelihood of Leslie Howard taking the role was never a serious one. However, he and Bogart were long-term friends, and in the past the older and more established Howard had lobbied effectively on Bogart's behalf to get the parts and the recognition he felt the younger actor deserved. When he suspected Hal B Wallis, the producer of *Casablanca*, might be wavering he spoke earnestly about Bogart's unique suitability for the role. So it came to happen.

Leslie Howard had one more connection with *Casablanca*, a tragic one. Not long after the film was released Howard flew in a civil airliner from Britain to Lisbon. His purpose was partly to publicize *The First of the Few*, a film about the development of the Spitfire fighter, in which he not only starred but had also directed. For this he went to preview events in Portugal, but also briefly visited Madrid. He was photographed there with his former co-star Conchita Montenegro.

A certain mystery surrounds this visit, because Conchita Montenegro had direct contact with Generalissimo Franco, dictator of Spain. Was Leslie Howard engaged in low-level espionage or an unofficial diplomatic mission of some kind? It is now impossible to know, but there were many theories later about what he was really doing in Madrid. The speculation about what happened to him afterwards was because he was thought to be a spy.

He stayed only two days in Madrid, then returned to Lisbon. He boarded a return flight to Britain from Portela Airport in Lisbon.

At the time, BOAC was running three or four civilian flights a week between Lisbon and Britain. This was one of the services that would connect with planes leaving Casablanca, as depicted in the film. It is likely that Ilsa Lund and Victor Lazlo, after landing in Lisbon, would have travelled to Britain on their way to the USA. They would therefore have flown on the same aircraft.

Throughout the second world war the Luftwaffe never made any serious attempt to attack these aircraft – the planes routinely carried diplomatic bags and prisoner-of-war mail, German as well as British, and civil servants, journalists, diplomats and their families, and other civilians travelling as passengers. Both sides in the conflict benefited from this unacknowledged connection. But the day that Leslie Howard flew back to Britain was the one occasion when the Luftwaffe fighters pounced. The plane was lost and everyone on board perished.

Insofar as we can translate the fantasy of a romantic film into the harsher realities of a real war, the fate of Leslie Howard and the other people on the flight with him underlines the risks potentially run by the fictitious characters.

Rick's farewell to Ilsa on the tarmac of Casablanca Airport is an emotional one, but they would both be aware of the dangers of wartime air travel. His toughly phrased words admit no thought of those. Their troubles were elsewhere, memorably insoluble, a deep agony. The tears welling in Ingrid Bergman's eyes, and her look of loss, devotion and hope seem to indicate that there might yet be a future for them. The film ends, but the magic of *Casablanca* endures, an eternal drama of escape and flight.

Justin Farmer

Sunday Times Arts Supplement, November 21st 1982

13

After some thought, and an unexpected attack of minor nervousness, Justin drafted a letter to August Engel:

Dear Mr Engel

I have been given your address by a colleague of mine called Andrea Connolly. I believe you worked with her when she was employed as a script consultant on Danger Within, *the adventure series made by Yorkshire TV. I know you directed three episodes. I greatly admired the show, which was broadcast as a re-run last year. Ms Connolly knows that you and I have interests in common, which I am eager to discuss with you. If you prefer not, of course I would understand.*

I have written and published several books about cinema. A few years ago I worked on a book called Goddesses of the Silver Screen. *It consisted mostly of photographs of many of the young actresses who made their names in Hollywood in the early 1930s. It was published in the weeks before Christmas that year, aimed at a popular audience. Although my job was to write continuity text, and captions for the pictures, I was working as a hired writer for a book packaging company*

and my name did not appear. I had no say over which
pictures were used. The published book was well produced and
the pictures were excellent, but it went out of print within a
few months.

One of the young stars who appears in that book was
Jeanette Marchand, for whom I have always had special
interest and admiration. I am currently working on a much
more serious and deeply researched book, which deals with the
period known in Hollywood as pre-Code. This was when
Ms Marchand was at her most successful and beautiful, and I
should like to be able to write knowledgeably and sympatheti-
cally about her.

I understand that you too take a special interest in Ms
Marchand's career, and according to a correspondent in Sight
and Sound *you might have particular or personal knowledge*
of her. Would you be willing to allow me to meet with you
and ask a few questions?

I hope you will not mind this approach, and I look forward
to hearing from you when convenient.

Yours sincerely,
Justin Farmer

Justin's link with August Engel was tenuous. Describing
Andrea Connolly as a colleague was only true at remote:
her name had been suggested to him by a friend of hers
called Matilda Linden, whom Justin knew only slightly
better.

Matilda Linden was a professional biographer, whose subjects were people in the film world. Several weeks after his
profile of Teddy Smythe appeared in the *Observer* he received
a note from her: she was planning a new book about Teddy,

and wondered if they could meet so she might pick his brain.

He recognized her name: Matilda Linden was the author of the book about Hugo Marshal Turnbull, director of *Auvergne*, which he had consulted while writing his profile of Teddy. He and Matilda met for a pub lunch, cut short on the day because they both had to hurry away to other commitments, but Justin had told her what he knew of Teddy, and the feeling of mild intrigue she created. Andrea's name came up somehow – Teddy Smythe had appeared in a children's play put on by Yorkshire TV, where Andrea worked. Later, Justin had discovered Andrea also had worked with Engel, although Matilda herself knew nothing about him.

Once Matilda had talked to Andrea and passed over August Engel's address, and Justin had drafted his letter, he thought he should telephone her before he mailed it. He read it to her.

'I think it sounds all right,' Matilda said. 'Andrea won't mind. The worst he can do is say no. Go ahead and send it.'

'Has Andrea ever mentioned him to you?'

'She did tell me once she was working with a director who had come to Britain from Germany. She probably said his name, which I'd forgotten, but I assume it was this man Engel.'

The address Andrea had given her was in St Albans, not far from the film studios in Elstree where the TV series had been made.

He posted the letter, then called Matilda back and said that he was going to be in the West End again the following week, and would she like to meet for a drink or a less hurried lunch?

'I'll be out of town all next week,' she said. 'Sorry, that

sounds like an excuse. Let's make it the week after – I'll call you when I'm back.'

'OK,' said Justin, suspecting it might be a brush-off in spite of that.

'But call me Matty,' she said, so maybe it was not.

After a week a handwritten reply arrived from August Engel. It was short and to the point, although not the reply Justin had been hoping for:

Dear Mr Farmer
I have now retired. You might be interested to read the enclosed. It is a photocopy, so you may keep it if you wish.
Yours
August Engel

Enclosed with the note was a sheet of white A4 paper, folded neatly in four. The piece of paper it had been copied from was smaller, and because it appeared slightly shaded in the copy it looked discoloured with age. The words *RKO Radio Pictures Inc.* were printed in black capitals across the top of the page. Next to the words was the familiar logo of a world globe with a radio mast transmitting lightning streaks. The date was *May 10 1933.*

Dear Mr Engel,
*   Thank you from the bottom of my heart for the kind and interesting letter you wrote me from Manchester in England. I am very happy here in California, thank you for asking. My next motion picture will be released later this year, it is called* The Devil Demands. *I am starring in it with Adolphe*

Menjou. I hope you will like it.
Yours sincerely,
Jeanette Marchand

Justin read this a dozen times, then stared at the clearly written signature at the bottom. He had never seen her signature before.

Two weeks later another brief note arrived from Engel:

Mr Farmer,
I will be in the Castle and King pub at the top of Wardour Street, next Thursday from about 12:00. If you would like to meet me there I will be pleased to answer your questions about Jeanette Marchand.
August Engel

14

The pub was a small one, close to where Wardour Street joined Oxford Street. Although Justin often attended screenings in viewing theatres in Soho, two of them in Wardour Street itself, he had never been inside this particular pub before.

He arrived early, but looked around to see if anyone who might be August Engel was already there. Many people were standing by the bar counter – Justin pushed politely past them and ordered himself a pint of bitter. While the beer was still being pulled he felt a touch on his elbow. He turned to look. A tall and thin grey-haired man was behind him.

'I think you are Mr Farmer?'

'Yes . . . you must be August Engel.' Justin was hemmed in by other drinkers, but half-turned and stretched out his hand. They shook – Engel's grip was firm. 'May I get you something?' he added, as the bar keeper placed his bitter on the counter.

'A chilled strong lager, please. A table has just come free. I will sit there.'

When he had paid, Justin carried both glasses to the table,

which was still cluttered with the empty glasses and traces of spilled beer from its previous occupants. They pushed everything to one side. Justin noticed that Engel had already bought another large glass of beer, half consumed. They nodded to each other, raised their glasses for a first taste, put them down, regarded each other.

Engel looked to be in good health, but he was obviously in his late seventies or early eighties. His hair was thin on top, combed lightly across his scalp, and his beard was tidily trimmed and white. His eyes were blue, slightly watery. Justin noticed a walking stick hooked over the back of his chair.

'Thank you for agreeing to meet me,' Justin said into the silence of their table, against the general background noise.

'I am pleased to meet you too.' Engel took another sip of the beer he had already bought, then swallowed more with several gulps. 'How are you?'

'I'm well,' Justin said. 'You have made several films, I believe.'

'I was the director of only one, but you won't have seen it unless you were in Germany at the time. It was not a great film, but there were problems with making it. I believe it has never been shown in Britain or America. When I moved into television, things were different. You probably have not seen much German television.'

'No, I haven't.'

'You make films yourself?'

'No – I'm a critic, a reviewer. And a film historian.'

'Yes – you told me you were writing about the Hays Code. That's a long time in the past.'

'The Code had a negative influence on film-makers for thirty years. A lot of films weren't made because of it. Others were lost, and all the rest were controlled by it. Most people in the film world today have heard of it, and most think it was a kind of censorship. It was actually more far-reaching than that.'

'And you have written this?'

'I am still working on it.'

Silence again.

'You said you wanted to ask me questions,' Engel said. 'I am happy to give you what answers I can.'

'I haven't prepared a list of questions,' Justin said, feeling already that this was not working out as he had expected. 'I wanted to meet you mainly because of Jeanette Marchand.'

'Yes, of course. A fascinating subject for us both, I think. More interesting than the Hays Code.'

'You sent me a copy of that letter she wrote you. That was a long time ago. Did you write back to her, did you learn anything about her?'

'No, I did not write back.'

'She was responding to something you had written to her.'

'Yes, that is so. I was a young man, I thought I was in love with her and I sent her a fan letter. That was her reply.'

'But that wasn't the end of it?'

'The end of what?'

'Your contact with Jeanette Marchand.'

'No, later I knew her better. A long time later.'

Engel had finished the first glass of beer, and now he started the second. Justin had still only sipped his.

'You are not telling me much. You don't owe me answers, of course.'

'You are not asking the right questions. But how could you? We know nothing of each other. Except when it comes to Jeanette Marchand, perhaps. I am happy to speak to you about her, but how I met her is a long and difficult story. I am German, as you know. I am also British, which you probably don't know.

'My life has been complicated. I was in Germany through most of the Hitler period. In my small way I dreamed of America, I dreamed of England, I dreamed of escaping what was going on. I was in love with the great American film stars like Jeanette, but my country was determined to start a war. I was trapped somewhere I did not want to be.'

'Did you become involved in the war? In the German army?'

'No, nothing like that. Not involved in the way you perhaps think.'

Justin was remembering something Florence Robeson had told him, an imprecise comment she heard when August Engel was interviewed on television.

'You knew Leni Riefenstahl, I believe?' he said, and Engel looked at him in surprise.

'Yes, I did. I worked with her for several years. She was how I was introduced to making films.'

'She was making propaganda films for Hitler.'

'That's what everyone said, and they still think it. But she was not a Nazi, she was never in the party. She was dedicated to making films, and she worked out how to get her way within the régime.'

Justin said nothing. August Engel looked away, across the crowded bar. 'Do you want to ask me questions about Riefenstahl,' he said, 'or about Jeanette Marchand?'

'I'm interested in film. Jeanette and Riefenstahl were both in cinema. Was there any other connection?'

'Only me. One woman led me to the other, but I've never been sure which was which. It's complicated.'

Justin felt they were fencing. Engel seemed to be defending, holding something back.

'I will tell you how it happened,' he said after a while. 'But it is not a short story. Do you have to be somewhere else?'

Justin glanced at his wristwatch. 'I'm due to see a preview in less than an hour. Not far from here.'

August Engel stood up. 'All right. But I am a man with certain needs. Please wait a couple of minutes.'

Leaning on his stick he walked unsteadily through the crowded bar room towards the toilets. Justin signalled to a passing member of staff, who cleared their table of the old glasses and emptied the ash tray. She came back a little later and wiped the table clean. Justin laid the copy of Jeanette's letter on the top. It had been written in a period that was for many people a lifetime ago.

When Engel returned he took a deep swallow of the beer, then began his story, promising it would lead to Jeanette Marchand. He told Justin he was an orphan. His father had been a soldier in the German army in the first world war, but was killed in France in 1916. He, August, had been born in 1912 – the same year Jeanette was born, he said. His mother died in the Spanish flu pandemic in 1918. He barely remembered his father – he had appeared at the house once in a grimy uniform and with a bandage around his head. He was then, and remained, a stranger. But August had never forgotten his mother, Stefanie.

There were no other relatives. After Stefanie died August was taken to Berlin and placed in an orphanage. Because of the terrible German casualties there were hundreds of other children there, and conditions were harsh.

The war ended not long after, and in 1919 a charitable relief organization came from Britain to visit Berlin. As a partial solution to a pressing social crisis the German government had agreed to allow married couples from other European countries to adopt German children. One day representatives of this organization arrived at the orphanage and August was one of the children selected. It was only then that he was provided with written details of how each of his parents had died. He was barely seven years old, and he still had difficulties with reading. It meant that for a long time he did not understand everything that had happened to him.

By then he had moved to the north of England and was established in his new family: he was adopted by a middle-aged couple called Harry and Elsie Winson, who had lost their own son, Tony, in the battle of the Somme. Tony was only eighteen. It was the same action in which August's father had died, but they did not realize this straight away. They took August in and gave him a safe and loving home. Here he started to grow up and change, learning to speak English, discovering his new family, recognizing the grief they felt for their lost son, feeling their tentative but growing love for him. They lived in a grimy industrial suburb to the north of Manchester and were not well off: Harry and Elsie's house was a cramped terrace, rented from a mill owner. The outside walls were black with soot, and the interior was draughty. There was no bathroom and the toilet was outside. Elsie worked as a weaver in a mill, Harry was a railway mechanic.

'I think you are also from the north of England,' Engel said to Justin. 'I hear a familiar accent.'

'Yes, I was born near Manchester,' Justin said, suddenly feeling mild discomfort. His middle class upbringing had not filtered the Mancunian accent away, which he discovered when he moved to live in London. He had spent his years since believing that all traces of it would fade. 'We lived in the south, on the edge of the Cheshire countryside. A place called Field Green.'

'I have heard of it. That is where the air is clean. And close to the airport, I believe.'

'Beneath the main flight path.'

'I did not know that part of Manchester.'

Engel said he had saved up his pocket money and bought a simple box camera, and learned how to use it to get the best pictures. When he was in his early twenties he read stories in the newspaper about what was happening in Germany following the rise of Adolf Hitler, although he now felt himself to be more British than German. One particular story caught his attention: the film director Leni Riefenstahl was going to make a film record of the Olympic Games, due to be held in Berlin in 1936. It was a huge endeavour, and Riefenstahl intended it as an international production. She was encouraging film technicians from all over the world to travel to Germany and work with her on different aspects of the Games. She was also setting up a training course for new or young film-makers, and would create an academy for them. They would work as apprentices or trainees on the film.

August had never heard of Riefenstahl but as soon as he read the story he wrote to the place that was mentioned, enclosing some of his photographs. He heard back from Berlin that he had been accepted. They would cover travel costs, induct him into the academy and provide him with a small stipend. That is how he returned to Germany.

Justin said, 'But surely you realized this meant you would be working for Hitler.'

'Leni Riefenstahl had a special place in the Nazi hierarchy.' Engel said this quietly, leaning his head confidentially towards Justin and speaking in a lowered voice. 'This is not easy to say, even now. I understand what her reputation was here and in the USA, but I had no knowledge of that then. To me she was a woman who was planning a major film. She had to be loyal to the Nazis, because they were funding the project, but they left her alone. Hitler liked her. She never talked about him to me.'

He said he had to sign up to work with the Reichsfilmkammer, run by Joseph Goebbels. Nothing at all could be done in Germany without involving the Nazi Party. Riefenstahl persuaded everyone on her film to treat it as a disagreeable technicality. Engel said this with an apologetic shrug.

'So you were working for Goebbels?'

'Those were different times. I did not see it as working for him. Like Riefenstahl, I was caught up by the thrill of making a major film.'

Both of them had emptied their beer glasses while Engel was speaking. He made to stand up to return to the bar, but Justin signalled him to stay put.

When he was back at the table with refreshed glasses, he said, 'The Olympics took place in 1936 – so when did you join Riefenstahl?'

'At the beginning of 1935.'

'You left when the Games were over?'

'No, I stayed on.'

'All through the war?'

'No – I stayed in Germany until 1939, just before Britain declared war. Let me tell you.'

August said he had become an orphan for a second time, this time as a young adult, when first Elsie died, then Harry. They had both suffered chronic illnesses related to the conditions at their jobs. Also because of the filthy air of the place where they lived, he said. He himself was now asthmatic, and all through his life he had suffered troublesome coughs.

After they died he had no ties in England. He was served notice to leave the house, and had no interest in politics. He was obsessed with photography and film. That was why, when he received the invitation from Riefenstahl, a month or so after Harry's funeral, he went to Germany.

From the outset Riefenstahl set a challenging round of work for all her young apprentices. They were given the latest equipment to learn on, with the highest quality German and Swiss lenses and film stock. The Olympic Games presented a deadline that could not be missed. From the moment of his first arrival August was swept up by the intense agenda. He was taught camera techniques, training at first as a focus puller. Later he learned how to operate the camera itself, and picked up an awareness of the importance of lighting and sound. He became interested in the editing of film. Because he spoke German he had a certain advantage amongst the other young trainees from overseas, but in fact many of the other film-makers who had come to join the Riefenstahl project were far more experienced.

As the date of the Olympics approached Riefenstahl

divided her volunteers into twelve crews, each of which was assigned to cover different events. She was devising many technical innovations: underwater cameras and slow-motion for the swimmers and divers, camera pits dug alongside the tracks, for instance.

'Have you seen the film?' Engel asked him.

'I've seen all of Riefenstahl's films. They were shown last year at the NFT, in a triple bill.'

'You do not sound enthusiastic about them.'

'No.' Justin had felt at the time he should not miss the films. In fact the screenings had been an ordeal that used up an afternoon and an evening, leaving him feeling flat and depressed.

'Technically, *Olympia* is a brilliant film,' August said.

'Of course.'

But that's not the point, Justin thought. He did not feel he was in a position to judge the man. It had been he who had approached Engel, after all.

'Hundreds of people in the German film world had already fled to Hollywood as refugees from Hitler,' Justin said. 'And many more civilians as well. Surely Riefenstahl knew she would be seen as a Nazi apologist?'

'I don't think so,' said August. 'Not then. Although after the Olympics I was desperate to leave,' he added. 'We were hearing rumours of other people who had managed to escape to France, America or Britain. But you had to have people outside Germany to help you. The Nazi régime wouldn't let you take anything with you – no money, or anything of value that you could trade.'

'So what did you do?'

'On my own I could do nothing. In the end I was helped

by Riefenstahl herself.' He seemed reluctant to expand on this further, saying only that in the end he had no other choice than to return to Britain. 'I was arrested as an enemy alien as soon as my ship reached Dover,' he said.

He was confined in a secure building, then a few days later transported to the Isle of Man. There, along with hundreds of other German nationals, he was interned for the duration of the war.

'You were going to tell me how you came to know Jeanette,' Justin said. He wanted to get away from the subject of Leni Riefenstahl and the Nazis.

'I knew her well.'

'This is what you said.'

'It is the simple truth. I came to know her well.'

'How well?'

'It was a long time ago, so remembering it doesn't hurt any more. Anyway, it's not a secret. I was in love with her and I was living with her in her house. We were together like that for only a short time, two or three months, but for me it was serious, it was a moment in my life that changed everything, and afterwards.'

'And you went with her in 1949 when she flew to Britain?'

'Yes.'

'You were on the plane with her? You accompanied her?'

'Yes.'

'But you left the aircraft in Ireland.'

'No. The plane didn't land in Ireland. It was diverted to Prestwick, in Scotland. That's where I left it.'

Justin said, 'That's not what Pan American told me. They said the aircraft was routed through Shannon.'

'You went to Pan Am and asked them about this?' said August. 'I am learning how interested you are.'

'I was trying to find out what happened to Jeanette March-and after that flight. It was Pan Am who indirectly led me to you. The airline has detailed records of every journey, every route. I saw the schedule, and one of the cabin crew told me there was another first class passenger who disembarked at Shannon. It turned out that this crew member had actually worked on that flight, and remembered Jeanette. So that was definitely you who was with her?'

'It was me, yes, but I left the plane in Scotland. Whoever told you it was Ireland was remembering wrongly. Maybe they misremembered other details too. These are the same people who claimed they saw Jeanette leaving the plane. Do you still believe them?'

'Are you saying they did not see her?'

'No – I am saying that is what they claim. I don't believe what they say happened. No one can disappear in the way they said. It's impossible. There's something incorrect about their story.'

'Why should they lie?'

'Maybe they made a mistake.'

'I've seen the Pan Am flight schedule. It's on the record that the plane landed in Ireland.'

'It's true the flight was originally intended to land there for refuelling, but because of bad weather the plane was diverted. It was a last-minute decision, not an emergency, but the plane could not reach London without taking on more fuel. The captain told us this when we were on the ground. I left the plane in Scotland. I can't be wrong about that. I watched it take off later, when it was continuing on to London.'

'OK, but why did you leave the plane?'

'Jeanette wanted me to.'

'Can you remember why?'

August shook his head. 'Not exactly – it's too long ago. Jeanette had personal problems, and much as I adored her she was sometimes difficult to be with. These problems were one of the main reasons she wanted to fly to England.'

'What kind of problems?'

'I cannot tell you, not exactly. You have to understand that Jeanette – there were things about her life she never told me. I think for a while at least I was important to her, but her years in the film industry had taught her not to trust people. There was her ex-husband, of course, the baseball player, who felt cheated after the divorce. He was trying to sue her for more money, but I know also there was something else, something she did not like to speak of to anyone. I did once hear something from the housekeeper – about a child called Natasha who died. Jeanette would never talk about that. She said she wanted to go on to London alone, but I should catch another plane in two days' time. She told me the hotel she was booked into. We were going to meet there.'

'And you went along with that?'

'After an argument, yes. I usually did go along with her, with what she wanted. I knew there would be no use in arguing, not once she had made up her mind.'

'But after you left the plane you didn't see her again?'

'I never did.'

'Do you know what happened to her after she landed in London?'

'No.'

'Is she still alive?'

'I don't know – I hope so. I tried everything to find her, but she completely disappeared. You must know this already.'

'Have you any idea at all of where she might have gone?'

'Anything is possible. All this was half a century ago. We are both now so old. We were about the same age. I am now in my eighties, so you can work it out yourself. Anything could have happened to her. I want her still to be alive and I hope the best for her, that she has had a good life. I spent a lot of time searching, contacting people who might know where she was, but I never traced her, not even a clue. The police couldn't find her, the studio in Los Angeles sent a private detective over to look for her. No trace was ever found. I spent months obsessed with trying to discover where she was. In the end I had to move on.'

He began talking about his arrival in London. The hotel, the airport, the airline, the police – no one could tell him anything. He was soon forced to realize that without Jeanette's financial support he was destitute. He tried to find a job in London, but the immediate post-war years were a period of austerity for everyone in Britain. In the end, about two years after the flight from New York, he moved back to Germany to try and find work as a film technician.

'But tell me about Jeanette,' Justin said. 'How did you meet her in the first place? You told me you were in Britain after leaving Riefenstahl's team.'

'I was arrested, and put in an internment camp. It was in Douglas, on the Isle of Man. I spent the whole war there. When we were released at the end I had nowhere to go. By then the authorities had checked my story and I was given a British passport. My adoptive parents were dead and of course I had no other relatives in Germany or in Britain.

We were given a little money in compensation for being kept prisoner and so I decided to spend it on a ticket to the USA. Riefenstahl had warned me that as a German I would not find work in Hollywood but the war was now over. I thought my chances would be better in America. Of course I was wrong.'

With his compensation spent he was forced to take on various menial jobs in New York: he became a janitor, he drove a street-cleaning vehicle, he painted store signs. During the first bitterly cold winter he cooked and served burgers and hot dogs on a street stall. He lived at the YMCA. In the following spring he travelled west, from one town to the next, found work for a while, then moved on. He always headed west. It was not until the early summer of 1948 that he arrived at last in Los Angeles. Once again he found casual work where he could. It was another burger joint. Few of his co-workers ever knew much about him, and even those who did asked few questions. Most of them had their own persistent dreams of becoming something in Hollywood: an actor, a stunt performer, a scriptwriter, a singer.

August too had similar ambitious plans, but he was in possession of real skills. Riefenstahl had trained him to become a cinematographer and film editor. He signed up with a couple of agencies who worked with the studios to recruit technical staff. He was sent for several interviews, but no offers materialized. Either the jobs he tried for were unsuitable, or, it turned out, he was. More often than not it was the latter. He had told the job agencies he was British, which was true and he had a passport to prove it, but his

Germanic name and the only other documents he carried told another story.

He eventually found work as a chauffeur for a private hire company that did business with the major studios. The limos belonged to the rental company but he had to buy his own uniform. The job paid better than the burger joint. For the first couple of days he was accompanied by one of the outfit's experienced drivers, who instructed him in the protocols and routines, warned him never to speak to the client unless spoken to. There was a voice link from the rear compartment: it was only to be used if the client spoke first. The man explained to him the sort of offences which would lead to him being sacked, told him to expect no gratuities. There were no advantages, no benefits, no chance to mingle with the stars. He was just a driver.

They drove together along most of the frequent routes so August would be familiar with them. Shortcuts were pointed out. He was given an address list of the fashionable restaurants, bars and clubs, and shown how to enter and drive into the celebrity pick-up lots of each of the big studios. He was warned one last time: a single complaint from a client would lose him the job. The stars of Hollywood had power in this town.

Then August was on his own.

He learned quickly. He made mistakes of course, and twice he was a few minutes late for a pick-up, but soon his record was good. Each car carried a large-scale street map, and the addresses he was likely to have to visit were highlighted or ringed by earlier drivers. Sometimes names, famous names, were pencilled in.

Most of the clients, male or female, took no interest in his driving or the route he was taking. They did not connect with him at all. He barely even saw them. They would emerge from the house, or the studio, or the nightclub, invariably concealed beneath a copious hat, or a scarf worn across the lower face. All wore sunglasses, often at night. They moved swiftly towards the car as he held open the door. Once they were inside the car he had no rear-view mirror to see into the compartment, and had to drive using external mirrors only. He was forbidden to turn around and look at who he was driving. On arrival the client would exit the vehicle swiftly and scurry inside, usually greeted and shepherded away by personal staff or studio employees.

In most cases he never learned who the client actually was. The novelty of picking up and depositing unidentified film stars soon wore off. Then one afternoon he was sent to collect a client from an address he had not been to before.

It was an anonymous large building in a poorer area of Los Angeles. He had to park the limo on the side of the road outside, the size and appearance of the shiny car attracting a small crowd of curious kids and passersby.

He had driven to the building following the map, using street directions, so had not realized what it was used for: but there was a drably painted sign over the door, describing it as a residential home for children. It looked a grim place for children to be living in, although the windows were decorated with brightly coloured paintings attached to the inside. He waited.

After about fifteen minutes the small figure of a woman came through the double doors and headed directly for the car. She was dressed casually, unremarkably, and wore large sunglasses. Her hair was tied back in a ponytail. As soon as August realized this must be his client, he climbed swiftly from the driving seat and held open the passenger door. She went inside without a comment, not glancing at him. He drove.

From time to time he looked down at the street map clipped discreetly beneath the dash. The address she was going to was one that had been circled. Previous drivers, users of the same maps, had faintly pencilled in names. When he had to halt briefly at a red light he pulled it away from the dash and looked more closely. Against this address two names could be discerned: McPherson and . . . Marchand!

He realized who the woman in the back of the car must be.

'I had not thought about Jeanette Marchand for a long time,' August said. 'But I still kept her letter from all those years before. It had been to Germany with me, I had it while I was interned, I brought it to the USA. I rarely remembered it, even more rarely took it out and looked at it, but I had never lost it or thrown it away. It meant so much to me when I was a young man growing up in England. It was a sort of permanent link with those days, when I was an orphan in a strange country, living with two well-meaning strangers. I had no special interest in most of the Hollywood stars, but with Jeanette it was different.'

'This was when?' Justin said. 'You arrived in Los Angeles in 1948?' He was trying to remember what he knew of Jeanette Marchand's film titles from that time. 'She had been making a couple of Republic serials, hadn't she?'

'One for Republic, another for RKO,' August said. 'She told me later.'

'So she was no longer a big star.'

'She was always a star, and she was still famous,' August said. 'The fan magazines reported everything she did or said. But she tried to keep her life as private as possible so her profile was lower than that of many other stars. The studios were no longer making romantic comedies, the kind of films that had made her name.'

'She had become a featured player,' Justin said. 'That's how people in the business describe someone like her. Still a top name, but not a box office draw any more.'

With less than a mile to go before he arrived at the house, August said he found it all but impossible to concentrate on his driving. Jeanette Marchand – in his car! A few feet away from him! He was star-struck, a fan, and for him she was the star of all stars.

They came to the hillside road where her house was situated. They came to the curving entrance to the drive. They came to the iron gates, which were closed against the world.

August halted the car then reached across to the radio transmitter. The gates slowly swung open. He drove through and past them, following the curving drive as it climbed through a stand of trees. The gates closed behind. The large house came fully into view.

As he slowed the car on the driveway he reached down and picked up the communicator device. To speak uninvited to a client was a transgression of every rule. He would be sacked instantly if she complained. And yet he could not resist this chance, the only one he might have, of exchanging words with the woman who had unknowingly ignited his passion for the cinema.

Before he could speak, to his amazement the voice tube made a click.

'Driver, look at me. I want to see you.' Her voice was attenuated by the device.

He had to turn awkwardly in the cramped driver's seat, holding the communicator. She was huddled in a corner of the wide seat in the rear compartment. Her sunglasses were off. Her face around her eyes was streaked with black mascara, from where she had been crying. Her ponytail had come undone and her hair was strewn untidily around her shoulders. She stared at him. She looked small, helpless, frightened, defensive.

'Have you driven me before?'

'No, ma'am. I am new—'

'You must never tell anyone what you are seeing,' she said.

August said to Justin he saw only an unhappy and vulnerable woman, but to Jeanette Marchand he merely said, 'Is there anything I can do to help you?'

She started to speak, but turned her face away. Then she spoke closely into the communicator, 'Please wait a couple of minutes. I can't go into the house like this.'

August noticed that a door to the house had opened. A large and muscular man, smartly dressed in dark trousers and a white shirt, had appeared. He stared towards the car. Jeanette had found a tissue and a hand mirror. She moistened the tissue with her tongue and was wiping her cheeks and eyes. At first she was making the mascara smears worse.

'Should I explain to that man?'

'No! That is Enrico – he works for me as a guard. Just wait! Don't make me leave the car yet.'

She sounded scared, unshielded, at a moment of stress. What had happened?

'Ma'am, that place where I picked you up – was it an orphanage?' August said he struggled to use the word.

The sob that followed was so loud he could hear it through the intervening glass, as well as through the communicator. August bit his lip. Although he had still not turned back in his driving seat he was trying to avoid staring at her.

An image was in his mind, the sign on the building where he had picked her up. *Saint Anne's – Residential Home for Children*.

She found a comb and began straightening her hair.

'Ma'am, I don't know if it helps if I say this, but I lost both my parents when I was six years old. I was placed in an orphanage.'

He was still holding the car stationary with a foot on the brake, but now he pulled on the parking brake. He turned off the engine. There was silence behind him.

Her voice, attenuated by the device, 'Excuse me – what was it you just said?'

'I said I think I understand something of what you are going through. I was an orphan. I lived in a place like that.'

She shifted position in her seat and her voice became stronger through the voice tube. She cleared her throat. 'You've some kind of accent. Are you British?'

'Well, yes.'

'I love the way you British people speak. I've always, *always* wanted to visit London. They show my films there. Did you grow up in England?'

'I was born in Germany, but when I was adopted I went to live in England.'

'Let's climb down from the car. I got to see you properly.'

She scooped her hair back, and wound a band around it. She pushed her dark glasses back on and already had her door open. August followed. As he stepped down, the man called Enrico looked as if he was about to stride across and take control of the situation. Jeanette Marchand waved a dismissive hand at him, and he immediately signalled his understanding. He went back inside and closed the door. Moments later the door opened again. Two Labrador puppies came dashing joyously across the gravel to be with her. She bent down to pet them. There was a flurry of energetically wagging tails.

'All right, let me look at you again.' She pulled off her dark glasses, and suddenly the beautiful face that was once so familiar to him was there before him. The tear-stains were mostly gone and she was lit by the sun. 'Did you say your name?'

'No – I'm August, Miss Marchand. August Engel.'

'Is that a normal British name?'

'It's the name I was born with in Germany. But I grew up in England and that is where I have come from.'

'So how long have you been here in the US?'

She was short, slighter of build than he had imagined. Her face – that was unmistakable to him, the large eyes, the brow, her perfect mouth, the corners slightly turned down when in repose. Without make-up she looked more mature, rounded, but still to him almost shockingly beautiful. When she spoke her expression was animated, and she delivered comments with the characteristic dryness, a mildly acid tone, her mouth aslant, the apparent attitude and style that made so many of the characters she played seem attractively witty and deadpan.

To be standing close to her made his breath run short – he knew his face had reddened. She was dressed like many women you might see about the streets, shopping or walking dogs or entering a restaurant. Her casual clothes were the perfect disguise of ordinariness.

But she was not in any way ordinary.

'The next day I was fired by the limo company,' August said. 'Jeanette spoke to them about me, said she wanted me to be her regular chauffeur, and that was the end of my paid job. I knew it was inevitable. No discussion, no arguments. I was canned.

'She made the mistake of thinking she was the client, but the courtesy cars were booked and paid for by the studios. Actors sometimes forgot that. But Jeanette wasn't obsessed with her ego, or not as much as you might expect of someone who was so famous. Some time later, when I knew her better, she admitted that her name was no longer up there in lights. She accepted that. When I met her she was in her mid-thirties, and she was acutely aware there was a new generation of young women actors who were taking the sort of roles she had played before the war. At the time I was with her she was filming another serial for Republic, called *Rocket Men Attack!* She was the woman in peril at the end of most episodes. She was realistic about it. Hollywood studios were going through a lean time, but she was earning money from the work. A lot of actors were finding it hard.'

Justin said, 'So when the limo company sacked you, what happened?'

'Jeanette offered me a job in her household. There was

a classic car in the garage she hadn't used for a long time. She had it fixed up and I put on a peaked cap and played chauffeur for her. I moved out of my lodgings and into Jeanette's visitor house, a small building inside the grounds of her mansion.

'For a while I was driving the old car for her, but it was clear to me that something else was happening. I know she was lonely and worried. I was a nobody, but I was young, still good looking in those days. I think she liked the idea of being with someone who had no hold on her, who would demand nothing and give everything in return. We were soon close together. I lived for those hours with her, those nights, when she was at home. The next day, I would again play the role of her driver if she needed to be somewhere. The other people on her domestic staff realized what was happening and they did not like it. More obviously they did not like me.

'I had outgrown my infatuation,' he said. 'I ceased to be a fan from almost the first day. It changed – of course it changed. Jeanette and I had become intimate lovers. She always had that charisma of fame and stardom about her and I adored her for that, but I also liked her, admired her, and soon I was totally in love with her. For a month or maybe two we were blissfully happy together. I was experiencing it, I was lost in it. I wasn't aware of time passing. All I know is that it was intense and it was brief. Then everything changed. One day a man in a business suit came on a visit to the studio. He represented a film production company in London which had some kind of distribution deal with RKO. He was introduced to everyone who happened to be on the set at the time.'

'Who was he?' Justin said. 'Can you remember his name? I can look him up.'

'No, it's too long ago. It doesn't matter – it wasn't about him. Jeanette told me this man said the British government had been making propaganda films throughout the war, and that the people who made them were now working as civilians, producing and shooting feature films. They were trying to persuade American actors to go to London and work with them. Americans were seen as big box office. They would usually be given leading roles, but they shouldn't expect Hollywood salaries, at least at first. Jeanette told me she didn't care about the money. Maybe it would work for her.'

'And you think that was what made her want to go to London?'

'All I know is that suddenly escaping to England seemed like the answer to all her problems. She was desperate for a fresh start. She was worried about her fading image as a Hollywood star. The sort of roles she used to get were going to younger actors. Although she had divorced him she was being chased through the courts by her second husband, Stan McPherson. The idea of looking for work in Britain was incidental, because like many people in Hollywood I don't think she had ever thought about films being made anywhere else. But it gave her a stimulus.'

By this time, August had learned a great deal he did not like about McPherson, the star pitcher of the Major League. In 1947 McPherson was probably more famous even than Jeanette. Whenever his name came up people instantly knew him for having made league-best strikeouts for the LA Dodgers two seasons in a row. But out of season he was a heavy drink and narcotics user, and a ruthless controller of Jeanette: during their short marriage he had dominated the household, and constantly criticized and undermined her in front of her friends and professional colleagues. He attacked her for letting her looks and figure go, taunted her for not being given starring roles any more, but most of all accused her of failing as a wife and mother.

She never said as much to August, but he was sure that McPherson had frequently been violent to her. In 1948, after eighteen months of private misery, she hired an expensive attorney and divorced McPherson, swiftly but efficiently, in the manner of many a Hollywood broken marriage. But now McPherson was aggrieved, making allegations about money he falsely claimed she owed him.

McPherson's cruel taunts about her first marriage had revived her long held and profound feelings of guilt, particularly about her daughter's death. August said he knew nothing about the child's death, which had happened years before. Jeanette told him she had been genuinely in love with her first husband Roy, but as her career took off his own had plummeted into obscurity. She did not at the time realize how profoundly this affected him. It led to a self-destructive spiral of drinking and gambling. He rarely worked. He had committed suicide in 1933, itself a major tragedy, but it happened while she was working endlessly under contract in one film after another. To cope, she buried herself in her work.

Because of court orders against her, Jeanette said they would have to leave America in secret, but that too became increasingly difficult. One of the fan magazines published an 'exclusive' story, that an unidentified man was believed to be living with her, widely rumoured to be the actor Dirk Halliday. Halliday had made two pictures with her in the past and their names were romantically linked for years, but Jeanette insisted there was no substance in anything the magazines printed. August knew that at least was true. She made no contact with Halliday at any time while he was with her.

With a decision made to escape from all this by visiting England, she and August left the house in a state of normality – the staff were told she would be returning within a week or two. They drove to the airport in two cars: Jeanette went alone in a cab, August in the car he had driven for her, in which all her copious luggage was carried. They arrived at Los Angeles Airport without attracting much attention – they had booked on the Pan American overnight flight to New York LaGuardia, the red-eye, which reporters and film people notoriously steered clear of. They flew first class, but Jeanette insisted on their having seats in different parts of the cabin.

August sat in the row behind her. He said he slept for much of the flight.

'Did anything occur while you were in LaGuardia?' Justin said.

'Occur?'

'Something that might have made her do what she did when she reached London. Were your flight plans changed in any way? You had to wait several hours before the flight to London took off. Were you hanging around in the airport all that time?'

'We were in a hotel. Jeanette wanted to stay away from the airport in case there were reporters waiting.'

'I think there were. I've seen press cuttings from the day the London flight started.'

'We had food somewhere, stayed in the hotel. Then Pan American called to say the flight would be boarding in half an hour, so that's when we went back to the terminal. We went into the airport separately.'

'Once you were on board, were there other passengers?'

'No – we were in first class and we were the only ones. Jeanette wanted me to sit away from her. One of the cabin crew said that no other first class passengers would be boarding so I went to sit in the seat next to Jeanette. She was tense, didn't want to talk.'

'Was she nervous of being on the plane?'

'I didn't know what was the matter with her. She wouldn't respond to me. After a while I moved back to one of the other seats.

'For a long time I blamed myself for what happened when she arrived in London. I believed I had failed her. I felt I was responsible for her, that she had come to rely on me utterly. I should have done more for her, but a man in love believes that love alone is sufficient for every need.

'I was wrong. After she disappeared I suffered feelings of guilt for many years, and even now I think of many small acts or decisions I could have made but did not. I became part of her problems, not as I thought a solution for them. As I sat by myself in the row behind hers, for most of that long wretched flight across the Atlantic, I simply guessed she wanted me to leave her alone. When the plane landed in Scotland, it was obvious she saw me as the most recent of her problems, but the one it was easiest for her to solve. I was abandoned. It took me a long time afterwards to recognize that, and it was painful. Yet here we are, half a century later. I have no hope of ever seeing her again and she still matters to me.'

15

Extract from *The End of Creative Freedom – The Hays Code, 1930–1934*, by Justin Farmer

Chapter 2 – Fay Wray and *King Kong*

Into the muddle created by the film studios' response to the Hays Code came one of the most remarkable films of the period: *King Kong – The Eighth Wonder of the World*. From this groundbreaking and innovative film we can see exactly what the code required, and the way in which film-makers either evaded it or ignored it. *King Kong* soon became one of the reasons the code was stiffened in 1934, and rigidly enforced thereafter, at least until the late 1960s.

King Kong was the most expensive film to date made by RKO Radio Pictures, then the smallest of the Hollywood studios. It was budgeted at around half a million dollars, but on release it became an instant hit and recouped not only the cost but made huge profits – it was the first Hollywood film ever to be re-released. Dozens of sequels have been based on it, many of them indirectly, and Kong the giant ape has become iconic, with an almost endless range of imitators, parodies, spin-offs, books and comics.

But from the outset it was a test of the Hays Code.

Three connected elements help explain the particular impact of *King Kong*: the personality and image of Fay Wray, the background to the way in which the script was written, and the economic, social and moral climate in which the film was made and sold.

Fay Wray, the iconic female star of *King Kong*, moved to California in 1919 while still a child. She had been born Vina Fay Wray in 1907 in Alberta, Canada, but her father moved the family to the USA in search of work, settling first in Arizona, then in Salt Lake City. She began working as a Hollywood extra while still at high school, and by the time she was nineteen she had appeared in more than twenty movies. All her appearances were in comedy shorts, playing bit parts or in crowd scenes.

In 1926 she obtained a six-month contract with the Hal Roach studio by walking brazenly one day into Roach's office and asking for work. Roach was amused rather than annoyed, and signed her for a series of two- and four-reel comedy westerns. While working for Roach she developed and polished the technique of playing the damsel in distress, which in any event was the common lot of many young actresses in the silent era. She made at least two films written and directed by a young and then unknown Stan Laurel.

Fay Wray's big break came when she was spotted by the expatriate German director, Erich von Stroheim, who cast her in the lead of a serious drama called *The Wedding March*. She was still only nineteen at the time.

Stroheim said, with some prescience, 'Fay has spirituality, but she also has that very real sex appeal that takes hold of the hearts of men.'

In *The Wedding March* (released in 1928, one of the last major silent dramas) Fay Wray played opposite von Stroheim, who cast himself in the leading role of an Austrian prince. Wray played Mitzi, a crippled Viennese harpist, who falls in love with the prince. Although the romance blossoms, Mitzi is made to marry a rich and lustful butcher, who treats her with great brutishness. The over-familiar 'beauty and the beast' theme was and still is a Hollywood staple. *The Wedding March* was Fay Wray's first venture into this familiar territory. It would not even be worth remarking on if she had not later made *King Kong*.

Wray was one of the relatively few performers of that era who transferred successfully from silent movies to the talkies. Her transition to sound was sensational. Famous in *King Kong* for her ear-shattering screams, Fay Wray made a number of extreme thrillers (the phrase 'horror film' had not been coined in her day) where her habitual role as the endangered, put-upon young woman gave her much practice in screaming. At least two of these thrillers pre-date the release of *King Kong* in 1933. Michael Curtiz's *Doctor X*, 1932, and Ernest B Shoedsack's *The Most Dangerous Game*, also 1932. In *Dangerous Game* Fay Wray and her co-star Joel McCrea were pursued through a tropical jungle, a set which was being used at the same time in *King Kong*, where similar chase scenes took place.

Wray was soon one of the busiest actors in Hollywood: in the three years leading up to *King Kong*, she was the leading lady in about twenty-five films.

This then is the background from which Fay Wray emerged, to take her most famous role. She was already a star, already a noted beauty, and had already shown herself to be adept at 'female in distress' roles. She was eventually noticed by the film director Merian C Cooper.

In a quote reported many times, Cooper told Wray that he wanted to cast her opposite 'the tallest, darkest leading man in Hollywood.' Wray guessed that he meant an actor like Clark Gable or the then up-and-coming Cary Grant, but of course Cooper was referring to the eighteen-inch model made of steel, rubber, cotton and rabbit fur which became the eponymous giant ape. Fay Wray's response to the reality of this hyperbolic promise is not recorded, but you can't help feeling that it must have come as something of a disappointment, at least at first.

Nor could Wray herself have foreseen how the elements of her particular acting background would blend into the part of Ann Darrow, the object of Kong's bestial affections.

Other female actors were considered at the time for the role, but either were not thought suitable or they turned down the part. These include Jean Harlow, Jeanette Marchand, Frances Lee, Ginger Rogers and Dorothy Jordan.

The main credit for *King Kong*'s screenplay is to Edgar Wallace, the prolific British thriller writer, hired by the production company to add a certain prestige to the project. In fact, Wallace died within a couple of days of starting work and it is unclear how much of the final film is his. In all probability, none of it at all. Even the title he was working with, *The Beast*, was changed.

From the outset, the film was the brainchild of Cooper,

who was to be co-director of the film (with Ernest Sho-edsack). They drew up the outline of what they intended, which was to use real animals photographically enhanced for the main action. When Cooper saw the stop-frame anima-tion work of Willis O'Brien he realized that it was a better technique for what he had in mind. Another writer was put to work: this was Ruth Rose, who was in reality Shoedsack's wife. Her screenplay is the final one, as used in the film.

In the meantime, this was the period in Hollywood of transition from silent movies to talkies, and the shadow of the Depression was deepening. In 1932, when *King Kong* was in the writing and planning stage, the need to make money would have been of paramount concern.

The films that Hollywood was producing at this time were of course nothing like modern output. Although there was a star system, and huge sums of money were lavished on many productions, the actual stories, the scripts, were for the most part conservative. Many writers had grown up in the world of formula fiction for the pulp magazines and had moved to Hollywood in the hope of bettering themselves. Writers were employed directly by the studios, and worked in tiny offices within the studio lots. Scripts were assigned to writers, who often had to pick up the work already started by another, while their own projects could be taken away and given to someone else. Writers frequently worked on three or more different stories at once, usually without credit and certainly without a percentage of the box office.

Although none of this is strictly true of *King Kong* – for one thing it's difficult to imagine the director's wife being made to sweat it out in a writer's cubicle – this is the climate in which the screenplay was developed. Stories had to be clear, uncomplicated and direct. Action and adventure were to predominate. Characters had to be stereotyped. There is no sub-plot in *King Kong*, no subtlety of motive, no plot-twists or surprise developments in the story. The screenplay is merely a straightforward exposition of the idea.

Early in *King Kong* there is a scene set aboard the *Venture*, the ship that will take everyone on the expedition to find the island where Kong is believed to be. A theatrical agent called Weston has come aboard, just before the ship is due to sail. He tells Carl Denham, the film director and leader of the expedition, that he can't find a female actor (a 'girl') to play the lead part in the proposed film. Denham has been told, presumably by his financial backers, that his next film requires a 'love interest.' Against his better judgement he has instructed Weston to find him an actress.

This is the key exchange between the two men, as it is played in the film:

WESTON   It can't be done, Denham.
DENHAM   What? It's got to be done. (*Weston shakes his head in silence*) Now look here, Weston. Somebody's interfered with every girl I've tried to hire. And now all the agents in town have shut down on me. All but you. You know I'm square –

Two suspicions that people have about Denham are implied throughout this scene. The first is that the young woman would be placed in physical danger if she went on location to make the film. The second is that Denham might be procuring her for sexual reasons, if only inadvertently:

she would be the sole woman on board the ship, otherwise crewed by many tough-looking and presumably sexually aggressive males.

Denham of course denies all this and asserts that an actress would be safe with him. At the end of the exchange, Denham decides he can't leave the problem to be solved by other people, and sets off from the ship intending to find someone by his own efforts. His departing remark is, 'I'm going to go out and get a girl for my picture – if I have to marry one!'

Again, there is a hint that sexual coercion will have to be used, not something that would arise if Denham was looking for a male actor.

In the exchange between Weston and Denham, Ruth Rose's shooting script has a slightly different emphasis, and includes a revealing extra detail. This is how she wrote it:

WESTON   It can't be done, Denham.
DENHAM   What? It's got to be done. (*Weston shakes his head in silence*) Look here, Weston. The Actor's Equity and the Hays outfit have interfered with every girl I've tried to hire; now every agent in town has shut down on me. All but you. You know I'm square –

Whenever you are able to compare a shooting script with the finished product that appears on the screen, dozens of tiny textual differences become apparent. These occur almost inevitably in many films: the director or the actors elide lines of dialogue, or make sudden improvisations, or simply get the lines wrong. No one (other than the writer, one assumes) either notices or cares.

In this case, though, it seems that the omission is fairly significant, and the result of a decision by either the director or the studio to leave it out, rather than an ad hoc alteration on the day of shooting.

'Actor's Equity' (Ruth Rose's punctuation) is an obvious reference to the actors' union, then as now a formidable presence in Hollywood. If Denham and his film existed in the real world, the Actors' Equity Association would certainly take a dim view of him trying to hire a young woman and transport her in a shipload of men halfway around the world to make a big-game movie without a proper script. The view would be even dimmer if they realized he was planning to pluck some homeless young woman from the streets, someone who had no experience of acting, and give her a starring role in a new movie.

It would be unlikely, though, that this remark about the union in a piece of dialogue would ruffle anyone's feathers. The mention of 'the Hays outfit' is a different matter. This is a reference to the MPPDA, the Motion Pictures Producers and Distributors Association, otherwise known as the Hays Office. For the film-makers of the time it was a controversial subject. It is no surprise that the remark was quietly removed from the screenplay, since it would have drawn wrath. Fay Wray's role in *King Kong* provides an interesting insight into the Hays Code.

After a series of scandals in Hollywood in the early 1920s, the studios had banded together to form the MPPDA (later abridged to Motion Picture Association of America, or MPAA). Initially, this was set up as a PR operation, to portray and foster a positive image of the movie industry. The MPPDA was headed by William Hays, who had previously worked for the Republican Party as campaign manager for President Harding.

At the time most of the film theatres in the USA were owned by one or other of the studios, but because they were scattered around in many different states they were subject to different state legislation. Moreover, the religious and moral patchwork of American life meant that what audiences would accept (or were assumed to accept) differed from one region to another. Prints of films were frequently returned to the distributors with whole scenes crudely edited out.

There was anyway a growing concern about censorship in many areas of the USA. The more popular movie-going became with the public, the more the moralists – religious groups, educational organizations, etc. – saw films as a threat to their values. Several state legislatures were under pressure to pass legislation that would strictly censor what was shown. Obviously, piecemeal censorship across forty-eight states would have made film distribution almost unworkable. Hays ran well-planned campaigns in a number of states, using the resources of the MPPDA as well as his own GOP connections, and after a state referendum in Massachusetts rejected the legislation by a two-to-one margin the battle was effectively won.

For a few years after this victory, Hays played a double game. On the one hand he was working to defend the movie industry against the continuing complaints of the moral guardians, while on the other he was trying to exercise his own moral authority over Hollywood. From time to time he would issue lists of Do's and Don'ts to the studios, but no one took much notice.

In 1930, as the introduction of sound brought fresh

complaints from the moral watchdogs, he published the first of his now notorious Production Codes, known forever after as the Hays Code. At first, the Hays Code had the opposite effect. The Depression was biting, and the studios were casting around to find what was certain to make money: the answer was of course the two hardy perennials, sex and violence.

The Code lacked the force of law. Its only power resided in the implicit threat of what might happen without it. For many, this seemed a vague concern.

By 1934, the MPAA felt that the Code needed strengthening, revised rules were published and a certificate of approval was required before a film could be released. Joseph Breen was appointed head of the new Production Code Administration. Under Breen, application and enforcement of the Production Code was unbending. Released late in 1933, *King Kong* falls squarely in the pre-Code period. The description is slightly misleading, because the 1930 version of the Hays Code was in place, but largely ignored. 'Pre-Code' really refers to the period of about four years before it was enforced.

Certain films of that period helped bring about the enforcement. Perhaps the best known is *Tarzan and His Mate* (1934). This is the film in which Maureen O'Sullivan went through most of the story wearing a flimsy tabard-like garment that provided titillating glimpses of her body, and which included in its first version a four-minute scene of Maureen O'Sullivan apparently swimming in the nude. In fact, the naked bather was a body double called Josephine McKim, who had won an Olympic swimming gold for the USA in 1928. By modern standards the film is tame stuff, and as in so many other cases you can't help wondering with hindsight what all the fuss was about. The German film *Extase* (1932) contained a similarly harmless nude scene with Hedy Lamarr, although in fact it never reached American screens. It was confiscated by US Customs – the mere fact of its existence was enough to send the moral watchdogs into a spin.

But then there was *King Kong*.

It's instructive to see just how far Cooper and Shoedsack went in defying the Hays Code. Playing devil's advocate, here are the relevant provisions of the 1930 Code. The description that follows the provision is what the film actually shows and the interpretation the Hays Office would probably have put on the material.

Under the heading of **Article II, Sex**:

2.b. Scenes of Passion. *Excessive and lustful kissing, lustful embraces, suggestive postures and gestures, are not to be shown.* Ann Darrow is twice shown in a suggestive posture, an 'abandoned' attitude, lying supine, through fear or exhaustion.

4. *Sex perversion or any inference to it is forbidden.* Bestiality (sexual contact between animal and human being) could clearly be categorized as a perversion. In the scene where Kong strips Ann Darrow of some of her clothes, Kong deliberately sniffs his fingers after touching her, underlining his animalistic nature.

5. *White slavery shall not be treated.* Although *King Kong* contains no scenes which might be mistaken for 'white slavery' in the sense it was usually meant in the 1930s, it does nonetheless contain many of the underlying elements: the concept of a vulnerable young woman from a civilized country being put at the mercy of some alien or uncontrollable presence, who

intends to make use of her for whatever purpose he wishes.

Under the heading of **Article VI, Costume**:

2. *Undressing scenes should be avoided, and never used save where essential to the plot.* Although Ann Darrow never purposely undresses, after Kong has torn off many of her clothes she does spend much of the second act of the film with what remains of them hanging away revealingly.

3. *Indecent or undue exposure is forbidden.* See above. After Kong has torn Ann Darrow's clothes she is in a state of semi-nudity. There are several short scenes where she is swimming, running, etc., in which her body is fleetingly revealed. In addition, there is a scene early in the film where Ann Darrow undertakes a screen test for Carl Denham, in which she wears a see-through dress. The sexual effect of this garment is underlined by cutaway shots to members of the ship's crew ogling her lasciviously.

Under the heading of **Article VIII, Religion**:

3. *Ceremonies of any definite religion should be carefully and respectfully handled.* The villagers on Skull Island are depicted as having built some kind of totemic religion around the presence of Kong on their island. They use a giant gong to announce or summon him, they perform propitiatory dances, they make human sacrifices, and so on. Whether this constitutes a 'definite' religion or not is unclear, but it is certainly shown to be central to their way of life. This is not respectfully handled. The villagers are depicted as uncivilized savages, coping with the dangers of Kong in only the most basic ways: throwing spears, running away, etc.

Under the heading of **Article XII, Repellent Subjects**:

5. *Apparent cruelty to children or animals.* At least one child is shown to be put in danger in the scene in which Kong is

rampaging through the village. As for cruelty to animals, the entire film is in essence about the discovery of a large animal living in the wild. This animal is hunted, chased, attacked with spears, shot at with rifles, knocked unconscious with gas bombs, shackled, displayed for the entertainment of others while in captivity and finally killed with aerial machine guns.

6. *The sale of women, or a woman selling her virtue.* Ann Darrow is captured, violently abducted and finally offered as a human sacrifice to propitiate Kong.

The second half of the 1930 Hays Code contains probably the most controversial material, as it presents its 'reasons' for the prohibitions. It justifies itself by way of argument: a discussion of various subjects including the meaning and effect of art, the motive of the artist, family values, respect for the police, the reaction of adults to films, the sexual responses of audiences to actions they might see on the screen, the absolute necessity of taking religion seriously, and much else.

Amid this pious nonsense there are further observations which have a bearing on the way *King Kong* was flouting the rules:

Impure love must not be presented as attractive and beautiful. The whole thrust of the story of *King Kong* is that the giant ape falls in love with Ann Darrow, and it is her beauty that leads to his downfall. This is stated on an epigraph screen card at the beginning of the film, and it is restated in the last words of the film, spoken like an automaton by Carl Denham. However, Kong is a giant animal, an immense ape or a huge gorilla. No animal is surely capable of appreciation of human beauty in any way that might be comprehensible to that human, and therefore its love is impure. *King Kong* certainly attempts to portray bestial love as attractive and beautiful.

It must not be presented in such a way to arouse passion or morbid curiosity on the part of the audience. As the film is obviously intended as entertainment, and is not at all a serious discourse on bestiality, the actions of Kong towards Ann Darrow must be seen in anthropomorphic terms by the film's human audience. In other words, when Ann Darrow is stripped of her clothes by Kong, the titillation of the audience is in human terms: an attractive young woman, held against her will, is seen having her clothes torn from her. It is a male rape fantasy, in other words. The intention of the film-makers is clearly 'to arouse passion or morbid curiosity on the part of the audience.'

Nudity or semi-nudity used simply to put a 'punch' into a picture comes under the head of immoral actions. It is immoral in its effect on the average audience. On this subject the Hays Code adds: *Nudity can never be permitted as being necessary for the plot. Semi-nudity must not result in undue or indecent exposures.* Ann Darrow is semi-nude for a large part of the second act of the film, and there are several glimpses of her body. There is in fact no reason for this that could be justified by the plot, other than to titillate the audience.

King Kong duly came in for moralistic criticism on its first release, but it was a huge popular success and it has gone on pleasing audiences ever since. After the Hays Code had been strengthened certain cuts were made to prints released after 1934. Clearly, the sort of points made above reflected the feelings in the Hays Office. In particular, the scene when

Kong removes some of Ann Darrow's clothes was cut, as was some of the footage of Kong rampaging through the village.

Those cuts have been restored in recent times, and the DVD versions currently on sale appear to consist of the complete film as originally released.

Tarzan and His Mate suffered a similar fate. The nude bathing scene was cut out in its entirety soon after the film was completed, and some extra footage was shot to replace the more revealing moments of Maureen O'Sullivan's skimpy costume. The original footage has been restored recently. Seekers after the sensational will be greatly disappointed by the clumsy innocence of the film.

The performance of Fay Wray as Ann Darrow made her a major star, or at least a star of *King Kong*. Although renowned throughout the world, never again was she to find a role with which she became so identified.

The film survives because of its unique niche in film history: it was the first major special effects movie, presenting a considerable novelty and a racy story to the audiences for which it was intended. For audiences who have discovered the film in the decades since it was made, *King Kong* still offers novelty, in spite of the immeasurable improvements since in animation, animatronics and other CGI special effects. Some of the animation might seem crude now, but it is still an extraordinary achievement. The film is of course a period piece, but it remains an amusing and fitfully entertaining one.

The greatness of the film can certainly not be attributed to Fay Wray's acting skills. When given a dramatic scene to play she is unconvincing and under-directed. She is not helped by the other actors. There is perhaps only one scene in the entire film free of the gaudy distractions of special effects, and therefore which can be judged as drama. That is the one she plays with Robert Armstrong.

Carl Denham (Armstrong) has taken Ann Darrow to a diner to tell her what he wants from her. Their exchange is excruciating: when Denham tells her his name and asks her egotistically if she's ever heard of him she says, 'Yes, yes, you make moving pictures in jungles and places.' Given that it's not one of the greatest lines of dialogue ever written, Fay Wray enunciates the words with all the emphasis of a shopping list. Armstrong is no better: his performance throughout *King Kong* is unconvincing, amateurish and ill-at-ease.

However, when called upon to run through undergrowth, fall over behind tree-trunks, be tied to a platform as a sacrifice, be carried around, scream, swim, lose clothes, Wray is as competent in the role as any other young actress of that era might have been. Her slightly bruised good looks and fair appearance added to the aura of vulnerability the film contrived around her, but did not improve her acting.

Fay Wray benefited more than anyone else in the film from the screenplay. Because it has the same trashy appeal as the pulp fiction with which it shares a tradition, she was called upon to do little more than be a damsel in distress. *King Kong* is a story told in a straightforward and undemanding manner, with no plot development or sophistication, and no efforts to fill out the characters except in the most unsubtle way.

This simplistic charm also lies in its opportunistic flouting of the Hays Code. In both of these, Fay Wray was seen at her best.

In 1990, when she published her autobiography, Fay Wray

began the book with an imaginary letter written to Kong. In this she said she felt she and the fictional ape had a tacit understanding. 'I admire you,' she said, and added a little ruefully that she had made nearly eighty films while he had made only one. That was the one which had made her famous.

16

Matilda Linden phoned Justin late one morning to suggest another meeting. She said she was planning to take a walk around her favourite park, near her flat in north London, and would he care to join her? He was surprised to hear from her.

Although she had said she would make contact with him after their first meeting, in fact she had not done so. He had liked her and she appeared to like him, but their brief lunch in a pub had created no undercurrent of feeling. He hoped vaguely that they would meet again one day. In the meantime he had met August Engel and afterwards spent a lot of spare time looking through his notes, checking up some of the matters Engel had told him about.

His story about Leni Riefenstahl's academy for new film-makers was certainly true, for instance, although it had never been widely publicized, at the time or subsequently. He had not previously known about the internment of Germans in the UK during WW2. It was also the case that in the years after the second world war the Hollywood establishment closed ranks against film-makers of German origin. Justin had no reason to disbelieve Engel's story, but it led to the moment of the end of Jeanette Marchand's known life, so it was of interest to him.

He remembered that Matilda was planning a biography of Teddy Smythe, and he had since given a second, close reading to her book about the director Hugo Turnbull, in which *Death in the Auvergne* was discussed.

During that brief lunch she had mentioned her current project, which was researching and writing a biography of the British cinematographer and influential cult horror director Keith Choriston, but she said she wanted to talk to him again about Teddy Smythe. She was still thinking of writing about her when she had some time: a book if that was possible, or perhaps a long essay.

The afternoons were often a slow writing time for her, she said when she called him. She felt like taking exercise and getting away from her desk for a while.

It was at short notice but his day was otherwise free. Justin readily dropped what he was doing and travelled across central London by tube to meet her. This time he remembered to take with him his copy of *One Hour of Murder*, Matilda's book about Hugo Turnbull. During the 1950s Turnbull had directed five one-hour films for Allied Studios, aimed at the support slot before the main feature. All of them were of interest, because they featured then-unknown young actors who mostly achieved fame later on, but the highlight was *Death in the Auvergne*. Justin had bought his copy of *One Hour of Murder* a few years before. At that time the name of the book's author meant nothing to him and he knew of Turnbull only superficially, but he loved collecting books about cinema. He had not read much of it until the day after his interview with Teddy Smythe.

A few months later the circle was unexpectedly closed when Matilda, who had seen his profile in the *Observer*, contacted him about Teddy.

He followed her directions to Abney Park Cemetery, which was a tiny part of north London he had not known about before. She was waiting for him by the entrance. Warning notices from the local council about unmade footpaths and a request not to leave litter or damage the memorials were attached loosely to the pillar.

On this warm day they were both carrying shoulder bags which turned out to be full of their own papers. They found it amusing when they realized they were similarly obsessive about not losing work in progress, and willing to hump it around.

Justin usually carried around several print-outs of his recent entries on his database, which he liked to check and annotate if he had time to spend while travelling. Matilda, Matty, had brought with her many pages of research material, as well as a hard copy of her draft of the Keith Choriston book in progress. She showed him the pages she had brought, and some of the stills she wanted to use: it was obviously a major project, with much more work to follow.

'I've made some progress with Teddy since we met,' she said. 'I went down to Seaford because when I contacted her she said she would be pleased to meet me. We drank tea and ate jam scones, and I learned everything about her cats, but I wasn't able to elicit anything new from her about her life. She corrected a few dates of films I'd been guessing at, and told me stories of how she met certain of the people she was working with, but she still wasn't giving anything away about her past. She maintains that what she was doing before she started acting is of no interest, not to her and certainly not to anyone else.'

'She more or less said the same to me,' Justin said.

The cemetery at Abney Park had been neglected for many years, with most of the ancient gravestones overgrown by weeds or crumbling away. In recent times the park's value as a wildlife sanctuary had been recognized, and it was now being sensitively maintained by council workers and local volunteers. Matilda and Justin were there on a sunny day, but it was cool and silent in the shade of the trees, and they found it pleasant to amble about on the uneven paths. They saw a couple of dog walkers while they were there, but apart from them they might have been alone in the place.

Matilda said, 'Being of no interest is one thing, but I live on the details of other people's lives. I've come to the conclusion that on one level Teddy Smythe is everything we think, everything we see. She's a pleasant old lady who had a good career in films, never famous, never rich, a jobbing character actor now retired, contentedly living by herself at the seaside. There's nothing wrong with any of that. But I agree it's clearly not all. She's so secretive about her early life that like you I feel certain she was up to something.'

'Such as what?'

'That's what I'm trying to find out. All lives are of interest to me. You can't live until you're about forty and not do anything! She says that's exactly what happened. I say she's hiding something. I wondered for a while if it might be war work? Something that's still confidential? She is of that generation. We know she was born in Leighton Buzzard, which isn't far from Bletchley Park. I wondered if she might have worked as a code breaker, as a lot of young women did. Everyone at Bletchley had to sign the Official Secrets Act, and those people have kept silent about it since the war. It's still difficult to trace them. I asked her about that. She smiled and shook her head, said nothing interesting had ever happened to her. She had heard of Bletchley Park, of course, but knew nothing about codes. So during the war was she working in an office, or in a factory? She said it was all long ago, another life. I wanted to ask her if she had been a spy, but I guessed what sort of answer I would get. She did let slip one thing, though. Did she talk to you about being married?'

'No – I saw a reference to a husband in a couple of old newspaper stories. She is obviously living alone now. I assumed that she must have gone through a divorce, or he passed on. Presumably she's not still married with a secret husband?'

'No, he died. She said it was a wartime marriage – she hardly knew him. They met while he was on leave, and married on an impulse. It's of no interest now, she said, as usual. He was in the army, took part in the D-day landings and never came back. The adjutant of the regiment he was in wrote to her about a month later. Killed in action.'

'So have you found the marriage certificate?'

'No way. There's nothing to go on. She had a different name then, which I later discovered myself. As she wouldn't tell me her husband's name, I couldn't trace it. She called him Bill – that's all I had to go on.'

'So she changed her name as well? I hadn't realized that. Is that when she became Smythe?'

'No, she was called something else before she married. I don't know her birth name – there's certainly no record of any Teddy Smythe being born around that time. Definitely not in Leighton Buzzard, and almost certainly not anywhere else. I can't even be sure that that's where she was born. The first mention of Leighton Buzzard was in a gossip column in a film-star fan magazine. Hardly an impeccable source. She probably took Bill's name when they married. It seems most likely she took the name Smythe as a stage name when she started acting in the 1950s. That is now her legal name.'

'Couldn't you get all this from Somerset House?'

'There's nothing there about her. I spent a long day exploring all the possibilities. Afterwards, I went to see a friend, a solicitor, for advice. He suggested something I hadn't thought of: most people who change their names do it by enrolling a deed poll, which is normally done through a lawyer. Or it can be done direct with Somerset House. But a deed poll isn't the only way. It's also possible to make a statutory declaration before a judge sitting in open court.

'To do that and to be able to change her name she would have had to declare on oath who she really was. So the court and anyone who happened to be there at the time would know everything about her, but on a typical day most court-rooms are usually empty of the public, especially at the end of ordinary business. That happens to be when most stat decs are sworn. The file would be held as confidential by the court managers. It would be up to them to notify Somerset House of the change, but my friend said that didn't always happen. It depended on someone on the court staff filing it. At the end of the war there was a rush of people making these declarations for one reason or another. The registrars at Somerset House often come across old papers which weren't filed properly, or which were put aside because of pressure of work. So a lot of post-war formalities went by without being correctly recorded. The file will still be there in the court, but there's no hope of getting to see it, even if I knew which court it was. If she'd gone to a solicitor and enrolled a deed poll that would be in Somerset House as a matter of course, on the public record.'

'So what's her game?' Justin said. 'It sounds as if she was planning this. Sometime after the war she started re-inventing herself.'

'It's entirely her business, Justin. That's why I say for now we should simply accept her for who she is, what she appears to be. No one is harmed by it.'

'But what about your biography?'

'I'll get to it one day soon. At the moment I'm busy on Chorrie Choriston. Teddy is an old lady. No one is immortal. Researching someone's background can actually be less complicated after they're gone, but I haven't the capacity to do it now.'

There was a wooden bench in an area cleared of much of the brush and undergrowth. They sat down, enjoying the green peacefulness of the place, a small patch of wild in the heart of London. Birds sang, insects flew. Justin slipped off his shoulder bag and balanced it on the ground between his feet.

'Before I forget – would you sign my copy of your book?'

He pulled out *One Hour of Murder*. It was still in almost new condition, although it had been published ten years earlier. Matty took it from him. The slip of paper he had left in as a bookmark opened the pages at the chapter about *Death in the Auvergne*. She turned back to the title page, holding the cover at an angle above it so Justin could not see what she was doing. She took a pen from the front pocket of her bag, stared away for a moment in thought, then scribbled something. She bent low over the book, her hair hanging down around it.

'I liked what you said about the similarity between Turnbull and Claude Chabrol,' Justin said, while she was still writing. 'Hugo Turnbull had been dead for several years before Chabrol made *Le Boucher* – but you can see the influence.'

'It wasn't just that.' Matty closed the book and put the pen away. She handed the book to Justin. 'Don't look at it now. I corresponded with M. Chabrol about that. He was quite open about it. A lot of people in France went to see the film of *Auvergne*. He said he was inspired by it, not influenced. It became a minor classic. Before that, Chabrol also made a film about the serial killer Henri Landru, which was a subject close to Hugo Turnbull's heart. Turnbull was trying for years to raise money for a film about Landru in Britain and America, but he died before anything could be done. Everything is circular, people think alike, coincidences don't exist, only connections.'

'Do you really think that?'

'Sometimes.'

'Well, what about Roy Tallis? Isn't he a coincidence?'

'Why?'

'Because Tallis was Jeanette Marchand's first husband, and Teddy has his photo on the wall of her living room. Did you ask her about that?'

'I did, but for her it seemed to be a sort of joke. She told me you had written to her after you identified the photo. She said the name meant nothing to her before then. Do we believe that? She had always assumed the picture was of an actor and thought it was probably going to turn out to be an early photo of a film star or celebrity who became better known. I think she was sorry it wasn't someone famous. The picture was still on the wall where you saw it. She repeated what she said to you – she just liked the guy's face.'

'That seems a weird reason to have an old photograph framed. The photo libraries are full of studio publicity shots. And isn't it a coincidence? Him being married to Jeanette Marchand?'

'A coincidence with what? Hollywood stars marry and remarry all the time. They leave trails of ex-husbands. Zsa Zsa Gabor—'

'I know – she married nine times.'

'But Teddy claims she never heard Tallis's name before you worked it out and told her.'

'Isn't Teddy about the same age Jeanette would be, if she was still alive? Do you really believe in coincidence of this sort? Both of them actors, a link with Roy Tallis? We know Teddy's hiding something.'

'What are you suggesting?' said Matty.

That stopped him. The words had spilled out of him un-prepared, the train of thought had a sort of momentum. Was he making too many connections?

'Well, not what I think I was about to say,' he said after a moment. 'Let's stay real. The link with Jeanette must be a coincidence. I've checked and double-checked everything about her disappearance. She almost certainly died or was killed soon after she got off the plane, or when she left the airport. I don't know how she got through the airport, or where she went to if she went anywhere, or what the explanation is – but there was absolutely no trace of her. There were intensive searches, no body was ever found and she never turned up anywhere. The world would have known if she did. She was famous everywhere. She was declared dead eventually. But why would Teddy have a photo of Roy Tallis on her wall?'

'It was next to a photograph of Richard Attenborough.'

'Which proves?

'Nothing, of course. Maybe she likes his face too.'

After a while they walked on, slowly moving back through the trees towards the park entrance close to where Matty said she lived. They said goodbye, agreed to meet again soon, then parted with a self-conscious handshake. They briefly kissed each other's cheek.

Justin walked to the nearest tube station, thinking about her, thinking about Teddy and Jeanette, thinking about co-incidences.

He was now in his early fifties, and guessed, because he could never have asked, that Matty must be somewhere around that age herself. He wondered interestedly about her. He knew so little about her. Did she live alone? She never mentioned a partner. What about the past? Had she been married before, or maybe still was? Had she too changed her name on marriage? Was there a Mr Linden? Still?

He hoped not.

Sitting on the tube as it rattled through the tunnels beneath London, he opened the book she had signed for him.

On the title page she had drawn a large circle. It was broken into three segments, with little arrow heads pointing in both directions at each of the spaces. In each gap she had written a name: *Teddy, Matty, Justin*. Everything connected.

In the centre of the simple drawing were the words, *See you again soon*? Then her signature, *Matty Linden xx.*

17

Justin was staying in a large motel in Baltimore, waiting for his flight back to London the following morning. The place was part of a hotel chain, modern, clean and utterly without character. It provided a sense of security and solitude, a feeling that he was the only person staying in the place, and that no one had ever used his room before. It was the first motel in America where he felt safe and anonymous. Apart from the clerk in the reception office he saw no one who might be on the staff, and saw or heard no trace of any other guests. Yet the parking lot outside was full of cars, and the motel was in a wide plaza next to one of the main feeder roads to Baltimore-Washington Airport, BWI Marshall. The motel had been set up to serve the airport, having been built just outside the perimeter and less than a mile from the vehicle entrance.

He was in contact with Matty, texting to and fro, sometimes by email. It was the first time since they started living together that he had stayed away from home for more than a day or a night. He had been in the USA for a week this time, and was anxious to get back to see her again. The trip was another film festival, well programmed but sparsely attended. He had been invited to be on the competition jury, but discovered once the festival began that the winners had been more or less decided in advance by someone on the organizing committee. A frustrating matter, which had he known about in advance would have made him cancel.

However, it turned out to be a blessing in disguise: there was a man called Charles Andrevon he wanted to meet who lived in the Baltimore area. That was only a couple of hours away by car from Harrisburg. Seeing Andrevon had been fruitful – when he first arrived at the motel he and Matty had exchanged several messages about him and what he had had to say.

In the evening Justin walked across the plaza to a steak restaurant, but after the meal he felt reluctant to return straight away to the air-conditioned room in the motel. The air outside was hot from the day, with smells of traffic and gasoline, and something else, the sort of untraceable airport odour he often noticed when he travelled. For him the humid night was still a novelty. He walked around the side of the huge open space, from one pool of overhead light to the next. He reached a line of shade trees planted alongside the road, where traffic went by in a continuous slow-moving stream.

Here he paused, the sticky heat of the atmosphere temporarily defeating him. He was on a slightly raised bank of ground, giving him a partial view across two of the airport runways. The one closest to him was for the moment not in use, but on the far runway one passenger jet after another trundled down towards the take-off position. The sound of engines drifted across to him. He watched as each aircraft accelerated away, then became unseen as it passed behind perimeter buildings, only returning to view as it lifted off. The sky was heavy with cloud, and there was a generally oppressive feeling of a storm about to break. Earlier he had heard rumbles of thunder, but they came from a long way away. Occasionally there was distant flash somewhere in the clouds.

Justin noticed that nearly all the departing aircraft did not climb steeply into the cloud base, but veered away, staying below, circling around to avoid the wind shear that could be created by large clouds. Some of the planes passed overhead, others disappeared off towards the west.

Their lights and noise created a sense of constant night activity, a web of purposeful travel spreading out across the continent. This was the vindication of the air terminal experience: escape, travel, seeking the sky, going the distance. How many of those passengers now flying out of Baltimore, those in the aircraft scudding away beneath the turbulent clouds, had been hanging around the terminal, enduring the feelings of nullity and endless waiting? As often happened to him, whenever he was in or near an airport, Justin remembered the way Jeanette Marchand's vanishing continued to intrigue him, while on a deeper level he completely understood it. He felt it was a psychic link between them.

A 747 in Delta livery came in low and landed on the runway nearer to him. Justin briefly saw the glaring navigation lights, the long rows of lighted windows, the polished metal fuselage shining, and then it was gone, thundering down the runway as it used its engines to slow it.

After that he walked back to his air-conditioned room and took a shower.

★

A few weeks earlier Matty had had what turned out to be a brainwave. While moving into the apartment she and Justin now shared she had discovered a book she had come across years before and long forgotten. It was the sort of paperback you sometimes bought on impulse if it was cheap enough: a book of recipes, anecdotes from the kitchen, memoirs of extravagant feasts with leading film stars. She glanced through it, her past interest in the early Hollywood days renewed by Justin.

The book, an old American paperback with browning pages and a creased spine, was called *Chef to the Hollywood Stars*. It was a culinary memoir of the experiences of a private chef who during the 1940s and 1950s made his living by renting out his kitchen skills to the houses and mansions of the famous in Los Angeles.

It was focused on cooking and dining, but the writer shamelessly dropped the names of Hollywood A-listers on almost every page. Justin, when Matty triumphantly showed him the book, was fascinated by the section about the dinner the chef cooked one evening for Jeanette Marchand and her invited guests. It was a lavish evening, with several well-known actors named with almost impudent relish. Hardly anything was said about them, apart from what they were given to eat and drink.

Their names came up at intervals throughout the book – it was a book of film stars, dozens of them at their leisure. Jeanette's name too. She also occasionally dined out as a guest at some of these home feasts.

Justin wrote a letter to the author, care of the publisher, using the most recent address he could find. Four or five decades had elapsed since the book was written so he did not expect an answer, but thought it was worth a try. About four weeks later, by which time he had almost forgotten about it, a reply came. The author, Charles Andrevon, was still alive, now retired, living in a suburb of Baltimore called Lansdowne. He signed himself Chuck. Justin wrote back, told him of his interest in Jeanette Marchand, asked if he had any memories of her or her life.

It was while this preliminary exchange of letters was going on that the invitation to sit on a competition jury came from the film festival in Harrisburg, which happened to be within reasonable distance of Baltimore. Once Justin had arranged that he wrote to Chuck and suggested he could visit with him after the festival closed. So it was set up.

In the interim Chuck had written back, saying he could not remember anything about Jeanette MacDonald, but he would ask his wife Hetty, who had sometimes taken part in his private chef gigs. Justin decided to wait until they met to sort out the misunderstanding.

In person Chuck turned out to be not at all vague or forgetful, although he claimed he was and made an old man's joke about the Jeanette confusion. He said he had long ago lost his own last copy of the book, and enjoyed thumbing through Matty's. He and Hetty had three kids and ten grandchildren, with their first great-grandchild expected later in the year. They lived in a pleasant suburban house with a huge garden, a small pool and a lot of dogs. Chuck was a natural gossip, and sat down with Justin on the shaded decking at the back of his house. They drank iced tea. From time to time Chuck went briefly into the house to check if Hetty needed anything.

Chuck said that the period covered by the book was his

own golden age, but the sheer excitement and endlessly exacting work eventually took its toll of exhaustion. And private chefs became less popular. By the mid 1950s the gigs became further and further apart, and some of his clients were slow to pay his fees. Then Hetty became pregnant, and they decided they needed a more stable way of life. Chuck found a job running the kitchen of a big restaurant in Chicago. They stayed in Chicago for about ten years, but moved on. Eventually they retired to this present house because two of their grown-up children had jobs in Baltimore.

Chuck said looking at the book brought back vivid memories of Jeanette Marchand – apparently the dinner at her mansion was a gig he would never forget. Not for good reasons, though.

He told Justin that once he received a commission his normal way of working was to visit the client's home a day or two before the feast. He would usually have a sous-chef and a commis with him. On that first visit they would check out the kitchen and the available equipment. They would then agree what dishes the client would like served and arrange for the provisions to be supplied. They would occupy the kitchen for the whole of the day of the feast while preparing and cooking. On the next day, the morning after the dinner party, he would send staff in to tidy up.

During the first visit he and the others were met by Jeanette and her housekeeper, a woman called Fran Goolden, who was mentioned by name in his book. Everything seemed calm and under control – a good kitchen, a spacious dining area, even a small dance floor for afterwards. Nothing seemed likely to go wrong. 'But you know,' he said, 'in Hollywood in those days you could never predict what might happen on the night.'

Jeanette and her husband Stanley presided. The dinner guests totalled fifteen people, including Barbara Stanwyck and Robert Taylor, Cary Grant, Humphrey Bogart and Lauren Bacall, and Dee Dee Cullen (an executive at Warner). They also cooked a separate feast for the staff at the house, including the housekeeper, Fran Goolden. All these names were in his book.

What was not described in the book was what happened during the meal. Chuck said, yes, that turned out to be a memorable night! He and Hetty had witnessed most of it.

Jeanette's husband Stan had been drinking heavily before everyone arrived, and over dinner launched drunkenly into what Chuck described as a prolonged and rambling attack on Jeanette. Stan claimed she was incapable of getting the right roles, but that he was now her manager and he alone could restore her fame and fortune. He also loudly proclaimed that Jeanette didn't take care of herself, that she was a drug abuser and alcoholic, and had cruelly neglected her daughter.

Jeanette was humiliated, her guests were embarrassed. When Jeanette started weeping the party broke up early: Grant, Bogart and Bacall made excuses and left. Stan McPherson began shouting abusively and wrecked the table. Jeanette screamed with anger and embarrassment. Barbara Stanwyck stayed on, leading Jeanette away into another room.

Justin said to Chuck, 'You heard all this?'

'We couldn't miss it. I was in the kitchen with the others, but Hetty had been serving and was in the same room.'

'What happened to Jeanette after?'

'I didn't see her again. I think she probably went to her room. I went back the next morning to supervise the clean-up. Everything was still a mess, but we couldn't replace stuff that had been broken. The only person I saw was the house-keeper, Fran Goolden.'

Chuck said that Fran was fearful of the household disin-tegrating, which would cause her to lose her job. She had worked for Jeanette for many years but was terrified of what McPherson might do next.

'I'm interested in what happened to Jeanette's daughter,' Justin said. 'I believe her name was Natasha. Did you learn anything about her?'

'I don't really remember. I know Fran said that McPher-son's taunts about her were the most painful. As I remember it, the girl was actually the daughter of her first husband.'

'Roy Tallis?'

'I never knew his name. He had died, and left Jeanette with the little girl. I think he must have been married before. This was back in the thirties, long before I was there. Fran told me Jeanette was devoted to the child but the husband apparently committed suicide. Jeanette was at the peak of her career, and with the chaos that followed his death was barely able to cope. Someone persuaded her that the girl needed professional care, and a place was found for her at a charity shelter in Los Angeles. Jeanette made a large cash endowment. It was intended as just a brief stay, but there was some kind of accident – if Fran Goold-en told me what it was I've long forgotten. It was a long time ago. But Natasha died soon after she arrived in the orphanage.'

'I think Jeanette kept up her support of the orphanage,'

Justin said, thinking of what August Engel had said when he first met her.

'I just remember that night. Fran Goolden said that Jeanette was haunted by her feelings of guilt. She said she wanted to turn the clock back.'

Early next morning Justin called Matty from the motel room before leaving for the airport. It was midday in London. He confirmed the flight details, which if everything went as planned would mean he could be home that evening.

He did not have time to speak for long, but Justin said, 'I feel I know Jeanette Marchand now. I was always interested in her, but I think I understand her at last.'

'After what you just told me I feel sorry for her.'

'Me too. It's now obvious why she flew to Britain that night. What I still can't understand is how she passed through London Airport without anyone noticing her.'

18

Justin flew to Varna, a city in Bulgaria. This was a short break from a sequence of planned journeys to overseas events, which he and Matty had spent several weeks setting up and arranging. They referred to it casually as his world tour, but it was a serious attempt to meet and speak to a number of film-makers outside the UK, some of whom had made long-standing invitations for him to visit, or film schools where he was to deliver lectures, or newspapers and magazines which wanted to interview him.

He had been putting off many of these events for a long time, but he had come up with the idea of making one huge trip, spreading it out over several weeks, in which he could not only accept and fulfil several invitations but also carry out some research of his own.

They had discovered that buying an advance multi-destination flight package not only gave him a real saving in expense, it meant he was able to change his plans at short notice if necessary. This flexibility of the package also allowed a chance to fill the gaps between other commitments with visits to places of personal interest. For instance, he had broken a journey for three days in Paris, a long wished-for opportunity to wander again around the streets on his own time. There were also several new French movie releases he wanted to catch up with. Less successful was a two-night stopover in Venice, which was blighted not only by a snap of freezing cold weather but by the fact that the cinemas in the town had been closed by a strike. He disliked Kyiv for other reasons, but had a memorably good time in Barcelona. The tour continued around these brief sojourns.

He saw the trip to Varna as a gamble: it was for him an unlikely destination, and could not be justified as serious research, but something that had recently happened there had made him curious. It was part of a project he had been pursuing privately for some time.

During July in the year before a group of four young men from the town of Uelzen in Lower Saxony had flown from Berlin Tegel Airport to Varna. They stayed at a hotel in the Golden Sands resort on the Black Sea coast close to the city.

Towards the end of their stay the four men went to a bar where they drank beer all evening. They were dedicated football fans, supporters of the team Werder Bremen. They ran into a group of fellow German vacationers, also football fans, but in their case supporters of Bayern Munich. Inevitably, perhaps, it was not long before feelings ran high and soccer's tribal differences emerged, and a long and boisterous argument began. The four men from Uelzen backed off before violence broke out. They left the bar and headed towards their hotel.

One of the four, a twenty-eight-year old named Heinz Ziegler, hung back from the others and walked away in the direction of the bar. The other three returned to the hotel.

They did not see Heinz again until the following morning.

He was in a bad way. He had obviously been physically beaten: his face and hands were grazed and one of his eyes was blackened. He said the Bayern Munich fans had encouraged a group of local men to beat him up. These thugs knocked him to the floor, kicked him hard in the head and on his back. He claimed his jaw was broken or dislocated and that his left ear had suffered a ruptured eardrum.

His friends helped him find a doctor in the town, where he was examined. The doctor confirmed the damage to his ear, but she said his jaw would return to normal with time. The other bruises and lacerations would heal naturally. She warned them that it would be dangerous for Heinz to fly and prescribed Cefprozil, an antibiotic used for ear infections.

Their holiday was coming to an end and they were preparing to fly home, but Heinz was reluctant to travel back to Germany with his friends. He was concerned about the doctor's warnings of the danger of flying with a ruptured eardrum. The others tried to persuade him to take the risk, saying the flight was only two and a half hours in the air. Heinz said he thought he should stay on by himself in Varna for a day or two longer, until he felt better. He insisted he would be all right.

After his friends went to the airport to catch their flight, Heinz checked into an inexpensive hotel in the town.

Later, when Heinz's movements during that time were being investigated, the hotel staff said that he acted strangely all through the one night he stayed with them. They heard him prowling in his room and seeming to collide with walls and furniture, he wandered up and down corridors, he talked loudly to himself. The CCTV camera behind the reception desk recorded him making several visits to the foyer, looking alternately frightened and aggressive. He never went outside, but peered repeatedly out through the tall glass doors of the main entrance.

He made one phone call from his room. He spoke to his mother in the middle of the night, waking her. She was already seriously worried because he had not returned from Bulgaria with his friends. What his friends told her about his encounter in the bar had frightened her. Heinz answered none of her questions, but speaking in a hoarse whisper he said that four men were plotting to kill him. He requested her to cancel all his credit cards.

The next morning he went to Varna Airport, carrying his luggage. He walked around the main concourse for a while, then apparently discovered the office of the airport medical team and went inside. He was in there only a few minutes. He suddenly cut short the consultation and left immediately.

His brief time inside the airport terminal was recorded on security cameras, and the police who were called in closely examined the footage from these. The clips were later released on the internet, where Justin saw them.

The cameras revealed that when he first entered the airport Heinz strode across the concourse in a normal way. He looked like any other traveller: he had a backpack and carried a large grip in one hand. He appeared to speak calmly to a woman standing alone on the side of the concourse. She nodded her head and waved her hand, as if giving directions. He walked away from her, moving out of the range of the camera. Nothing more could be seen of him at this stage.

The same camera picked him up later: it could be a minute later, or five minutes or half an hour – there was no date/time stamp on the footage. He was no longer carrying his luggage. Now he was running – not just hurrying, but sprinting across the concourse towards the exit. He seemed desperate to escape, to get outside.

Other security cameras tracked him after he went through the doors. Once outside the building he ran more slowly, firstly across a levelled area used as a car park, then he jogged alongside the terminal wall until he reached one of the access roads. The last camera to record him captured him in the distance, apparently now outside the airport boundary. He was walking across a field where sunflowers were being cultivated.

As he climbed over a fence a shadow of an overhead aircraft passed briefly over him. Once he was across the fence he was out of sight of the camera. The shadow was later established to be from a passenger aircraft on its final approach to the runway – Heinz was directly beneath the flight path.

Heinz Ziegler was never seen again.

Of course, there was a logical explanation for what happened. Heinz had been involved in a street brawl, and suffered what were likely to be serious head wounds from a kicking. The medical examination was superficial, and concentrated on damage to his jaw and ear. At the very least he would have been suffering from concussion – it's also possible he received critical brain damage. Such injuries, if not treated as a matter of emergency, are known to lead progressively to disorientation, amnesia and psychosis. It was also likely that he would enter a fugue state, which would account for his erratic behaviour and wandering.

On a less critical level: he was in a country where he did

not speak the language, he was alone, he had no personal contacts. He had only a little money on him, but neither of the two credit cards, which his mother had not in fact cancelled after his last call, was used after he disappeared.

Justin knew that it was most likely that Heinz Ziegler had died as a result of the beating.

Nearly two years had passed without news of him. He never reappeared or made contact with his family in Uelzen. This was in itself unusual. At the time he flew to Bulgaria he was still living with his parents and everyone said how close they all were. But he did not return home. If he had died his body was never found in spite of extensive searches, first by police and volunteers, the second by a sophisticated aerial scanning system in a helicopter, funded by an insurance company. There was no trace of him anywhere within the airport. The area of the flight path, under which Heinz had last been seen, was systematically searched without anything being found.

After the story was publicized on the internet, a more informal wider search began. Police in Germany started contacting and eliminating other men of Heinz's age who had the same name: 'Heinz Ziegler' was not uncommon. Reports started coming in of encounters with men who might have been Heinz. Most of these were quickly eliminated from the enquiries, although one sighting of a man did cause hope to be awakened: a man of Heinz's age and general appearance was noticed sleeping rough on the beach of the Greek island of Naxos. His clothes were dirty, his hair unkempt, he spoke only German and he turned out to be deaf in one ear. Questioned intensively by Greek police, the man was soon able to prove he was not Heinz.

Heinz's disappearance could not be entirely explained: why, for instance, was he seen sprinting across the terminal concourse to escape? Many passengers are keen to leave an airport as soon as possible, but not to the extent of running flat out. What happened to his luggage? He was recorded arriving at the airport with two bags, but he was later seen without them. They were not in a left-luggage locker, and they never turned up anywhere else in the terminal. It was possible they were discovered after Heinz had left but before it was known there was a mystery to his disappearance, and taken to a storage depot off-airport, still there, unrecognized and unclaimed. Or the bags might simply have been put down somewhere by Heinz, and later stolen.

For Justin, the weirdest detail of the incident was contained in the final few seconds of the security footage. The last sighting of Heinz was under the flight path, as an aircraft came in to land. Justin had become interested in the story of Heinz's disappearance because of its similarity to the disappearance of Jeanette Marchand. Jeanette, like Heinz, had gone missing at an airport. Both had vanished without warning and without a plausible explanation. The more Justin researched the story, the more stories like it began to come to light.

People disappear from airports, but only occasionally is evidence left behind. Jeanette could not hide from her celebrity; Heinz could not elude the CCTV cameras. Most airport disappearances are silent, unseen, unnoticed. Many of the people do reappear later, with stories, apologies, excuses, explanations, but it was the moment of disappearance that intrigued Justin.

Some people disappeared in the days before they were due to board a long-distance flight, before they went to the airport. Some others vanished not long after arriving back from a flight.

Company managers and business representatives sometimes went missing, and in the cases he was able to investigate Justin was astonished by the many air miles such people accumulated. Most of them collected tens of thousands of air miles on short and long flights, indicating how often in their lives they had passed through the airport environment.

Financial or career problems were often part of what was behind the traumatic upheaval, but the real common thread was being in or passing through airports. This occurred with a regularity that to Justin felt uncanny and somehow significant.

Many people who disappeared from their homes were living within a radius of two miles of a busy airport. Statistically, such a person was about five times more likely to disappear from the neighbourhood of an airport than someone who lived further away.

There were suggestions of a similar pattern concerning people who regularly stayed in airport hotels, or hotels close to airports, but this was harder to quantify.

Justin routinely followed several internet pages or websites which catalogued people who were recorded as missing. He had originally discovered these as use of the internet began to spread, and one day his search for Jeanette Marchand's name brought him to one of the largest listings.

The overall numbers came as a shock to him. Thousands of people, many of them below the age of twenty-one, disappeared every year in Britain and Europe. Around the world the number of similar cases must have been in the hundreds of thousands.

Few of these stories became known to the wider public as the majority of them involved family crises and ended soon afterwards with a reunion. Only the outstanding cases, the ones with a bizarre or seemingly inexplicable element, or which involved someone famous, or those that led to the discovery of a grisly murder, were the ones reported in the press or on television, or discussed in social media. Many of the disappeared were rootless. Cities large enough to have an airport are also the sort of places that attract the itinerant, the homeless, the casual worker. Most of these people have troubled pasts, or have lost contact with the families and friends who once cared most for them.

The reasons people go missing are varied. There are people of either sex who are trying to escape from a controlling or abusive partner. Children at risk, children hiding, children abducted. Teenagers rebelling. Lovers separated. Suicidal thoughts and attempts. Mental health issues, including dementia. Desperate efforts to escape from authority or political persecution. An accident or other violent event far from home, as happened to Heinz Ziegler.

In almost every case it is the families and lovers left behind who suffer most. They believe that it is their fault: they must have been too unloving, critical, inadequate, bad-tempered, insensitive, neglectful, and they assume these failings, almost always magnified by the sense of guilt, were the main reason for a sudden departure. The guilt sometimes obscures other clues they might have picked up on, while there was still a chance to remedy everything. Many of these people say that the worst of it is not knowing what to do, who to turn to, not understanding what they did that was wrong. Most of all was not knowing where the missing person might have gone, and what new dangers they now faced.

In the two years since Heinz Ziegler went missing in Varna, Justin's researches had led him to the cases of eleven separate young people, living in Britain, who had run away from home. They were all unknown to each other, so there was no link or influence between them. Some of their stories were reported briefly in the press or on TV, others were discussed online. All of these young people had been living in the London area, immediately beneath or close to the flight path of aircraft using Heathrow Airport. On average, one of these unhappy youngsters disappeared almost every month. Most of them had since been accounted for or had returned home, although one died in tragic circumstances.

Similar flight-path clusters were detectable close to other busy airports in the UK, but the data were not so clear. Heathrow was unusual because it was surrounded on three sides by densely populated suburbs. Manchester Ringway Airport had been built in the Cheshire countryside, but because of post-war redevelopment housing estates and business areas crept out towards it, just as the airport, in its tentacular way, was also expanding. Justin came across several people who had been close to the Ringway landing zone and were reported missing.

Other large airports in Britain – Gatwick, Bristol, Birmingham, Stansted, Glasgow – were built away from conurbations. The same was true of many of the hubs around the world, although the fact that an airport came into existence led to a swift accretion of business parks, hotels, restaurants, parking lots, wide highways and so on, soon followed by houses and high-rise accommodation. Airports require staff: Heathrow Airport was the largest single employer in the London area.

There were, though, some major airports in built-up areas. Lisbon Portela Airport was close to the centre of the city, surrounded on all sides by residential blocks and business estates. A landing at Lisbon Airport, as Justin had discovered on a recent visit, involved a breathtaking final approach skimming above many tall buildings. Kai Tak Airport in Hong Kong was another extreme flight path experience which included an approach turn between two tower blocks, followed by a short and steep final descent – not for the nervous. There were doubtless many other hubs with similar problems, but with an estimated forty thousand or more airports in use around the world, it was impossible to gain a global view.

Some other cities, such as Paris and New York, banned passenger jets from overflying the city. In those places the incidence of missing persons, at least those traceable to flight paths, was lower than elsewhere. Justin felt that even the small samples he was able to tabulate indicated that there was a connection of some kind. The main airports in Paris and New York City suffered the opposite problem. Some people, often homeless or evading justice or for some other reason, gravitated to the airport buildings. There they could find anonymity, warmth, a place to rest, shops and restaurants. People like this were routinely looked for and discovered, and removed by the airport security teams, but soon they or others drifted back. It was a permanent feature of the blank spaces created by a society always on the move.

*

Justin flew in from Vienna, landing in Varna in the early afternoon. Once he had gone through passport and customs checks Justin went straight to the lockers and put away his baggage. He wanted to be able to move about freely. Although it was an international airport Varna was a provincial town and the airport was not large. There was a single terminal, recently built but still somehow looking down-at-heel. The signage was in the Cyrillic alphabet, with familiar logos.

The place was full of noise. Construction work was going on: hammering, drilling, the sound of generators. Scaffolding had been erected across one high side of the concourse, and building workers were everywhere. Dust hung in the air, billowing thickly where masked labourers were working by windows or other gaps in the wall. Huge sheets had been hung to try to control the flying grit, but they were ineffective. Yellow-black tapes on the tiled floor, as well as metal partitions and many small signs in Cyrillic and Roman letters, steered people away from the work areas. The fine rubble crunched under his feet.

Naturally, he had emerged into the arrivals area of the Varna terminal, whereas Heinz's time in the airport was recorded in departures by closed circuit cameras. The way from one part of the terminal to the other was signposted, but the signs were out of date and led to a wall being rebuilt. Justin headed for the main doors. The place seemed completely different from the way it had appeared in the security footage online.

He went through the doors into the hot sunshine, glad to be out of the dirty atmosphere. He could feel the grit in his mouth against his teeth, and his eyes felt sore. It was not high summer but the outside air was humid and warm, with a strong unidentifiable signature smell. He often experienced this when he arrived in new places: the scents and pollens of local trees and plants, the road surfaces simmering under the sun's heat, the ground itself, soil or dust, sometimes the outspill of industries. For some reason this kind of smell was always most noticeable on arrival at an airport – one stopped being aware of it after a while, and local people were so used to it that if questioned they had no idea what caused it.

Justin walked along looking for the other entrance, past the cars and small trucks parked or waiting outside the terminal, past a line of taxi cabs. Reconstruction work was going on outside too and contractors' vehicles were parked untidily, with building materials and pieces of loose equipment standing in the way. It was not possible to follow the line of the building: he had to cross the parking area at a diagonal, push through an area of planted bushes, walk back along a short paved path, and only then could return towards the terminal building. The sun was beating down on him.

Justin knew that he must be crossing the area outside the terminal where Heinz was filmed running away. Obviously, the presence of the builders was a recent change, but in his memory the video of this area looked different. There were no parked cars on that day, and he had no recollection of the spreading bushes, which now he was there looked mature, as if they had been planted some years ago. Had he simply edited them out of his recollection, or had the security film been taken from or looking towards a different part of the airport? There was no way of knowing.

He reached the departures entrance, hotter than ever in the reflection of the sun from the half-mirrored glass doors. A constant trickle of slow-moving cars and taxicabs was arriving, disgorging passengers and their luggage, then leaving. Backpacks, rolled sleeping bags and wheeled suitcases littered the ground as people exited the cars.

Justin went inside. It was noticeably cooler once he was through the swing doors. Remodelling work was going on in this part of the airport too, although the noise level was lower. Less dust drifted.

As soon as he was inside he realized that changes were already in place. He had assumed that once he was able to orient the position of the likely security cameras then he would recognize the scene as it appeared in the footage, but the part of the concourse he was in was narrower than it had looked. There was a McDonald's franchise bulking out of one side, and next to it a pharmacy and a magazine stand. Other stores and stalls on that side were closed and shuttered, presumably a response to the ongoing building work. He remembered none of them from the video, taken within what was in reality recent memory, and last viewed by him shortly before he left home.

Justin was familiar with the phenomenon of airport renewal. The buildings and the layouts within seemed never to be left alone. This was certainly true of the two airports he had to use most often: London Heathrow and London Gatwick. Remodelling went on continuously. Was it caused by necessary expansion to deal with the increasing numbers of passengers passing through? Or to provide more space for commercial franchises? Or was it a security matter, a means of channelling the movements of airport users, restricting their freedom to move about?

Nothing ever seemed to improve, from a traveller's point of view. Security issues caused lengthy delays. Reactions to increased social fears about immigration, and official concerns about terrorism, created long queues at passport control. But these features of travel were not themselves stable: the procedures, the rules, were never quite the same twice. Even the commercial areas, the bars and restaurants and perfumeries and electronic gadget shops, seemed inconsistent. New brand names were displayed, new signage, different staff. There were always small but uninteresting surprises.

Were these things really changing, or was it because he simply never noticed them properly?

In recent years Justin had become a regular flier. Whenever he passed through an airport building, waiting for a flight or leaving one, he knew he was in an altered state of mind. He felt his normal self ebbing away from him as he approached the terminal buildings. He assumed many people must feel the same.

Other travellers usually looked passive, patient, accepting, weary. Those waiting for connecting flights often seemed unusually tense. For a long time he attributed at least some of this to a fear of flying, but he was no longer sure of that. Few people met each other's eyes. A lot of passengers sat in the waiting area, asleep or pretending to sleep. Some people looked at magazines, flipping the pages but not reading. Mobile phones were held by almost everyone, but few calls were being made: those who were speaking revealed a sense of urgency, the making of last-minute arrangements or sudden changes of mind. People gathered where the flight departure or arrival boards could be seen.

Flight announcements in foreign airports, often in several languages, were a constant mental intrusion. Everywhere people were walking about – they were restless, not purposive.

They wanted to be done with the terminal, and either out of it and on the aircraft that would take them elsewhere, or out of it and on the way home.

It was a negative environment. It pretended to welcome you with suggestions of good food, a civilized drink, a place to spend time with family or friends, a promise of comfort and relaxation. The reality was the opposite. Being in the airport induced low-level distress and anxiety, so that you would not willingly stay. Food was prepared in line with convenience, not quality, and had to be eaten hastily. Drinks were usually taken standing up or leaning against high stools. Conversation was virtually impossible because of the noise everywhere: announcements, music, the sheer pressure of crowds. Flight connections were often delayed, or missed, or difficult to reach in time.

The only certainties were movement around or movement away. An airport embodied temporary stasis, the nullity of transit.

Justin looked to see if he could locate the security camera that had filmed Heinz during his brief visit – in fact he spotted four darkened perspex globes attached at various positions high on the walls. One was above the entry doors, and the camera hidden behind this was almost certainly the one that had recorded Heinz as he first entered the terminal, his grip in one hand and his backpack over his shoulders. Another was further along the same wall, looking across the same part of the concourse, a longer view, a different angle. Justin moved across to stand beneath it.

From this perspective he could see how Heinz had walked through part of the concourse, and then had spoken to the woman standing alone. She had been waiting where now there was a magazine stall. Justin was certain the kiosk had not been there when Heinz was passing through. Until he had another chance to view the video he could not be sure. Heinz had then moved on, passing what was now the McDonald's concession, and disappeared off to the right through a sort of arch or opening in the wall.

Justin walked in that direction. According to several witness accounts, including the staff involved who had been interviewed early on in the police investigation, Heinz located the medical centre and entered to seek the advice of a doctor. The consultation had only just begun when there was an interruption. A man in work clothes suddenly entered the surgery. The doctor said that he had ordered the man to leave, but Heinz looked frightened and fled the room.

Justin discovered that there was no trace of a medical centre in this part of the terminal, nor anywhere it might have been. The opening led directly to a wide corridor lined with pictorial advertisements for the Golden Sands resort, with two more small, boarded-up concessions, and beyond those some public toilets. Justin walked the whole length, then turned back.

For the next few minutes he wandered around all the parts of the concourse to which he could gain access, but to get through to the inner area, the airside, he would have to check in to obtain a boarding pass and go through security and passport control. He had a flight out of Varna later in the day, but was not yet ready to commit to it. He went to the check-in area, where there were long queues, then walked around the rest of the public space. He looked in all the bars and magazine stands.

He went up to the next level where the building work was less intrusive, and where a restaurant was open. The menu displayed on large boards by the entrance was in Bulgarian, Turkish, English and Spanish, and included coloured photographs of every dish. The prices were in Bulgarian leva or American dollars.

At the end of the hall was a viewing window across the aircraft handling zone. Three large passenger jets were standing on the apron, hooked up to passenger access ramps, with baggage trolleys and refuelling tankers in attendance. While he watched, another aircraft flew in low from the west and made a landing. It was painted white and had a red, green and white flash on the tailplane. It belonged to Bulgarian Airlines.

The feeling of mild tension that had been gripping him since he entered the terminal now eased slightly. It was as if the sight of the big jets coming and going was the valid business of the airport, the rationale, an ultimate provision of the social function of escape.

He took some photos of the view from the window, then of the rest of the upper level. Downstairs he took several photographs of the area of the concourse he believed Heinz had dashed across, although by now he was sure the whole area had already been remodelled, with further changes to follow.

His incoming flight had not provided a meal so he returned to the upper level, tempted in spite of many past airport meals by the coloured photographs of the professed international cuisine. The reality did not live up to the image. It was airport food, the same as everywhere else, over-priced, unimaginatively cooked and served, and only marginally qualifying as international because of the multitude of languages describing it.

Two hours later Justin collected his baggage and boarded the plane for his return flight to Vienna. He was due to interview a documentary film director named Joachim Messer, now retired to Austria, the country where he had been born. During the 1960s, Messer had been recognized as a formative figure in the New German Cinema, associated with such well known names as Werner Herzog, Rainer Werner Fassbinder, Wim Wenders and Volker Schlöndorff. He was also known to have had professional links with Leni Riefenstahl. He directed only one feature, but worked as film editor on several more. Eventually he had set up his own production company, which made well received documentary films for German television, and a series of unusual and idiosyncratic experimental short films.

After meeting Messer in Vienna, Justin was to attend a festival of fantasy films in Ingolstadt, where he was to moderate the festival jury. Beyond that – he was going somewhere else. He was momentarily hazy on details of some of his upcoming gigs, many of which had been arranged weeks earlier. His itinerary was on his laptop. He knew that in ten days' time he was booked to fly to Toronto, but for the moment he could not remember exactly who he would be seeing. There was also an upcoming convention somewhere in the Netherlands.

He had accepted these invitations during the last few months, partly because he was interested, partly because he enjoyed some aspects of foreign travel, but also for the money. Two or three of the gigs were well paid, and the rest had attractive benefits. He and Matty had chosen them to a planned schedule: he would be away from home for about six weeks, with gaps between each date to allow a short break or a rest.

This hectic schedule had seemed like a good idea at the time, but after the first two weeks Justin was starting to regret it. He was already looking forward to returning home, to a long period of catch-up with the film openings he had missed while he was away.

Meanwhile, the life he was leading was becoming a tiring blur of airports, planes and hotels, distances, long waits and longer flights, problems with languages and currency, sights seen from afar, places left behind. And a thrilling but exhausting discovery of film events around the world.

As his plane lifted away from the runway Justin was able to glimpse for three or four seconds the area of farmland next to the airport perimeter where Heinz Ziegler had been spotted. It was the last place in the world where he was known to have been.

Where there was said to have been a field of sunflowers, the soil was now bare. Justin could see the shadow of the plane he was on, speeding across the ground. Then the plane banked away and all he could see was sky.

He managed to doze for most of the flight to Vienna.

19

A comedy without laughs

Playtime (Jacques Tati, 1967), reviewed by Justin Farmer

Jacques Tati's long-awaited magnum opus, *Playtime*, has finally arrived in Britain after a long and famously troubled production. It is already being described as a masterpiece.

Filmed on 70mm stock, dressed in various muted shades of grey and pastel, the action takes place on a vast modernist set specially built by Tati's team on wasteland at the edge of Paris. Most of the scenes are inside a lavishly constructed building, the true star of the film, with a few short scenes taking place in the traffic-jammed narrow streets outside. The blank faces of glassed-in skyscrapers surround the setting. Perplexingly, it appears to be in the centre of Paris: reflections in glass doors give the occasional glimpse of the Tour Eiffel, Sacré-Coeur, and so on.

The film certainly has a unique look. In its two and a half hours of plotless inaction most of the snatches of dialogue (in English, oddly) are all but inaudible or swamped by background sound. There is no central character to speak of, no crime, no chasing about in cars other than those driven so slowly they can be overtaken by pedestrians, a brief flirtation but no sex or love, no suspense, no firearms, and crucially no laughs.

It is the most expensive film ever made in France. It is a loner: it will set no precedent for other films to follow. It is, in the sort of cinematic terms we can apply to recent French films, the last widescreen gasp of the nouvelle vague, an impressive if null space.

It begins in Orly Airport. A group of American tourists, all women, arrive on a crowded bus. They serve the function of a chorus: they drift through most of the action, inseparable and unidentified. They have a leader of sorts, a woman called Barbara (played by Barbara Dennek), who is sometimes addressed by her name and given specific things to do by the director, unlike the rest. The women disembark from the bus and enter what looks like a terminal building, with areas for departures and arrivals, and a glimpse of a jet passing outside one of the vast windows. This reminds us we are in Orly Airport, but we have been taken into a place that is like no other airport building.

We are quickly made uncertain of what the building is for. It is almost deserted. A man strides around in a military uniform, a patient seated in a row of chairs waits nervously for treatment, a cleaner goes by with a broom, a nurse appears, two nuns walk in step. Doors open and close. Is it in fact a hospital of some kind? Most of the space is empty, glossy, glassed in. The feeling of an inert, passive ambience spreads out to the audience.

Tati's signature character, M. Hulot, appears briefly here and throughout, but this is not another Hulot comedy, either in the meaning of the word that suggests a drama with a fortunate outcome, or a story that makes you laugh. It is a Tati enterprise but Hulot is incidental, often in the background or passing through, waiting, observing without comprehending. The real central character is the film set.

What we are briefly led to believe is an airport terminal, or maybe a hospital, turns out to be an endless office block, then a hotel, then an exhibition hall, then a block of apartments. All have the same ghostly feeling of grey anonymity, impermanence, soullessness. There is no comfort, privacy or logic. The tour group passes through most of the iterations, as helpless and transitory as passengers waiting for a delayed transatlantic flight.

The second half of the film is set in one place, an upmarket restaurant which has opened before the builders have finished their work, with a horde of waiters, a tyrannical maitre d', an overworked chef, at least a hundred well-heeled patrons (the tour group is now dressed for dinner), a dance floor, a cha-cha ensemble and, ultimately, a hot jazz band. This is at first a refreshing change from the icy neutralities of the modernist blocks, but it is all apparatus for a series of comic accidents.

The word 'comic' is used tentatively. Although Tati's purpose is clearly comedic, in practice the film contains nothing in the least funny. At best it provokes a wry smile from time to time, an acknowledgement that something we have just seen was at least intended to be amusing. Tati finds hilarious such things as padded chairs that deflate and make a long puffing noise when they are sat on, a ceiling falling in, rooms that turn out to be the cages of elevators, waiters tearing their trousers on the sharp metal backs of chairs, office workers trapped in solitary booths, people dropping umbrellas, slipping off bar stools, colliding with glass doors.

The star of the show remains the extraordinary purpose-built set, which became known to Parisians as 'Tativille' while it stood there during the long months of filming. Although some of the imagery was achieved with perspective cheats using detailed miniatures, and in several scenes many of the extras glimpsed in the background are in fact cardboard cutouts, you soon believe in the surreal urban horror implied and depicted by Tati's camera.

In true modernist fashion, as soon as shooting was completed the Parisian authorities, clearly not admirers of this last widescreen gasp of the nouvelle vague, grimly bulldozed the whole place to make way for a freeway interchange. One nullity replaced another.

Justin Farmer, *Time Out* (London), September 15th 1967

20

It was after his day in Varna, Bulgaria. It was after he went to Vienna. He had been to Sitges, in Catalonia. He had been back to Paris for a day and a night, then had flown to Toronto. Then somewhere else. Athens, Interlaken, Geneva, several more. He was full of regrets, missing home.

Now Justin woke up somewhere. He had been dreaming, but now he was awake. Or slowly waking. As he stirred and moved his back, turned on his side, he sensed the dream images fading. He rarely was able to remember his dreams. He often wished he could, because he loved the vague but pleasant after-sensation. This dream, whatever it had been, was also slipping away. His eyes remained closed. He was halfway between waking and sleep, hoping to doze for another half hour before deciding to get up. The mattress was soft beneath him, the sheets or quilt or whatever was over him moulded comfortably around him. The room was dark. The building was silent, or if it made sounds none of them reached him. Nothing was wrong. All he had to do was lie here in temporary luxury.

Then of course the sense of false security struck him – what was he forgetting to do, or had planned to do? There would be someone to meet, some film to watch, an interview to conduct, another plane to catch. He tensed up and was soon wide awake, but as he lay still and ran mentally through his plans no urgent matter occurred to him. He was due to board another flight the next morning, but he couldn't remember where to. Later – he would look it up later.

He stretched his legs full length and he felt the pressure of the sheet or quilt above him pressing down. He was in a hotel – the bed covers at the end were tucked in with military tautness. At home he always kicked the covers loose, but hotel beds were usually made up unconquerably tight. A hotel, then. Another hotel. The most recent of hotels, a whole string of hotels behind him, a blur of them. All of them much the same, but different in small ways, forgettable ways. Never the same twice, but never anything unusual or memorable.

He lay in the dark, trying to visualize the actual room he was in this time, the one in which he must have fallen asleep the night before. Justin thought back to where the last one had been. He had started from London, then to Bordeaux, then after that to . . .?

And not just hotels, but cinemas and films and viewing theatres, interviews and festival panels, directors and writers and camera operators and film editors, and actors inevitably, countries and visas and interventions by ticket offices. Also of course planes and airport terminals, a long sequence of airport terminals, with their vast inner spaces, shining floor tiles, row after row of hard seats designed for short-term use, expensive consumer advertising, numbered gates, canned music, channels to wait in, paperwork to produce, prohibitions to obey and obligations to accept, officials to listen to or seek information from.

He had realized early on in this long adventure that it was a kind of madness, that he was taking on too much, and at one point (after Toronto?, after Cologne? – both of the events were unsatisfactory for different reasons) he thought seriously about abandoning the rest and simply catching the next plane home. But he always found time and enough interest to keep his notes up to date and on occasional days when there was no travel, or not much, or there was no one to meet or no festival to attend, then he worked assiduously on updating his online database and preparing his next interview or panel appearance.

So he stuck it out, flew tens of thousands of miles, acquired hours of taped interviews, had seen on average at least one new film a day, had met and grown to know superficially those directors and other film professionals, some famous and influential and unwillingly giving their time, others in mid career with time to spare, still others retired by age or choice, or because the work ran out. Most of them at every level were optimistic: the next film, the next screenplay, the next role, was always going to be the breakthrough. Sometimes it was likely, or at least possible, but mostly he suspected it might not be.

Justin had tried to establish a routine but was rarely able to keep to it. Meals were often taken in haste, or postponed, or missed altogether. He endured constant dryness in the mouth, with a choice of drinks, some with too much alcohol and others with too much added sweetness. He carried bottled water everywhere. There was often a rush to get to the next airport, or a long delay while in it. Connections were missed, or involved tiring dashes from one end to the other of an unknown and overheated transit terminal. Seats were double booked with other travellers. Weather was bad. Airports were invariably crowded or noisy or both. Exhaustion almost always attended a flight, sometimes mid-journey, always at the end.

Now, though, this morning.

He opened his eyes, but the room was profoundly dark. A small digital display next to the bed revealed the time: 08:17 am – not therefore the middle of the night. He was fully awake so he moved, sliding his legs out from under the bedding then sat up. Apparently triggered by his movement the curtains across the window slid open with a slow, smooth motion. The sudden burst of light into the room surprised him. It was daylight out there, a sunny morning: sunshine poured into the room. Heavy net curtains diffused the light so it was difficult to see outside. Justin pulled on the white hotel towelling robe that he must have used just before he fell into the bed the night before. How long ago was that? He had no memory of looking at the time. He sat down on the side of the bed and looked at his wristwatch, but it was showing 11:18 pm, clearly unadjusted after the last stopover, or perhaps the one before.

Where had that been? Justin had only superficial memories of the airport from which he had taken off the previous day: the usual lighted direction signs in the terminal, the taped-off stockyard queues, concrete walls and carpeted passageways, an immensely long travelator full of other passengers and their hand luggage. He remembered a killing heat and humidity outside, a breathtaking walk across a sun-dazzled apron towards the aircraft, accidentally touching the metal side of the fuselage as he boarded, burning against his fingers. The plane had taken off with the window shades pulled down on both sides of the cabin. An announcement came from the cockpit that the crew had received a warning of tropical storms ahead. The plane passed into night not long after take-off.

They landed hours later. Now he was here in his room. It was the most recent flight, the latest room.

The room contained no clues as to the name of the hotel or the city it was in. There was no familiar logo, hotel or corporate, anywhere in sight. The desk had a pad of paper for guests' use, but there was no printed hotel name or address. The ballpoint pen that rested beside it carried no marque, not even the name of the pen's manufacturer. There was a vase of cut flowers, but he could not identify any of them. The towelling robe he was wearing had no crest or name woven into it. The room was luxurious, more so than he could normally afford, so he wondered briefly how he had come to be allocated it when he checked in.

He was tempted to return to the known and familiar: to go back to bed and postpone the problems of orientation.

An array of several unlabelled electrical switches were mounted on the wall next to the bed. There were too many of them to be only for the lights, so they must control something else. He threw one experimentally and the entire bed began to vibrate and ripple. A humming noise emanated from below. He switched it off and tried another: the lights over the desk came on. Another: this time the pillow end of the bed started to tilt upwards, but only on one side. He switched off and the bed silently subsided.

He needed to use the bathroom so he walked across the

wide room, again glancing around for a sight of a logo or marque. The sensation of the thick pile of the carpet against the soles of his bare feet imparted a sense of luxury – he felt the pile squeezing up between his toes. He passed a minibar, a big one, and pulled the door open to peer inside: the bottles and miniatures were familiar brands but with a range of choices: whisky (two well known blends and a single malt from a Scottish distillery), gin (two brands), vodka (one Polish, one Russian), a bottle of pre-mixed cocktail of some sort, wine (one small white, one small red), orange juice, apple juice, cola, soda water, beer (regular and non-alcoholic, large size and small), nuts, chocolate bars, an ice compartment. A range of other wines was suggested. The printed price list on the top of the fridge had no heading, just the brands and prices, written in English and priced in US dollars.

Lights came on as he opened the bathroom door, and an extractor fan began whirring. Again nothing identified the hotel or the city he was in: no brand names anywhere. He wondered if he had inadvertently been moved across into a high-price business hotel, or had made an error when making the booking several months before, at the time he and Matty were planning the trip.

He used the toilet, then showered – a sweet and steamy fragrance of rosewater surrounded him. Afterwards, when he had put on his underclothes, he went at last to the window: was he in a hot climate or a cold one? The net curtains shading the windows were thickly woven and held tightly against the frame. They were strung top and bottom on metal rods. They admitted the bright sunlight and he could see through them to the extent that he saw the outline shapes of buildings, but no details. He tried sliding the curtain to one side, but it resisted him. He finally managed to lift one edge, pulling hard, so that he could peer around it into the outside world.

The sun was shining brightly from a sky of glossy, un-clouded blue. It looked hot out there.

Tall commercial blocks stood opposite his window: the expected concrete, mirror glass, a few minor embellish-ments, the same sort of buildings you found downtown almost anywhere in the urbanized world. They towered above him and the hotel in which he stood. Nothing to identify them was visible. One immediately opposite was the tallest of all those he could see. If there were corporations and offices inside, as almost certainly there would be, their names and brand images were displayed a long way beneath or above, out of his sight, close to street level or up in the sky.

Justin craned to one side, hoping for a view perhaps of sea or mountains, anything to help him locate where he was. The thick net curtain put up stiff resistance. The street ran right and left outside the hotel, traffic driving slowly, or temporarily held up, on the right. On the ground: many traces of snow. Snow! There were heaps which had been pushed or shovelled to the sides of the traffic lanes. It seemed he had come to a cold but sunny climate, or a winter zone. Reykjavik? Somewhere in Canada? Surely not Russia – he had no recollection of attending anything in Russia. He felt lost again. No pedestrians moved on the narrow, partially blocked sidewalks.

Then he noticed: a couple of hundred metres from where he was standing the monoliths of modern buildings pressing close against each other were interrupted by a small park:

there was a glimpse of bushes and some trees. The ground was snow-covered. Set back a short way from the busy road there was a pagoda.

Because it was lower than almost every other building in sight he could see down on to its square, concave-pointed roof. Thick snow lay there.

A pagoda obviously meant he was somewhere in the East. Japan? China?

Japan was a possibility – ages ago he had tried to arrange an interview in Osaka with a screenwriter called Kondo, but there was a difficulty with dates, the need to book an interpreter. Unexpectedly, production of the most recent film Kondo had written was put back until the following year and the magazine in London lost interest. The planned encounter fell through.

Vietnam? Thailand? He had made no arrangements in either of them, and anyway the wintry weather made them unlikely. Perhaps he was in Taipei – he was planning an article about the successful Taiwanese cinema, but again he didn't remember making any plans for a visit.

A name came into his mind: Kim Su Bong, a young director who had made his mark the previous year at the Berlin Film Festival, screening a minatory feature of extraordinary violence and unexpected beauty. He was Korean. He had agreed to an interview with Justin at the studio complex in Seoul, where he was shooting a new film.

Justin felt the world around him reshape itself understandably, suddenly return to focus. He regained memory, identity, awareness, purpose.

He continued dressing, putting on winter clothes.

★

After interviewing Kim Su Bong (whom he now knew to call 'Hap') Justin spent another three days in Seoul, mostly eating, sleeping, seeing films and transcribing several earlier recordings. The sense of dislocation, the lack of orientation, never really left him. The transcribing of interviews was a priority, because they were generally timed to appear when the interviewee was known to be having a new film released, and he had slipped behind. He usually transcribed an interview tape soon after recording it while he could still recall informal details. In addition to the interviews he had been taking detailed notes for some theoretical essays he wanted to write on film structure, the intention being that one day he would collect them into a book.

He had scheduled his stay in Seoul for two days, but he decided to extend it. The hotel turned out to be an inexpensive upgrade: his original booking was with another place, but a month ago there had been a fire or some other catastrophe, and the company had transferred all guests to other hotels in the same chain. He was comfortable and felt spoiled in the semi-automated room with its switches and auto-responsive sensors, so he could afford a short extension.

It took him a couple of hours on the first afternoon to reschedule the next flight, and make alterations to the dates and times of meetings ahead. He replaced his existing flight with the only non-stop service to Bombay he could find for that day, a Singapore Airlines flight. With that all sorted out he went to see as many films as possible. Hap had fiercely urged him to sample the current output from several young South Korean directors, none of which had yet been shown outside the country.

Justin did his best, but naturally the films were screened

in Korean, with no English translation available. Two of the films were shown with subtitles in French, so he managed to follow those to a certain extent, while realizing he was probably missing subtleties, nuances, jokes and so on. He tried hard with the others, but knew that to understand them properly he would have to wait for them to be released in the USA or Britain.

During his second night in the hotel, unable to sleep and roaming in a desultory way through the dozens of TV stations, Justin came across a movie channel. To his surprise and pleasure he discovered that one of the films he could select was the 1942 release *Casablanca* – it was being shown in English with Korean subtitles available as an option. He welcomed it like an old friend and watched while sitting on his luxurious armchair with a feeling of guilty pleasure.

At the end of his stay he checked out of the hotel, arranged for a taxi to collect him, and headed for the airport to catch his flight to Bombay.

21

Seoul Airport, more accurately known as Gimpo International Airport, was about ten miles from the centre of the city, towards the border zone with North Korea. During their interview Hap had sounded surprised Justin was departing from there, because he thought the new airport in Incheon had already replaced Gimpo for long-haul flights – Justin later double-checked that he was going to the right airport, in case. The person he spoke to on the phone sounded puzzled that he needed to check – Gimpo still number one.

He had begun to find his luxurious hotel room oppressive, and he barely slept during the night before the flight. He kept thinking about all the travels that still lay ahead, and in the darkest hour of the night he made a definitive decision to cancel the rest of the trip. Once he was out of bed in the calm light of day he could not face the upheaval that would cause, so carried on. His insomnia had left him feeling traumatically alert, his limbs sore and his joints aching, with a sense of physical exhaustion in bizarre opposition to his busy but aimless mental state.

He maintained an upright posture in the rear seat of the taxicab, but in fact it was difficult to keep either his eyes open or his mind alert. The ground was frozen, the sky was dark with heavy clouds. The cab driver said he was worried he wouldn't be able to get back to the city if the threatened snowstorm began.

Justin thought ahead through the next couple of hours, during which he would have to endure the usual drudgery of delays at the airport, but at the end he would be seated in the aircraft cabin and able to make himself relatively comfortable for the long flight ahead. He had flown with Singapore Airlines before, and found their cabin service sympathetic and excellent.

He was deposited by the taxi at the entrance to the departures area, and went in to look for the check-in desk for his flight. The place was crowded and the heaters were working overtime against the deep winter chill, so it was hot inside. He stared at the departures board but could not see the flight to Bombay. The day before, when checking the airport was the right one, he had also confirmed his flight and seat.

Through the windows out to the parking areas Justin could see that it had started to snow, as expected.

He wheeled his heavy suitcase to the information desk and was politely told by a uniformed young woman that his flight had been reassigned to the satellite area of the airport. This was where flights to India now departed. She smiled a great deal. He should check in at the satellite desk, she said, but if he preferred he could check in here at her desk, and deposit his luggage. It would be loaded automatically on his flight. Justin was tempted by this suggestion, but in the past he had suffered lost or mislaid baggage. He said he preferred to keep his bags with him for now and check in at the satellite. She smiled and said that was a very good idea.

She handed him a complimentary booklet with a voucher for a free introductory drink at any of the airport's many bars.

He asked her for directions to the satellite. She said it was not far, and laid a little map in front of him. The satellite appeared to be a large circular building away from the main terminal. She pointed to it with a special stylus as she talked him through it. He should walk across to the elevators at the far end of the hall, which she pointed out to him, descend to the next level down, then follow the signs to the satellite. She assured him it was not a long way. Very easy walk. No problem. No, he did not have to go outside, and could access the satellite from here. Yes, there was a bus to the satellite instead. Very reliable, but the walk was more enjoyable.

He thanked her effusively and trundled his suitcase away. He was to remember her words.

When he reached the elevators it turned out that none of them went down to lower levels, so he read the symbols engraved into the call-button display, and experimented. He went up to the floor above, then to the level above that. Neither of them led to signs directing towards the satellite.

He returned to the floor he had started from, intending to go back to the information desk and check what she had told him. A crowd had gathered, though, and the young woman he had spoken to was no longer there. She had been replaced by two others, who both smiled all the time. He waited, but the passengers at the front of the crowd were two Americans wearing business suits who were aggressively demanding a refund of some sort. One of the young women was speaking on a telephone, watching the two men and smiling at them, holding in her free hand the special stylus.

While he waited he glanced around the hall and noticed that he had been deposited by the taxi driver in a part of the airport that appeared to serve only destinations in North America. He had not spotted this when he first arrived. He saw long lines of people waiting at check-in desks for United, Delta, American, Air Canada, Korean Air, British Airways and Qantas.

He was still in plenty of time to catch his Singapore Airlines flight, so without any feeling of urgency he dragged his case across the concourse to the opposite end of the departures area. Here there was another bank of elevators, all of which served a lower floor. In front of them was a direction sign in English: *Satellite Arrivals Lounge, Level 0.* He assumed that once he was in the satellite building it would be a simple matter to move across from arrivals to departures.

He descended one level, saw another sign indicating the satellite arrivals and set off along a straight and brightly lit corridor. Many other passengers were already crowding along the passageway, most of them walking in the opposite direction to him. Some, looking flustered, were hurrying and trying to overtake others, weaving and dodging.

Illuminated advertisements for resorts in Bali, the Swiss Alps, Indonesia and the Caribbean were spaced at regular intervals. The slogans were in many languages. On the floor was a carpet made of some kind of acrylic material whose static charge made it feel as if the hairs on his arm were standing on end. It was woven in a continuous, repeating design, a zigzag of dazzling bright colours that he could not stop looking at and which gave him feelings of vertigo. The corridor seemed to extend forever. He trudged on, the small wheels of his suitcase not working well on the stiff carpet pile. Several times he eased the load of the heavy case by swapping the arm with which to tug it.

Finally the corridor opened into another terminal concourse, which at first Justin assumed must be the satellite. It was not. It was an interim security check at which he would have to produce his boarding pass. Although he had not yet checked in and so had not been issued a boarding pass, Justin lined up in the huge press of other passengers, but when he finally reached the barrier and this omission was discovered he was turned back.

Following instructions from a member of the security staff he had deposited his suitcase on the conveyor belt to the X-ray machine. It had already gone through and was on the other side.

Separated from it, Justin experienced the first sense of alarm. He could see it beyond the barrier, lying irretrievably at the end of the X-ray system. People were all around it, picking up their own luggage, having to reach over his. One man pushed Justin's case aside with an irritated movement. Another brusquely moved it out of his way, lowering it neglectfully to the floor, where it fell on its side. Now it was forcing people to manoeuvre themselves past it, while stretching over to reclaim their own luggage.

Justin tried to explain the problem to security officials, but either they did not understand or chose not to. Someone's child climbed on top of his case, then sat down on it − a parent lifted the child away, and used his feet, one kick, two kicks, to push the case further to the side.

Finally, one of the uniformed security people listened to Justin's anxious requests.

'It is in the security zone,' she said. 'You can remove it but we must search it to make sure it is safe.'

'It has already passed through the scanner!' Justin said, but to no avail.

After a wait of several minutes one of the officials retrieved the case and carried it through to a long metal table outside the security zone. Justin stood by as two guards gingerly opened the case with the key he was forced to pass them. They removed everything that was inside. They laid out his personal possessions one by one in plain view – his clothes and underclothes, both clean and in need of laundering, shoes, socks, books, toiletries, prescription medicines, his files of handwritten notes, his diary, his chargers, his spare laptop. When the suitcase was empty they checked its sides, lid and base in detail, scanning with an electronic device. Then they took his backpack and emptied that too. They looked through his notebooks, one of the officials exclaiming with a laugh and pointing something out to his colleague. They booted both his laptops, complaining at how slow they were, and scanned his mobile phone.

After about half an hour of this, while other travellers surged around, the two guards walked away without a word.

Justin repacked hurriedly, cramming everything back in. He was now at risk of missing his plane. The overheated hall and lack of fresh air were making his head swim.

He made a quick decision: that he would return to the area where he had first arrived, check in at the information desk and deposit his suitcase, obtain a boarding pass to secure his seat on the plane, then demand reliable instructions for the quickest route to the satellite terminal and the departure gate.

He hurried back towards where he thought he had left the long corridor to enter this hall, but the dazzling design of the carpet was different: patterns of variously sized multi-coloured circles, snaking to and fro across the width of the corridor. He backed away, crossed the hall, tried another passageway, and found what he was looking for. He set off back towards the main terminal, almost at home with the familiar zigzag, and now in the company of many other people who had presumably just landed and passed through arrivals.

The heavy suitcase weighed on his arms and shoulders as he tugged it along. Again, the two small wheels dragged against the stiff pile of the carpet, a constant exertion. He was over-dressed, still wearing the quilted jacket he had put on before leaving the hotel. At intervals he passed beneath ventilator grilles in the ceiling, from which warmed air was being pumped down. He paused, removed the thick jacket then carried it over his arm. Now he felt cooler, but it was more of a strain to propel the large case with one hand.

Although this time he was moving in the same direction as most of the other people, there were a few coming the other way. Justin frequently had to step aside or tiresomely weave to make way for them. He soon felt certain that this return walk was taking longer than before. Had he walked past an exit without noticing it? Soon after this he saw a printed sign, indicating the way to the satellite, and it was pointing back the way he had come. That was a reassurance of sorts.

He saw a toilet so he went inside quickly, relieved himself and washed his face and hands in cold water. A sign by the door, which he noticed as he was leaving, warned him in English that a boarding pass must be carried at all times. Security delays to his own flight and those of others might otherwise be caused. Anxiety returned. He took hold of the handle of the suitcase – his hands were already once more moist with perspiration.

He continued on down the long corridor. The crowd of other passengers had thinned noticeably while he was in the toilet. Where had they gone? Suddenly unsure of where he was he returned to the washroom, wondering if in his confusion he had exited by another door, but no. He carried on.

A door set in the side wall opened a short way ahead of him, and a tall man in a cap and braided uniform entered the corridor. He walked towards Justin. He was wearing dark glasses, and exuded the sort of assured aura Justin associated with flight crew. He was self-confident and businesslike, and was carrying a small case.

Justin said, as they passed each other, 'Excuse me, do you speak English?'

The man did not break his stride, looking straight ahead. But then he turned back, his face breaking into a good smile.

'I guess you're British, right?' he said.

'Yes.'

'Well, how may I help you, sir?'

'You're a pilot?'

He nodded assent. 'Do you need something?'

Justin quickly explained his problem, asking if the man knew the way to the satellite, and if he did, preferably a quick way. The captain stared towards him steadily. Justin could see a tiny reflection of himself in the golden convex lenses of the dark glasses. He kept waving his free arm agitatedly whenever he spoke, but could not stop himself.

'May I see your boarding card, sir?'

'I don't have one yet. I was told to check in at the satellite.'

'This is airside. Passengers are not allowed to cross into this part of the airport without a boarding pass. If a security guard stops you it could cause big problems. You'll have to get back to the check-in area and be allocated a seat. Strictly speaking I shouldn't be talking with you.'

'I don't know how this happened!' Justin said. 'I'm simply trying to reach the departure gate for my flight.'

Justin pulled the printed booking confirmation from an inner pocket, and brandished it. The captain backed off.

'Sorry, sir. I can't look at that. You need to be landside. I can't help you until you have been cleared for airside.'

'Is that where you just came from?' Justin pointed towards the door the man had used, a short distance further along the corridor. It was painted the same colour as the wall and was hard to notice. A small keypad device was beside it.

'Flight crew area. You'll have to visit a check-in desk. The satellite is back there.' He pointed behind him, which confusingly was the direction Justin had been taking.

'I saw a sign pointing—'

'No, there has been a restructuring program. Extra access options have been introduced. Now excuse me, sir, I have a long flight ahead of me.' He edged around Justin, looking away. A small cluster of other passengers was passing.

'Thank you for your help,' Justin said politely, but there was no response.

He changed the weight of his jacket from one arm to the

other. He looked back to see the captain striding confidently down the long corridor, heading into the humid distance. Passengers stepped meekly aside as he approached them. Electric heat billowed down on Justin from a grille above his head.

He went to the door from which the captain had emerged, but the coded keypad lock defied him.

He pressed on along the corridor. He was again feeling detached from the reality in which he seemed to have found himself. The hideous carpet was like a psychedelic nightmare from which he could not look away. He was stunned, tense, feeling blurred.

Until this, Justin had believed that because of his experience of making many flights abroad he had become an old hand at airports, could read them and understand them, and easily negotiate the various quirks and obstacles put in the way of travellers. Many inconsistencies − physical layout, rules about what might be carried on to the plane, differing procedures − were never explained, but he was used to that. To him, airport syntax was like a puzzle with slightly different rules everywhere, usually solved easily but sometimes requiring persistence. This meant that many people travelling were put on the defensive, were made submissive and became unprepared to challenge or question anything. Most of them were anxious nothing should go wrong.

Justin himself, braced against the airport experience, was never entirely at ease, often slightly stressed by the anticipation of a long flight or one with transits to other flights in foreign airports, but at least he usually felt confident of knowing the way to parse movement through an airport, how to resist unwanted retail opportunities, or freedoms that were channelled into permitted zones, and restrictions that often seemed arbitrary.

He knew this was a coping strategy, a form of denial.

He could see the end of the long corridor approaching and he accepted that this time denial had failed him. He was now deeply immersed in the blur of alienating architecture of concrete, space with no purpose, artificial light, synthetic carpet fabrics, advertisements for things he could not afford and did not want, junk food, unreliable signage, obsessions with security, rites of passage determined by the anonymous people who ran the airport and who were not there to justify their decisions.

He was living the familiar waywardness of a bad dream, the sort he always remembered but could never learn from.

The corridor came to an end.

He was in a stairwell. He had arrived earlier at this place by descending in an elevator, one of a bank of lift-shafts, but now he could not see where the elevators were. A flight of stairs stood in their place. He clambered up towards the level above, dragging the heavy suitcase behind him, the wheels drumming and halting against each step, the handle twisting awkwardly in his hand. It was a steep climb, and a long one. The final ten or fifteen steps were a physical ordeal.

He emerged, perspiring but thankful, into the familiarity of the check-in hall. When he had been here before all the desks bore illuminated signs for mostly British and American carriers, but now every single one had changed to Korean Air.

There was a window to outside. A full-scale blizzard was in progress.

He looked around for the information desk, and hurried over to it. A new sign had appeared, warning in English that passengers should proceed to the boarding gate as soon as possible, as all aircraft required de-icing before departure.

The desk appeared to be the same one as before, but he could not be sure. The smiling women he had seen and spoken to were not there, replaced by two young men, but he waited in line with other passengers.

Soon, one of the smartly attired young guys behind the desk beckoned him forward. He smiled courteously at him. 'Which airline are you flying with, sir?'

'Singapore Air.' Justin thrust the booking confirmation and his passport across the desk.

After a glance at the booking, the clerk tapped something on his keyboard, then looked up at Justin.

'You fly to Bombay? No check-in here. Korean Air passengers only. You must transfer to Terminal 2 or the satellite.'

'I tried to go to the satellite, but I found out I was supposed to check in first.'

'Terminal 2 for check-in.'

'I was told I could check in here,' Justin said.

'All baggage drop-offs at this desk are now closed. Terminal 2 for check-in.'

'I have to get to the gate soon,' Justin said, waving his hand towards the sign about de-icing.

'De-icing at Gimpo Airport always very quick.'

'So how do I get there?' Justin could feel his heart starting to race, the familiar confutation of purpose returning. Anxiety swept through him. It was going wrong.

'Short walk, no problem.' The clerk looked reassuring. He waved the hand holding his special stylus towards the far side of the hall, where there were several doors. 'Through there. Then take shuttle bus Number 7 to satellite. Very easy.' The clerk typed something else on his keyboard, which was concealed on a lower shelf of the desk. He looked at the monitor. Then he said, 'Singapore flight to Bombay will be slightly late departing. One hour. For you good news, and plenty of time. Have a complimentary drink at one of our bars. Gimpo Airport wishes you a lucky and successful day.'

Justin hastened away.

Halfway across the wide concourse he felt his vision blurring. The sound of his own heartbeat pummelled his ears. He pressed on, trying to avoid other passengers, but now he felt unidirectional, set on his way. He brushed hard against some of the people, and muttered apologies. He made sure not to meet anyone's eyes. He saw a sign indicating the direction towards Terminal 2. He put on speed in spite of stiffness in his legs and an aching back.

He reached a set of glass-panelled doors, pushed through and entered what he presumed was Terminal 2. No signage confirmed this. None of the check-in desks displayed the logo for Singapore Airlines.

He steadied himself against disappointment, forced himself to be calm. His heart was racing, so he took two deep breaths. He went slowly towards the nearest desk, then saw a small but clearly illuminated message board.

This thanked him for using Terminal 2, and added the information that passengers for the airport satellite should check in at desk no. 20. This was the one at the furthest end, a long walk.

Relief swept through him. Justin went across as quickly as he could to desk no. 20, waited for the two passengers ahead of him to be dealt with. He tried to calm his heavy breathing. He was giddy with anxiety. At last it was his turn. He stepped forward and handed over his passport and booking confirmation.

It went smoothly. The woman clerk handed him a boarding pass and a seat docket, but she then told him that baggage items as large as his could only be handed in at the satellite. However, she ran off an adhesive label printed with fluorescent Day-Glo orange, and secured it around the handle of his case. The code for the destination airport was printed in large black letters: BOM.

'Proceed to Gate 22b in the satellite terminal,' said the desk clerk, but not looking at him. 'Very easy to find. No problem. From here all will be automatic. Shuttle bus carry your bag for you.'

'Shuttle bus Number 7?' said Justin.

'Yes. All arranged.' She tapped her stylus against the boarding pass.

'What about the weather? Is the bus likely to be delayed?'

'No delay. Gimpo Airport rated number one for shuttle passenger satisfaction.'

Justin scooped up the papers and his passport. 'Where may I catch the shuttle?'

'At shuttle depot. Short walk, close to the terminal.' She pointed towards the main doors to the outside. He could see now that while he was in the closed world of the terminal building outside it had continued to snow heavily. The sky was thick and dark, and the wind was already piling drifts against the stanchions and frames. The clerk looked at her computer terminal. 'Plenty of time. Next shuttle bus departs in thirty-five minutes.'

'Are we talking about shuttle bus 7?'

'That is correct.'

'I need to get to the satellite more quickly than that,' Justin said. 'Is there another way?'

'Shuttle bus 3 serve the satellite terminal. That leaves in five minutes.'

'Then I'll get that one.'

'Shuttle bus 3 only for passengers on domestic flights,' the clerk said. 'But it is a short walk to satellite. Very easy. No problem.'

There was a door behind her station. This was clearly marked *To the Satellite*. Justin thanked her, grabbed his bag and jacket and hurried to the door.

Beyond was a carpeted corridor, brightly lit, heading off into infinity.

At first he was trudging along in a crowd of fellow passengers. Some of them were rushing to catch their plane, or were travelling light, so they could move along faster than the others. These people threaded their way, dodging through the throng, half running with their luggage. Others were moving slowly, especially those carrying babies or herding groups of children, and Justin himself became an overtaker, leaving many of them behind. Gradually, the crowd around him thinned out.

The carpet dazzle in this corridor was different from the others, but just as bright. It was composed of brilliantly coloured geometric shapes, lines and solids, polygons, adjacent to each other, or overlapping, or concentric. Seemingly placed randomly in fact they were in a repeating pattern, which once it had been rationalized by the eye became a maddening sequence which could only be blurred, not looked away from.

The back-lighted advertisements were the same ones he had seen all over the terminal, just as repetitive in their depiction of images thought to be alluring: catamarans on blue seas, roulette tables with players in dinner jackets and evening gowns, complicated meals on crowded tabletops, lovely young people in swimming pools, darkened dance floors with disco lights, palm-lined beaches, ski slopes, again and forever again.

Justin simply wanted to reach Bombay. He had no visual preconception of the city, or even of the places he knew he would be visiting. He knew only the names of the people he had appointments to meet: a director of Bollywood musicals, and two young actors who were as famous and celebrated in the Indian subcontinent as any Hollywood stars, but much less well known around the world.

After struggling with his case for a long time Justin glanced at his wristwatch. If his flight really had been delayed there was still enough time for a short break. When he reached another toilet area on the side of the corridor he went in. He washed again with cold water, dampening his hair, cooling his body. Because he had been forced to repack he knew there was a clean shirt close to the top layer inside the case. Justin removed it and swiftly changed into it. The one he had been wearing was stiff with sweat. He saw a faucet of drinking water, so after he had swallowed several gladdening mouthfuls he used it to refill his plastic bottle.

When he returned to the corridor he found he was more or less alone – the only other passengers he could see were a long way in the distance, ahead of him.

He was worrying again about getting to his flight in time. Even assuming that the hour's delayed departure was real, it could not be much longer before the boarding of the plane started. But he knew from experience that boarding a busy intercontinental flight could take a while. There was probably still time enough to be there, join the end of the waiting line. How much further would it be? The long corridor stretched interminably ahead.

He briefly put on a spurt, fuelled by anxiety, but his legs and back were aching and after a few frantic paces he slowed down, feeling depressed and resigned.

He headed on doggedly, staring down at the monstrous carpet. The minutes ticked by. The carpet seemed to move beneath him, a repetitive, hypnotic dazzle. The intermittent glare from the illuminated advertisements was like a slow shutter release: each one shone brightly on him as he passed. Every now and then one of the panels would be unlit, as if the power had failed or the lights had burned out.

The failure always attracted his interest, making him look at nothing to see.

Justin struggled on as long as he could, but it was no good. He knew it was becoming impossible. He would never reach the departure gate in time. He gave up.

He slowed, he came to a halt.

The padded jacket fell from his arm and he let the suitcase go. It tipped away from him, leaning with its handle against the wall. Justin squatted on the carpet beside it, exhausted and demoralized. He had trouble focusing his eyes. He was out of breath.

He drank a lot of the water from his plastic bottle. He usually carried chocolate in his backpack whenever he travelled, so he found that and ate several chunks of it. It had softened up in the constant blast of heated air, but it tasted good and the sugary content lent him a restorative surge of quiet energy.

He sat down properly, stretching his legs out in front of him and leaning back against the wall. His case was beside him. On the wall immediately opposite was one of the lighted advertising panels, so familiar, so repellent. It depicted a restaurant in Paris, apparently noted for its seafood. The interior of the place was conventional and classical, with dark wooden panelling and what appeared to be several Impressionist paintings on the wall. Four attractive young people were seated around a table, which was already laden with numerous dishes of oysters, lobsters, crayfish, crabs, mussels, sauces and salads. They were raising glasses of white wine to each other. A maitre d' stood by, beaming proudly at the perfectly arranged table and its admirable diners. Justin had staggered past this picture of epicurean fantasy an uncountable number of times, and had grown to hate the people depicted. Now they were almost everything he could see.

After a while he took some of his cleanest clothes from the case and bulked them into a temporary pillow. Although the corridor remained warm he placed the jacket on top of himself as a makeshift cover. The carpet was soft beneath him. When he closed his eyes the shocking pattern no longer had the power to dazzle his mind and dull his senses. Soon he was asleep.

And then he was awake again.

His sleep had been deep, apparently dreamless. He had not stirred at all – he was still in exactly the same position as he was when he first lay down. He peered at his wristwatch. Something like seven or eight hours had passed while he slept. He roused quickly, aware that this was a public passageway.

Justin stood up, blinking and stretching, easing his body into verticality. He returned his clothes to his suitcase, and snapped the locks shut. Hearing a distant noise he looked back along the corridor in the direction from which he had come. Made tiny and stick-like by the immense distance, but clearly visible because of the unforgiving lights, a horde of passengers was hurrying along towards him. He felt an irrational terror of inclusion, that he was threatened by them, that they would surge towards him and surround him and sweep him up. He was suddenly anxious to flee and be ahead of the mob.

It was still warm in the corridor so he again carried his padded jacket over his arm. He pulled his wheeled suitcase over the resisting pile of the carpet.

Ahead he saw light. He had noticed this almost as soon as he was awake, but assumed it was more of the same, more lighted panels in more of the endless corridor, but now that he was striding as fast as he could towards it he could see it clearly. The light was of a different quality. It was bright and clear rather than artificially intense.

The corridor was coming to an end. Open air was ahead. The sun was shining. The closer he came to the mouth of the corridor the warmer the air seemed. He marched towards it, refreshed.

As the passageway ended so the carpet gave way suddenly to a floor constructed of concrete slabs. He walked out into hot, brilliant sunshine. The wheels of his heavy suitcase emitted a familiar rumbling noise.

Low walls on each side allowed him to see where he was. He had emerged on to a pier, a jetty, the roof of a long terminal. There were a few wooden bench seats on each side. Small roofed platforms gave shade from the sun. Lights on gantries bulked overhead. A few people stood in groups, staring away. It was an aircraft viewing platform.

On each side, right and left of him and slightly below, was the flat expanse of an airfield. The heat made the air shimmer and distance was lost in haze.

There was a smell of kerosene, a constant whining of turbine engines. He could see the high tailplanes of several big jets, obviously parked on the apron below to take on or discharge passengers. There were more aircraft standing away from the terminal, and at least two huge aircraft were out on the access runways taxiing slowly towards the take-off zone.

While Justin was looking in that direction he saw a Boeing 747 approaching, already close to the ground with its undercarriage deployed. It landed with what looked like easy precision. Waves of heat billowed in from the sunbaked ground.

A young woman, her hair blowing lightly across her face, was standing alone by the rail, her interest divided between watching the movements of the aircraft below and looking across whenever someone walked past her on the pier. She stared towards Justin as he trundled his suitcase past her – he returned her gaze, saw her face clearly, felt a rush of interest in her and an irrational desire to get to know her, but in the same instant she flicked her loose hair back from her eyes and turned away again.

The moment died and whatever might have passed between them was lost forever.

A boy was standing on the other side of the viewing area accompanied by his parents. He too was looking across at the woman, but the parents had not noticed.

A man brushed past Justin: he was tall and thin, with a shock of untidy hair. His face was gaunt, with prominent cheekbones. His eyes were hidden by impenetrably dark glasses.

The crowd of passengers who had been following Justin along the passageway were now emerging behind him into the daylight. They were all heading in the same direction, along the viewing platform towards a tall concrete and glass building some way ahead. A few of the men were in Western business attire, but most of them were dressed lightly in open-necked shirts and casual trousers. Many of the women were wearing sarees.

A large sign ahead said in English: *Passport Control – Please have all documents ready.* It was repeated in a few identifiable European languages, but also in Hindi or Gujarati script, which Justin recognized but could not read.

He swung his backpack around and groped inside for his passport, suddenly realizing he needed it. The passport was where he normally kept it, but the boarding pass and his booking confirmation had disappeared. He found them screwed up and stuffed into a pocket of his bulky jacket but he had no recollection of putting them there. The bright orange baggage identifying tag was wrapped around the handle of his case: the letters BOM were clearly visible.

Also in his pocket he felt a smaller, softer ball of crumpled paper which had not been there before. He pulled it out, uncrumpled it: it was a paper napkin with the name and insignia of Singapore Airlines printed in one corner.

He stepped aside from the walkway and leaned against the low wall to smooth the napkin completely flat with his fingers.

There was no mistake. He folded it neatly and returned it to his pocket.

He was momentarily distracted by one of the big jets flying overhead. The sound of its engines caused many people to look up to watch it pass over. It was directly above them, spilling its noise, turning steeply, presumably to avoid flying across the main runways. One of the other planes was now at the end of the runway, waiting to start its take-off run.

In addition to the wheeled suitcase and his backpack, Justin realized he had the strap of a third travel bag hanging diagonally across his chest from his shoulder. He did not remember putting it there, and in fact had not noticed it until now. The bag was small, dark blue and made of stiff fabric. He swung it down to have a look at it. It too bore the Singaporean insignia. He wrenched the zipper open.

A printed card was inside:

Singapore Airlines hope you have enjoyed your flight with us today. Please accept this useful tote bag with our compliments. The voucher attached to this card may be used on your next Singapore Airlines flight to purchase any of the inflight Lancôme® luxury products at half price.

Inside the tote was a small package contained in a transparent wrapper. There was a toothbrush, a small tube of toothpaste, a white face flannel, two pieces of soap wrapped in paper and a pocket comb. All of these bore the airline's insignia. There was also a pack of paper tissues, eye masks and a tiny cellophane envelope containing noise-cancelling earplugs.

At the bottom of the tote Justin found his Nokia, safely stowed away. He had no memory of putting it there. The battery was flat.

He walked with the crowd into the terminal hall, waited for ages in a jostling and noisy queue, but in the end was smoothly granted permission to enter India. He called Matty on his hotel phone to tell her he had safely arrived. They talked for several minutes, very expensively and on a noisy line. He kept his appointment with the Indian film director the following day.

His world tour continued.

22

Hanks in Waiting

The Terminal (dir. Steven Spielberg, 2004) – reviewed by Justin Farmer

In 1988 an Iranian man named Mehran Karimi Nasseri arrived in Charles de Gaulle Airport near Paris, having been deported back to France after he landed in London. He was not carrying a valid passport. He had claimed to be half-British with a Scottish mother and that his papers had been lost or stolen en route. He said he could not return to Iran and was a refugee. British officials sent him back whence he came. Although his return to the Parisian airport was legal he was not allowed to enter France itself, could not go anywhere else and therefore remained in the airside of CDG's Terminal 1. To the present day Nasseri is still permanently living at the airport, without passport, identity papers or any legal status. He is inescapably in transit, waiting and waiting.

His plight was made into a French film, *Tombés du ciel* (1994), directed by Philippe Lionet and starring Jean Rochefort as the Nasseri figure, and now his predicament has been given the full-on Hollywood treatment by Steven Spielberg.

Unlike Lionet's film, *The Terminal* is likely to be shown and viewed all over the world.

Just as Jacques Tati could not find a convenient modern office block in which to film *Playtime* (1967), Spielberg was unable to locate an airport willing to sign away one of its busy terminals. The presence of his huge technical film crew and their intrusive equipment, not to mention the many actors and several hundred extras, would have made normal operations unworkable. Like Tati, Spielberg therefore had his own set built for him, in this case an entire terminal was constructed inside a vast hangar formerly used for servicing Boeing 747s. Unlike Tati, Spielberg appears not to have been bankrupted by his grandiose designs.

Both directors had the same idea in mind: to recreate the alienating neutral space of an airport, where people constantly come and go, where no one belongs or would choose to be, where the motivating interest of everyone present is to be somewhere else, but where some become permanently marooned. Or where at least one person is marooned.

The physical ambience is again the unacknowledged star of the film. Spielberg's mock-up of a terminal at JFK Airport looks just like the real thing. You accept it as 'real', probably even think you recognize it from your own travels, or are reminded of a dozen other airports like it. But where Tati depicted the chilling abstraction and surrealism of modernist architecture, alien to human existence, three and a half decades later Spielberg and his production designer, Alec McDowell, have made the place US-friendly, a liveable area of reassurance and familiar safety.

All the signage is in English. Popular brand names are displayed everywhere. There are shops and fast food restaurants, a Starbucks coffee house, a bookstore, a fashion store – these were made practical by the set constructors, so the film crew could take lunch in a Burger King, and browse books during their spare moments in a branch of Borders. Our stateless, marooned passenger buys a designer suit from Hugo Boss to clinch his amorous intentions. Things could hardly be more different from Tati's icy vision. For perhaps the first time ever we visit an airport terminal where life goes on as normal, where it is even possible to have a good time.

The actor who takes the Nasseri role is the much admired and bankable Tom Hanks. His love interest is the beautiful Catherine Zeta-Jones. Around them is a gang of airport employees who seem at first threatening and rather sinister, but who in Disney fashion soon turn out to be goofy and amiable allies: a janitor who leaves puddles on the tiled floors so that people will amuse him when they slip and fall on their backsides, a love-struck passenger transport driver, an overweight security guard, an immigration official whose passion out of hours is going in costume to *Star Trek* conventions. Their role is comedic, comforting. The closest thing to an enemy these lovable people have is the boss of the terminal, played with great zest by Stanley Tucci. Even he is an honourable and unthreatening man, hard-working, conscious of the law and fair to his staff.

Seriousness breaks out from time to time. The word 'wait' recurs with interesting frequency. It is argued that airport terminals are not for transit, nor for arrivals or departures, but for waiting. We learn eventually that Viktor Navorski (the name of the character played by Hanks) has been in the airport for nine months, waiting for release. Although the real incarceration of the unfortunate Mr Nasseri has been for a much greater period, nine months is a long time to wait, even in the tame circumstances of a shopping mall offering an inexhaustible supply of cheeseburgers.

We see Viktor Navorski's many actions but we only glimpse the interminable other hours he must have spent wandering the retail opportunities and the bland passages, seeking some kind of release from the tedium. His new friends do not grow or change in this time: they too are waiting for Hanks to escape, trapped by the doings of this likeable hostage over whose destiny they have no control.

As Tom Hanks at last finds a way out of his dilemma he leaves not only the terminal behind but abandons his allies too. There could be real human drama in this, but *The Terminal* is feelgood cinema where the positive outcome is calculated to be heart-warming. His amiable friends are at the front of the crowd who gather round to smile and applaud as he makes his way to freedom. In the real world most passengers feel pleased, or at least relieved, to escape from an airport terminal, but Hanks induces a few smiles too many.

It is said that Mr Nasseri was paid a quarter of a million dollars for the use of his 'story'. That must have given him the feelgood factor too, although his status remains unchanged. He is still waiting for exit papers in Charles de Gaulle Airport, Terminal 1.

Justin Farmer, *New Statesman*, 24th September 2004

23

For reasons not adequately explained to him, the journey to Australia began with a short first flight from London Heathrow to Paris. Justin assumed the fare was cheaper for the festival organizers in some way. In Paris he had to connect with an Air France flight, which advertised only one other stopover on the long journey, and that would be in Singapore. He was told by the ticketing agency that the connecting flight in Paris would be reached from one gate to another within the same terminal, that the change of planes was routine and straightforward and that the rest of the flight would be uninterrupted and comfortable.

That was technically true, but the terminal in Paris turned out be the same size as a small city, or felt as if it was. Justin's long trek from one side of the vast building to the other made him experience in full the bleak concrete and glass caverns of Charles de Gaulle Airport, blighting the countryside to the east of Paris. Finally boarding the flight to Singapore came as a relief, the brutalist terminal left behind. A day and a half later he was in Melbourne. He had flown from a cool

European spring to a hot Australian autumn, and he was glad to be there.

In the usual meaning of the word, Justin had hardly slept at all for the last thirty hours, roughly from the time of take-off from CDG Airport, through a long wait during the stopover in Singapore, until finally clearing the fearsome customs checks at Melbourne. An intermittent state of mental immobility had sufficed as relaxation, but was not enough. The flight seemed interminable while it was going on, but telescoped into a single bad memory almost as soon as it was over. As he walked through the Melbourne arrivals area with his luggage he felt wide awake and fully alert. But also in a state of dreamlike unreality.

He paused to send another text to Matty. They had texted to and fro at various stages of his journey, but she had asked him to tell her when he landed safely, and he was eager to do so. She was already in Melbourne, having flown out from Britain the week before to stay with her father. Her parents had moved to Australia at the end of the 1960s. Her mother died about a decade ago, but her father, Dan, now in his eighties, was in good health and still active. He lived in the north-eastern Melbourne suburb of Bundoora, close to the university where he used to teach.

Justin was met at the exit area of the terminal by two young men, one of them carrying a large placard with Justin's name written in black capitals. The other held a slightly smaller board aloft – this carried the logo for SKIFFF, and underneath the name, St Kilda International Fantasy Film Festival. He was greeted warmly, helped with his luggage, taken out into the warm Australian sunshine.

Once in their car, with him in the front passenger seat,

they enquired politely about his flight and if he had enjoyed it, then they enthusiastically rattled off a list of the names of other guests and speakers, and when they were expected to arrive, and those who were already there. One of the names they mentioned was that of the film biographer, Matilda Linden – Justin did not show a reaction. Then they said that the American director Spencer Horvath and a team of his assistants had flown in from Los Angeles the day before, a matter of intense interest and excitement for the festival organizers, and a focus of unceasing demands for access from the media.

From the point of view of the festival committee the fact that a usable print of Horvath's new film *The Sator Meaning* had gone missing en route was much more alarming. They were waiting for a replacement to be sent from the studio, or failing that were trying to get hold of another copy of the film that had been with the Australian distributors since the previous week. They were excited and worried by this: the first real crisis to threaten the festival's plans.

Horvath himself, apparently now at his hotel sleeping off the jetlag, had seemed calm about it, they said. He's totally zen, they added admiringly. Justin, temporarily in a similar state of time and body displacement, felt much the same. Things would work out in the end, he thought vaguely, aware that a certain redness of mist was occluding his vision.

He stared straight ahead at the road as they drove towards St Kilda, feeling grateful not to be on the aircraft any more, relieved that these amusing and dedicated people had come to remove him from the airport terminal without any delay, and looking forward to being shown to a hotel room. His mobile vibrated in his pocket: a text from Matty, happy he had arrived safely, promising to join him the next day, saying affectionate things. He tried to send a reply, but his fingers were fumbling and he dropped the phone. He had to lean forward to retrieve it from the car floor. Straightening again turned out to be an effort.

Another list was recited as they named several of the films due to be screened out of competition, they asked him if he would like to stop somewhere to crack open a tin of beer, if he wanted some tucker, they pointed out some of the sights of Melbourne.

Justin was preoccupied by the discovery that if he looked at something for more than about five seconds his gaze became locked on it. His eyes felt sticky. The mist was still there.

It was hot and sunny and Melbourne looked like a beautiful modern city, but the car dashed past everything. He commented blandly on the warm weather. One of the guys said, 'This is Melbourne. It changes without warning. We tell people if they don't like the weather, wait a minute.'

Justin said a few things in response, but as soon as he uttered the words he couldn't remember what he had said. What were those films they had mentioned? Why were they discussing the weather? He dropped his mobile phone again. His mouth felt numb and he was having trouble focusing. One of the guys was called Bernie, the other was Harry, or maybe Harvey, he wasn't sure which, and a little later he could no longer tell who was who.

They drove him to a huge modern conference centre, which incorporated a hotel. It was adorned with banners and flags for SKIFFF. He glimpsed people moving around in reception, thought he probably knew some of them, but not right now. He was shown to a room. He threw off his clothes and lay thankfully on the bed. Sleepy oblivion swept up and consumed him. And that was the end of that until halfway through the next day. He woke up then with a full bladder, a terrible thirst and an aching hunger. There were five texts waiting from Matty. He replied, and she replied back, and he went downstairs to find some food.

She joined him at the festival that evening.

The formal opening of the festival followed on the next day, in the early afternoon. It was held in an open area of the centre, sometimes used as a dance floor, sometimes for conference meetings, or banquets. The wide windows gave a panoramic view of Melbourne Bay. The launch event was slightly chaotic: several of the invited guests or competition jurors or speakers were yet to arrive, there had been problems with an overflow hotel with delegates unable to find their rooms, but above all Spencer Horvath failed to show up for the launch session. This was the only problem that seemed to matter. He had sent two young assistants to speak for him, but they were clearly not the same thing. They explained that Mr Horvath was visiting the distributors' office in downtown Melbourne, to try to straighten out an issue concerning the use of their copy of *The Sator Meaning*.

Matty had been invited to preside over the competition jury, because of the success of her book *Chorrie*, a biography of the legendary Keith 'Chorrie' Choriston, published the year before. The recently deceased Choriston was a hero figure to fans of horror and supernatural films, and Matty's book was doing well. When it was belatedly realized by someone on the committee that Justin was Matty's partner, a temporary but to them embarrassing oversight, they had invited him to come to the festival too and act as a celebrity interviewer. He did not yet know who he would be interviewing, or when the interviews were to take place. He was content to go and see as many of the films as he could. He did not mind at all playing second fiddle to Matty, and he was enjoying being in Australia.

Teddy Smythe was introduced by the festival organizers at the introductory session as a special, surprise guest. One of the men on the festival committee propelled her on to the raised dais in a wheelchair. He paused her beneath an overhead light. She was wearing a beautiful gown, sat erect in the seat, still looking much as she had done the day Justin interviewed her. The crowd standing around applauded her, but politely.

Justin whispered to Matty, 'Did you know Teddy was going to be here at the festival?'

'No. Did you?'

'Spencer Horvath is here. That must be why she was invited. Obviously someone in the festival made the connection with Horvath.'

'It's common knowledge now, I suppose,' Matty said. 'We should try to spend some time with her.'

But the brief round of applause suggested that not everyone present realized who she was.

Teddy remained on the low platform for the few remaining minutes of the opening remarks. She was positioned behind the people from the committee, the light shining down on her. She looked at ease, smiling around as the speeches went on. Her silver hair was longer than Justin remembered, but she had that familiar half-smile. He realized he was staring, and experienced a surge of affection for her.

Immediately after the opening ceremony, which was in reality a long straggle of semi-audible introductory remarks by members of the committee speaking through a poor PA system, the first of the competition films was to be shown. Matty and Justin headed down to the superbly well equipped theatre in the building's sub-ground level, where the celebrity interviews and some of the press conferences would be mounted, and where most of the films were to be screened.

This opening film was a misjudged gang-warfare film from the Netherlands, with a fantasy element: a sort of Merlin figure appeared to be controlling the outcome in some unexplained way. The violence was unremitting, but the many action scenes were unconvincing.

As usual, Justin scribbled notes in the dark. He wrote them on the printed handout on which the names of the cast and the most important members of the crew were listed. Matty also took notes, after the film was over, on her phone.

They had dinner later, sharing a table with two others from the competition jury, a young director from Poland who had enjoyed a success the previous year with an unusual vampire film, and an Australian actor called Brigitte McWillson. Brigitte was new to the cinema of gross-out horror: two years earlier she had acted in a film in which a group of socialites wander into a forest where a homicidal maniac is lurking. She made everyone at the table laugh with her accounts of what the film's inexperienced writer-director tried to make them do. The film had never achieved cinema release.

Down in the sub-floor theatre another film followed – this was an animation from Ireland about a leprechaun. Justin, still recovering from after-effects of the long flight, fell asleep less than halfway through. He made no notes of his own, but he kept the info handout. He and Matty went straight to bed immediately after the film finished.

The following morning Justin and Matty were walking along the hotel corridor, heading for the elevators, when they saw Teddy Smythe approaching them in her wheelchair. She was being pushed by one of the committee members, Bernie or the other one who had collected Justin from the airport. She was looking down, not ahead.

As they came near, Justin said, 'Good morning, Teddy!'

She did not look up, but raised a hand in a weak gesture. As the wheelchair went past, they stepped aside to make room for her, and they heard her say in a trembling voice, 'Hello, dear.'

They walked into the elevator, heading down to the breakfast restaurant. Matty and Justin looked enquiringly at each other. Justin shrugged.

'Maybe she didn't see it was us,' he said.

'Maybe she did.'

'Remind me of the name of the guy who was pushing her? Have you met him yet?'

'That's Harvey Hanting. He's on the festival committee, responsible for the jury, making sure we view every film and discuss it properly. He's a grad student at the University of Canberra. Film grammar and structure.'

'An expert in film theory.'

'Not yet, but probably soon will be. He's a nice guy, good to know.'

After breakfast there was a press conference with the director and producer of the Dutch gang-warfare film, and two of the actors. Then they went to the next film in competition: an American indie about an AI robot gaining a sense of identity, learning the satisfactions of revenge and running rampage. The day went by: two more films, one after the lunch break, one after dinner.

The next day, two of the movies Matty had to view for the competition Justin had already seen in preview in London. He took the opportunity to watch two of the out-of-competition films, one of them on a DVD in the hotel bedroom. He caught up with Matty again during another press conference.

That afternoon they went out to the terrace, which enjoyed a view across to Melbourne Bay. They sipped margaritas beneath the shade of a festival parasol. The conference centre was built on the coast. They revelled in the warm sunshine: many of the festival delegates were splashing around in the centre's swimming pool.

Teddy Smythe was already outside on the terrace when they arrived, her back towards them, her wheelchair pressed up against the table. There was a microphone on the table, several books and papers. Two journalists were asking her questions. Justin and Matty were too far away to hear anything, but Teddy repeatedly shook her head, looked away, looked down. One of the men leaned back in his chair and made a loud hoot of sarcastic laughter. Teddy pushed back her chair and stood up, holding on to the handle at the back for support. She turned away from the men, as if about to walk. She kept hold of the back of the chair for support, looking unsteady on her feet. Justin glanced across at Matty, who was watching as closely as him, and stood up, thinking he should go across to her and offer to help. Then one of the journalists said something calming to her and she sat down again. The situation resumed after some quiet words.

Justin and Matty waited for the conversation to finish, intending to walk across to her and say hello properly, but things had been smoothed over. Soon, Matty had to depart for the sub-level cinema once again.

This new film was an Argentinian fantasy which Justin had heard much about, and also wanted to see. It was cool indoors, air-conditioned with a chilled draught blowing across them. They missed the pleasures of the sunshine.

The following morning Justin was taken aside by Bernie Williamson as he was heading down to the theatre to try to find Matty. She was viewing the programme of short films, also in competition. Bernie asked if he would he be able to conduct an interview with Spencer Horvath that afternoon?

Justin was surprised to be asked – this was the first he had heard of it. He had been waiting to find out which interviews he was supposed to conduct, but nothing so far had been said. Bernie told him that the Horvath interview had originally been planned for the final evening of the festival, when his new film *The Sator Meaning* was to be given its first public screening as a finale to the festival. But Mr Horvath needed urgently to return to Los Angeles. His private jet would be leaving after the interview.

'I haven't seen his new film.' Justin said. 'I know nothing about it.'

'No one does,' Bernie said. 'It's under embargo. But one of his assistants says they have prepared a list of questions that Mr Horvath will answer.'

'I don't like someone I'm interviewing knowing in advance what I'm going to ask.'

'I'm told they're only suggestions. You're presumably aware of his other work?'

'Of course – I've reviewed all his films as they were released, and I wrote a long chapter about him in one of my books.'

'Yes – I've seen that. We thought that was probably the case. You can pick the questions you want to use. Or none of them. It would be entirely up to you.'

'OK,' said Justin.

'Mr Horvath's temporary headquarters are in the executive suite, on the fifth floor. His people are waiting for you now. The interview will start after lunch, at 2.00 pm. Mr Horvath will join you on the platform. We have been asked to tell you that you must be ready to start at exactly 2.00 pm. Punctuality is important to Mr Horvath.'

It was already nearly 1.00 pm.

'Couldn't he and I have an informal meeting beforehand, in the green room?'

But Bernie's mobile rang. He clamped it to his ear and turned away.

Justin went to the elevators. None of them travelled as high as the fifth floor. He found someone from the staff of the conference centre, and they directed him to the private executive elevator, placed inconspicuously in a corner of the entrance hall. The access code was whispered to him.

As he travelled swiftly upwards Justin had only enough time to think nervously of being unexpectedly in the company of the single most powerful producer and director in Hollywood, when the doors opened with a silky sound and he stepped out into the suite.

Not having any idea what he expected to find, Justin felt

at once that he had entered the newsroom of a busy metropolitan newspaper. The area was filled with noise. Bright lights shone down from the ceiling. There were many desks laid out in rows, all at an apparently measured ergonomic distance from each other. Every desk had one or more laptops. Some of them had huge monitors connected to desktop machines. Every desk had someone sitting there working the keyboards. Most of the people were wearing headsets, and communicating with someone else, somewhere else.

A bank of TV monitors stood against one wall, with news stories from American channels showing on most of them, but one of the screens was running an animated feature, with the soundtrack turned down. Violent action flickered intermittently on all TV monitors, both news bulletins and fantasy animé. No one appeared to be looking at them. Next to the TV monitors was a gaming area: three separate consoles were there, two of them in use as Justin arrived. Electronic music was being pumped from speakers. There was also an array of automats: ice water, cola, soft drinks, iced tea, chocolate bars, protein bars, vegan bars, bubble gum, corn and potato chips, chilled salad portions, wristbands, headbands, memory sticks, mobile phone recharging station, caps and sweatshirts. A basketball hoop had been fixed to the highest wall. At the far end of the long room was a selection of cross-trainers, treadmills and exercise bikes.

Although the blinds on the windows had been lowered to filter the bright sunlight, Justin glimpsed through them a large satellite dish that had been set up on the balcony outside.

No one looked towards him. He stood by the doors

to the elevator, wondering who to speak to. As he stared around he noticed that there was no paper anywhere, not a shred of it, not on desks, not being read or carried, there were no paper files, no newspapers or magazines or books. Nothing.

Finally, a young man with a buzz cut turned away from one of the automats, noticed Justin standing there and walked across to him. He was in training gear and sweatband, and a white towel was draped around his shoulders. A dark patch of perspiration lay on his chest. He wiped his face as he came across.

'Hi, you look like you might be the interview guy. I'm Larry.'

'Yes – I'm Justin.' He extended a hand, but Larry merely knuckled it lightly.

'You have your mobile handy, Justin?' he said. 'Let me use it for a moment?'

Justin passed it over. Larry glanced briefly at it, and produced his own phone from a back pocket. He pressed the two handsets together, screen to screen, then handed back Justin's. Wet fingermarks lay on each side of the screen.

'OK, you now have the questions for the interview. You may ask any of them or all of them, but do not deviate into questions of your own. Mr Horvath will not answer any questions of that sort. You should not try. Is that understood?'

Justin nodded.

'I need you to say yes, Justin.'

'Yes, it's understood, Larry,' he said politely. 'Thank you.' He glanced across the extent of the suite. 'Is Mr Horvath here at the moment?'

'He's unavailable right now. May I take a message?'

'I thought we might say hello to each other before the interview.'

'Spencer Horvath does not like to say hello.'

'I wanted to ask him about Teddy Smythe, and how she came to appear in *The Silent Genius*.'

'Spencer Horvath never discusses his past features.'

'OK,' said Justin. 'But I noticed Teddy Smythe is here at the festival. '

'What name is that? I'll have to check if he's on the list.'

Larry turned from him. He ambled away, passing between the desks. He paused to speak to someone else.

Justin waited for a while, but then walked back to the elevator, remembered the access code and the doors swished apart.

Justin stepped out on to the terrace, intending to take a seat in the sun and glance through the questions that Horvath would allow. He thought if he could select a few that came close to his own interests he could structure the interview around them. The only interviews with Horvath that he remembered seeing were in print media. He had never seen him interviewed live, on TV or even online, but the run of Horvath's box office hits in the last two decades suggested a restless intelligence, a good mind and a wide-ranging imagination. Justin felt inspired to make the best of this opportunity to obtain an interview that would gain attention throughout the world of film. It was a stimulating prospect. And Teddy Smythe was also here: intriguingly, Horvath had said he knew who she really was.

As he walked down to the area of decking he saw immediately that something was going on. All the seats, the tables and the sunshades had been taken down and members of the conference centre staff were folding them and stacking them inside a concrete shelter situated to one side. The cocktail bar had already been closed and shuttered. In the pool, the many people who had been swimming were now levering themselves up and out of the water, and wrapping themselves in towels as they gathered their belongings. Staff were standing by, making sure the whole area outside the main building was cleared.

One of the women on the staff approached Justin and asked him if he would please return to the building and wait inside.

'What's happening?' he asked her.

'A storm is forecast, sir. Guests are obliged to stay inside the building if atmospheric pressure falls below a certain reading, or if there's a big wind. We've received warnings of both.'

Justin could not help glancing at the peaceful scene of a sunlit midday, with scarcely the breath of a breeze. No dark clouds loomed. A low bulking of white clouds was on the far horizon.

'Are you sure the forecast is right?' he said.

'This is April in Melbourne – the weather can change in a matter of minutes.'

She raised an arm impatiently, indicating he should move back and into the building. He obeyed.

He waited around in the general area inside. He sent Matty a text saying he had to interview Spencer Horvath at 2.00 pm in the auditorium, but if she was free there was still time for them to meet for a quick lunch.

He then moved to a spare chair by one of the windows

that overlooked the terrace. He took out his mobile phone, and searched for and found the questions Larry had placed there.

Justin read them. It did not take long. There were only three.

'Oh shit,' he said aloud.

24

Because the terrace had closed, the main restaurant was crowded, but Matty and Justin were able to grab some sandwiches and coffee. Justin took his to the auditorium, where he mounted the stage. Two chairs and microphones were already in place, so he sat in one of them.

Staff from the conference centre were getting the theatre ready. They said he wasn't in the way, and it was OK for him to sit there. The cinema screen and sound equipment were being winched up and out of the way. This revealed the bare rear area of the stage – two wooden crates had been left there, a coil of wire, a workbox of tools. A metal staircase led up to somewhere in the loft. Soon, the guys lowered a curtain upstage, making an intimate setting for an interview. From above, the stage lights were tested, on and off, targeted on the chairs, the table between them. They asked Justin to do a sound check.

Justin had wanted some space to think, but he felt bare of thought. He finished the sandwiches quickly, then sat with the paper cup, sipping the coffee. His ears suddenly popped, as if he were back on the long-haul flight again. He swallowed to clear them.

He was daunted by the prospect of this interview. He sat in a depressed and worried state as the workers cleared up and left. The audience began to arrive. At first there was just a trickle but the numbers built up. With only about ten minutes before the start time almost every seat was taken. Soon there was standing room only. Matty had taken one of the reserved seats in the centre of the front row. Harvey Hanting wheeled Teddy Smythe in. She went past Matty's seat without looking, then sat staring around while Harvey locked her wheelchair in the allotted mobility position at the end of the row.

Justin looked deliberately towards her, hoping for a response or a sign of recognition, but nothing came. Once again, he felt the magnetism of her presence.

There was no sign of Spencer Horvath.

Justin had removed his wristwatch and placed it on the small table beside his chair. He kept glancing at it. His ears popped again, puzzlingly. Then, with three minutes to go, a loud crack of thunder came down from above. Justin at first wondered if it was a sound effect, an announcement, but the familiar sound rumbled on for a few seconds, followed by silence. The auditorium was below ground level, with no daylight admitted anywhere.

Two minutes before 2.00 pm the main access doors to the auditorium swung open, and a group of half a dozen young men strode in with almost military precision. The doors were then closed, with one of the men standing before them. The other five men walked briskly to the front of the auditorium, where they spread out and stood facing the audience. One of them was Larry. He had his arms folded, and he kept scanning the audience like a security officer protecting politicians.

The house lights went down. Spotlights lit the stage.

Alone in the glare Justin felt more self-conscious than ever before in his life.

With precisely one minute to go, a burst of familiar music roared out of the sound system: it was the famous triumphal march from the climax of *Space Warp Heroes*, Horvath's ground-breaking science-fiction film, made when he was still in his twenties. At the sound of the first exultant notes the audience erupted into applause, many of the people standing up in excitement and cheering and clapping. Justin, almost paralysed until this moment by his attack of nerves, felt the same surge of thrill and anticipation. Everyone loved *Space Warp Heroes*. He too rose to his feet.

As the extract of music approached its climax, Spencer Horvath walked out on to the platform from somewhere upstage. His arms were raised, his hands waving in encouragement to the audience. The cheering increased to a deafening level. Horvath moved into the centre of the main spotlight beam, arms still raised, smiling and waving to the audience.

A second crack of thunder burst forth above, much louder and more sudden than the first. Horvath clearly relished the sound that continued as the thunder died away, the renewed cheering, whistling and yelling.

Justin sat down again, reflecting that if that roar of thunder had been dubbed into an action scene in a film, it would be mocked as a tired cliché. Horvath seemed unaware of such a thing, and stood in happy receipt as the extravagant ovation continued.

Finally, it began to quieten down.

Horvath strode across to the second chair. As he did so there was third rumble of thunder, this one loud and long.

In normal circumstances, when interviewing someone on a stage, Justin would make some introductory remarks:

a personal appreciation, then a list of titles, or awards, or a summary of the critical reception that had been earned over the years. In this case he had had little time to prepare. Anyway, Horvath, he felt, had set up his own introduction, and anything Justin said now would be superfluous and seem like an anticlimax.

So he simply said, 'Spencer Horvath, it is my sincere pleasure to welcome you to this film festival in St Kilda.'

'Well, thank you, Justin. I'm a great admirer of your work. I love everything you do, and it's a fantastic privilege to meet you.'

Another round of applause followed, this time brief. Justin looked at the screen of his mobile phone, and read aloud the text of the first question.

'Mr Horvath, your films are famous for drawing uniquely on the existential conflict between self-doubt and the modern agony of life. Would you care to enlarge on what most people agree is an irreconcilable dilemma?'

'Well, that's an interesting question, Justin, and I am pleased to explain. You see, I was born on a small farm in Idaho, the nearest town more than an hour's travel away. We were dirt-poor. From an early age I observed the movement of the stars and the ebb and flow of the seasons. The mysteries of nature enthralled me. The love of my mother and father inspired me to meet with my maker. I knew even then that I held in my small hands the key to a higher form of enlightenment, and—'

The audience was silent. Thunder rumbled loudly again. Horvath had come to the platform wearing bright-blue sports shorts and a T-shirt emblazoned with his own name and a photograph of one of the women actors who had played a leading role in two of his space films. He was wearing rope sandals. On his head he had a bright orange cap with some sort of corporate logo on the front. He was wearing huge round sunglasses with mirrorshade lenses, which made it impossible to see his eyes or read his expression. Most of what could be seen of his face was his nose and mouth. He wore a goatee beard, starting to turn grey. He was thin. His bare knees jutted upwards from the way he was sitting. His hands, which he waved as he spoke, were almost skeletal.

But he was poised, his body language evinced confidence, his speech had been perfected.

As Horvath reached what seemed to be the end of his peroration, another clap of thunder came again, this one louder and more terrifying than any that had preceded it. Justin could see many members of the audience reacting uneasily to the sound of the storm. It sounded as if it was directly overhead.

'Thank you, Mr Horvath,' he said, and, feeling he should press on, looked at the second question on his smartphone screen. 'Would you kindly share with the audience the key to your personal psychology? In other words, what is it that drives you, what opens your personality to your great and unique visions?'

'Well, Justin, how interesting that you should ask me that. In my small way I feel I have understood the supreme wisdom of God, and this has created the lifetime mission on which I have embarked—'

There was now a distinct roaring sound. It was not more of the thunder. This was something else, something material, heavy, broken, loose, intermittent, falling or collapsing, closer than the outside atmosphere.

While Horvath droned on, Justin looked around to see if

he could locate the source of the noise, but because of the darkened house lights and the glare of the spotlights focused on them on the stage it was difficult to see into the depth of the hall. He could just about make out the people in the front row, including Matty. They were looking around and up, clearly distracted by the ever-increasing racket from outside. Another crack of thunder was followed by a louder, more alarming and destructive rumbling sound.

Horvath continued.

Suddenly, all lights in the hall were extinguished, throwing the entire place into pitch darkness. The PA system died – Horvath's words were silenced. Many people in the audience immediately shouted their frightened reactions and some screamed. Voices were raised everywhere. The racket outside grew shockingly louder and closer. The dark was impenetrable, but after a few seconds emergency back-up lights came on: the bland radiance filled the hall, flattening the scene, illuminating the crowd in a frigid, shadowless way. Signs over the main doors and the emergency exits glowed brightly, flashing on and off to make their presence known.

A deafening warning signal began: a loud electronic bleating, two notes repeated endlessly, drilling into the mind.

Most of the people in the audience were already standing, looking around, starting to shove away from their seats. Many were pushing towards the exits. Everyone seemed to be shouting at once. Beside the platform area, over to the right, but not far from where Matty was sitting, a heavy cascade of water was pouring unstoppably down the wall and jetting towards the audience seats. Justin saw Matty trying to stand, then being overcome by the flood. She staggered to her feet, managing to recover. He was out of his seat, trying to leap down towards her. A large section of that wall fell catastrophically away, and the torrent plunged in with a terrible roaring sound. Deadly cold water gushed against him. A group of people who had been scrambling away from their seats in that area were overwhelmed, swept helplessly along by the surging wave. Rubble-filled water spread muddily across the area. It flowed rapidly on the sloping floor, flooding into the well in front of the first row of seats and immediately before the stage. People in the front row were attempting to move back and away from it. Some fell over the seats as they tried to climb to safety, others fought and elbowed. One aggressive man fought to get away, overbalanced, fell backwards and landed in the muddy flood. He struggled to his feet and splashed angrily away.

A recorded announcement, maximum volume: *'Please leave the building immediately. This is an emergency. It is not a drill. Use the emergency exits as soon as possible. Take your time, and do not rush. Help anyone with mobility issues. Use the stairs only. Do not attempt to use the elevators. Do not run.'*

It was immediately repeated in several languages.

The torrent of floodwater increased, now breaking into the sub-ground auditorium with horrifying force from other sides. Panic was rising with the flood.

In the chaos of what followed Justin never saw Horvath again, nor even thought of him.

He managed to scramble down from the stage, half propelled by the turbulent inflow of rubble-filled water. He waded through the flood, stumbling, terrified of falling over. Matty was there, stretching her arms towards him. He reached her. He briefly held her, she held him. The sound of the rushing water was terrifying, but the shouts and screams from the hundreds of people still trying to escape the hall overwhelmed everything. The water was rising fast.

'Backstage!' he shouted to Matty. 'There are some stairs there!'

But the flood between them and the stage was spreading. Matty pointed to the far side, where there was a short flight of access steps up to the platform. They waded through the edge of the flood, which had already almost overwhelmed the first three rows of seats, but people were going the other way and in the pandemonium many bags and other pieces of property were in the water, floating and blocking. Several people were floundering in the water, bundled along by the violent inrush, which was now circling like a maelstrom.

They managed to reach the end of the row. Teddy Smythe's wheelchair was there, lying on its side, almost submerged in the muddy torrent. A woman, presumably Teddy, was lying face down in the turbulent water next to it. She had one hand on one of the metal legs, and was using that to try to lift herself out of the water. Most of her head was submerged. Her struggles were weak. She was trapped between the fallen wheelchair and the fixed seat at the end of the row. She was soaked through and covered with mud.

Justin leant down in the water, thrust his arms beneath her. Matty lifted her head, pulling her face into the air. Teddy choked and spluttered. Her grey hair was a streaky mask across her face. Dark water burst from her mouth. They managed to raise her out of the flood as she yelled with pain, but the wheelchair was trapped somehow beneath the theatre seat it was beside. They pulled hard to shift it, but it was impossible. She threw up more water. They dragged her away from the wheelchair while she gasped.

There was a roar, and another part of a side wall collapsed. A huge new surge of filthy water rushed in.

They abandoned the wheelchair but now they had to wade through the currents of the dangerous flood and all the debris it was carrying. The stage was still not inundated, but the steps up to it were almost swamped. Justin and Matty splashed and struggled, dragging Teddy between them, her arms limp across their shoulders, their drenched clothes making every movement a massive effort.

They scrambled across the stage. Teddy was a deadweight between them. When they reached the steep service stairs behind the stage they seated her on the lowest steps. Her eyes were open but she slumped forward, belching and groaning. Water still came from her lips, but now in a series of trickles. She gasped as she tried to suck in air. Justin looked up at the climb they had to make: twenty-five or thirty metal steps, so narrow that only one person at a time could ascend. A handrail and a wall defined them. Floodwater was pouring down from above, a forceful cataract.

Matty went first, dragging Teddy up towards her one step at a time. Justin was below, taking her weight, lifting and pushing. Debris-laden water continued to flood down on them in a terrible deluge. It was gaining strength. Every step was an ordeal. Somehow they managed to reach the top. They emerged into daylight, where the storm still raged.

The alarm siren continued to blare. The disaster went on.

Teddy Smythe was rushed to the emergency room, first at a hospital in Prahran then later into St Vincent's in Melbourne. She had suffered multiple cuts and bruises, and a badly sprained knee and hip. Her lungs had to be drained.

Because of her age she was judged to be in a critical condition, but she was resilient and quickly started recovering.

She was one of the several hundred people seriously injured in the tropical storm that suddenly swerved inland and hit the eastern coastal strip of Melbourne Bay. Hurricane-force winds coincided with an extreme drop in atmospheric pressure and a high tide, creating a powerful tidal surge. It was a zone of devastation. Sixty-seven people died in the St Kilda town area – twenty-three of those fatalities occurred in the conference centre involving attendees at the film festival, and fifteen of those were of people unable to escape when the auditorium was violently flooded. Dozens more were injured in the stampede to escape. Several of them were to die later in hospital.

Buildings in many parts of the town were damaged or destroyed. Hundreds of trees were blown down. The conference centre itself became unusable, although many of the guest rooms on upper storeys had survived undamaged because they were at the rear of the building. The executive suite was devastated when a large satellite dish was thrust by the gale through the balcony windows. All the accessible levels on the ground floor were beyond use. The admin offices occupied by the conference staff and the temporary information centre of the festival were overwhelmed by the violent wind and the associated flood.

The floodwater did not entirely disperse until three days after the storm. Matty and Justin suffered cuts and bruises, but did not require hospitalization. The festival was abandoned and the conference centre closed.

Eight days after the storm Justin and Matty boarded a Qantas flight, one stop to London, calling only at Bangkok. Teddy Smythe travelled with them.

25

Justin, Matty and Teddy were airside, in a huge transit lounge in Terminal One, Charles de Gaulle Airport, near Paris.

The passengers had been told that they would not have to wait long, and that as soon as replacement planes to London could be cleared for take-off they would be informed. Their luggage was somewhere else. Ground staff working for airport services had brought them to this lounge and left them there. The lounge was equipped with automats offering snacks and drinks, which would accept credit and debit cards. The carpet was woven with the Air France logo. There were rows of bench seats, padded with tough-looking flat cushions. Brought in first, because of Teddy's wheelchair, they moved to a corner position where there was a low table. The room was lit flat white by overhead strip lights. It was made for waiting, not for comfort.

They had not intended to be in this airport. They were no longer flying. They were not travelling, not arriving, not leaving. They were waiting in null space.

★

Their flight home had gone normally until they were some-where high over Russia or Finland, coming towards the end of the long second leg from Bangkok. They were seated in a row of three, Justin at the window, with Matty beside him. Teddy was on the aisle seat because of her mobility diffi-culties. From time to time Matty or one of the flight attend-ants would help Teddy along the aisle if she needed to use the bathroom. She had been offered a special ambulance plane with medical attention on board, paid for by the festival's liability insurance, but she insisted she was well enough and preferred to fly home with her friends.

They were on a scheduled Qantas flight, a big Airbus, all seats taken. Several of the passengers were survivors of the disastrous storm and flood tide in St Kilda, a few even who had survived the catastrophic flood at the film festival. For that reason the cabin crew were giving all passengers extra attention if needed. It was otherwise an unremarkable journey, two long uninterrupted flights.

Teddy slept for most of the way. Justin watched the inflight movies, then dozed, intermittently attaining real sleep, but only for short periods. The bruises on his back and legs made him uncomfortable, but the cabin crew gave him a neck rest and noise-cancelling earplugs. Matty was a better flier than him: she read for a while, watched a movie, read some more, listened to music on headphones, then fell asleep twice, once before the stopover in Thailand, once in the hours since.

Their calm exterior concealed the emotional impact of the disaster in the underground auditorium. Apart from what turned out to be the relatively minor injuries they had suffered they were overawed, shocked, by the tragic serious-ness of the event. Even so, compared with what happened to many other people they had come through it reasonably unscathed. No one they knew closely or had worked with died in the flood, or as a result of the damage caused by the violent storm wind. All the members of the competition jury, who for the Horvath interview were occupying the section of seats reserved for them at every event, made their escape before the water rose too high. Matty, being in the front row away from the others, was the only jury member to have had to struggle to get out. Harvey Hanting suffered minor bruising and a soaking; his colleague Bernie Williamson escaped without injury. Spencer Horvath had been immediately surrounded by his people, and spirited away to safety. He had departed Melbourne in his private jet at the end of the same day. Several members of his executive staff suffered various degrees of injury. None was critically hurt.

Even so, the images of darkness, the tempestuous thunder and the screeching wind outside, the inrushing cold water and the flooding mess of broken masonry and soil, the fear of being overwhelmed, still haunted both Justin and Matty.

They wondered about Teddy, who said little. At first, while she was recovering in hospital, she was withdrawn, perhaps under the influence of painkilling drugs. She recognized them when they visited her bedside. She smiled a lot, that symptomatic half-smile, but said little. Justin was concerned about her mobility for when she was discharged. He made it his business to investigate what had happened to her wheelchair, to recover it if possible, to arrange for a replacement if not.

When the theatre auditorium was pumped out her chair was found close to where they had last seen it. Emergency crews and volunteers pulled it clear. Once it had been dried, cleaned and repaired it was more or less as she had known it before. If it had carried any of her personal effects those were lost. She said nothing about that. Everyone in the disaster-hit hall had lost something.

Before they were driven across to Melbourne airport she had started using it again, although she was hardly strong enough to propel herself. Now it was folded and stored somewhere in the cabin, out of the way while the flight went on.

Looking along the row at where Teddy was leaning back in her seat with her eyes closed, Justin wondered what she would have to do to reach her home on the south coast after the plane landed in London. She looked frail, vulnerable, an old lady slowly recovering from a life-threatening accident. Should he and Matty try to arrange a car or a taxi for her? Or help her find a hotel room in London? Before boarding the flight he had vaguely raised this subject, but then Teddy brushed it aside. She could manage, she said.

Maybe she could, or maybe she knew of someone who was going to collect her. She was proud of her independence, but her life had been changed by the accident. What would be done if there were no arrangements for her? These questions were for Justin like the dreadful waking thoughts of the early hours: awareness of plans and decisions that had to be made, their importance magnified by darkness and isolation, a sense of desperation and urgency.

Then a voice from the cockpit, the captain. Everyone stirred, listening. Matty nudged Justin, and he whipped off his earplugs. The pilot began speaking with Aussie informality, but quickly became serious. They were going to have to make a change of route, he said: all airports in southern

Britain capable of handling heavy passenger planes had been closed by some kind of action. This included the two main airports serving London.

The phrase was chilling: what kind of action could close several airports? Why didn't they say? Suddenly wide awake, Justin thought about the acute and specific risks of modern jet travel. Was it some act of terrorism? Had there been a major aviation accident? Surely not bad weather in Britain at this time of year? Perhaps something as unthreatening as air traffic controllers or baggage handlers on strike? They would probably find out after they landed somewhere. Matty, beside him, was wide awake and alert. Teddy did not move.

The plane was going to have to make a diversion to an alternative airport, the pilot said, one which could accommodate their heavy aircraft. There was no cause for alarm. It would probably mean only a short delay. Air traffic control had suggested diverting to Brussels, Amsterdam or Paris. They would land, then complete the flight to London Heathrow as soon as possible afterwards. The voice spoke calmly and blandly, intending to reassure.

The plane flew on.

An hour later, the pilot confirmed that they had been cleared for a normal landing in Paris. Still no explanation. The cabin crew would soon be coming round to make final preparations for arrival. Soon after there was a change of engine note, a feeling of the aircraft slowing down, gradually losing height. The atmospheric pressure increased and ears popped. Somewhere else in the long cabin a baby started crying.

★

'I'm going to take a short walk,' Justin said in the transit room, now crowded. 'I need some fresh air.'

'In this place?' Matty said.

He knew he was starting to get on Matty's nerves – he could read it in her manner. All three of them were worn out after the long flight. He was tense, and his sore back was hurting. He had not slept enough on the plane and was restless and touchy. This unexpected delay in the journey home was galling.

Much of his irritation was unreasonably focused on Teddy, who was passive and mostly silent. She hardly responded when he asked if she would like something from the automat. She claimed she needed nothing, although when Matty bought a bottle of mineral water she accepted it. She simply sat with her back stooped in her wheelchair, seeming to avoid his gaze. He was probably irritating her too. She was looking and acting as he had now seen her several times: allowing herself to sink into the role of an irascible old lady. He knew that was not typical.

Something was not being said. Matty was also quiet. His restlessness was making things worse. He left the room.

He entered the corridor that ran past, went to look around. Knowing they were still within the airside zone of the terminal he made sure he had his passport and the original boarding pass with him. Just in case.

When he continued along the corridor where the room was situated it led nowhere – there was just another transit area with a locked door, and a wall at the end. He went back. They had been led away from the ramp by a member of ground staff, so he retraced the way they had come.

There was a landing, with stairs up and down, but beyond

that was where they had come from: a long walk back to the passenger landbridge. He went down the stairs to the floor below: after walking a fair distance he came to a large passenger waiting area, a shuttered bar, a closed snack bar, two automats, a stand bearing many free copies of that day's early editions of the *New York Times*, *Le Monde* and *Le Figaro*, several signs in French and English about where to wait, where to queue, what identity and travel documents to have ready. Portes 27B, 27C, 28, 28A were identified with lighted signs – no one was there.

He walked through. After passing along a lengthy corridor he came to another waiting area, almost identical: there were dozens of people here, many of them standing in line, others sitting around. These were Portes 15, 16, 16A, 16B. All the passengers had hand baggage and most were holding cellphones. Two members of airline staff were standing by a desk. The refreshments bar was open, although no one was using it.

Seeing an escalator he rode up to the next level, where a spacious hall led off into the distance. He glimpsed a travelator: a way out of the building, or a way to somewhere else inside, or just a way that led to another way?

Justin was starting to sense a familiar emotional dysfunction: a kind of irrational inner determination to solve the building, as if it were an enigma, a challenge to be faced down. It was a feeling he was accustomed to from his many flights around the world, with long periods spent waiting in terminals. He still never liked the sense of alienation in terminals, never quite knew how to deal with it. It manifested itself in him as a desire to explore, to seek the limits, but it was always a futile thing. The only certain remedy was to leave the airport complex, to re-enter the world. That was not an option this time.

It was wrong to have walked away from Matty and Teddy like that, his reaction to the unease of limbo. He glanced at his replacement wristwatch – he had already been gone for nearly half an hour. What if the onward flight to London had been announced while he was not there with them?

The familiar tension wrapped itself around him.

He started retracing his steps but he took the wrong escalator down, arriving in a part of the airport with signs to the RER connection to Paris – *Centre Ville*. Checkpoints and barriers leading to landside stood in the way. Uniformed staff or officials were on hand. He saw a gendarme standing at the back of the area. He had the sense to realize at once that he had reached an unwanted extreme, so he rode up on the second escalator. He soon recognized where he was and walked quickly back along the way he had come, trying to remember what he had passed, which gate or porte numbers he had seen, or direction signs. He found the flight of stairs he had used before and climbed up to the next level.

Soon, thankfully, he found the right corridor and the transit room. He did not go in straight away, but paused outside for a few moments to catch his breath, to try to shake off any signs of tension in his body or face. He stretched his back to ease it. Then he opened the door.

The mood in the room felt transformed. There was a smell of food. Most of the crowd of passengers, dispersed about the hall, were sitting down and eating. Teddy had left her wheelchair and was sitting on the padded bench seat against the wall. Matty was on one of the wooden chairs across from her, with the low table between them. There were dishes of cold food and plates, wine glasses as well as a bottle of wine inside a cooler jacket. Matty was holding a glass of white wine. Both women smiled at him as he walked across to join them. Matty raised her glass towards him.

'Santé, Justin! Compliments of Qantas. It has become my favourite airline.'

'When did this arrive?'

'About fifteen minutes after you left.'

'Did they say how much longer it will be before we can leave?'

'In less than an hour. They'll come and collect us in a motorized passenger transport.'

'How are you feeling, Teddy?' Justin said. 'You look a lot better.'

'I was hungry, tired, needed to use the toilet. I'm fed up with being stuck in a wheelchair. Mostly, I was hungry.'

'Better, then.'

'Yes. Much better.'

He pulled up one of the spare chairs. Teddy offered him a platter with several pieces of cold roast chicken. He took two pieces, then some greenery, potato salad, sweetcorn, dressing, cold rice. Matty poured him a glass of wine.

Not much was said until they finished eating. In a while, airport staff arrived to help move away some of what was left. One of the men told them he did not know how much longer they would have to wait, but air traffic control had cleared extra flights to London. Two replacement aircraft were being prepared. Because of Teddy and her wheelchair they would be allocated seats on the first one to leave. Probably not long now.

They sat facing each other, waiting. The large hall was quiet, most of the other passengers dozing or reading or looking at their smartphones. Everyone must be feeling the same: the long journey from Melbourne behind them, a delay now, more flying to come.

Teddy suddenly began speaking, her voice low and intense, looking across at Justin and Matty.

'I have to say something before we get back on the plane,' she said. 'I still haven't thanked you.'

'There's nothing to thank us for, Teddy,' Matty said, but the older woman interrupted her almost immediately. She sounded tense, energized.

'I wouldn't be alive now if it weren't for what you did. You put your own lives at risk to help me, both of you. I can't stop thinking about it, how I almost drowned in there.' She hesitated, stammering a little. Her breath seemed to catch in her throat. 'There are things you don't forget. The terror I felt, afterwards, when I was in the hospital. I haven't felt like that since the war.'

She fell silent, looking down at her lap. Justin looked across at Matty, who touched Teddy's fingers briefly then glanced up to meet his eyes. Justin experienced a sensation he had had before, a kind of déjà vu. There were other people sitting near them. Matty leaned forward, closer to Teddy. She said quietly, 'Where exactly were you during the war, Teddy? I don't think you said.'

Teddy looked surprised. 'Why would I? It isn't important.'

'Come on, Teddy. I need to know. Were you in London during the Blitz?'

'I talked to you about that when you came to visit me.'

'So you were there during the bombing? All those lives

lost. The incredible damage. Was it a reminder when the theatre flooded – you'd seen something like it before?'

'Yes.' Teddy was looking away. 'But I was never directly affected during the war. Not like that.'

'Where in London were you living?' Matty said, persisting. 'Were you alone? How did you meet the man you married? Most women had to work – did you? Did many bombs land near where you were living?'

'Why are you asking me this? You know what I told you.'

'You wouldn't tell me anything.'

'You didn't ask me.'

'I'm asking now.' Matty spoke softly but with determination, apparently trying not to be confrontational. 'Teddy, you know what we've been through together. All those people died around us, people who were at the festival for the same sort of reasons as us. You know I mean the best for you, and you know what I do for a living. You've had an extraordinary life and a fascinating career.'

'You know nothing of my life,' Teddy said.

'Well, I'd like to discover it, write about it. One day, when you're gone, people will want to remember you for what you did, discover how you lived, read about the people you knew and what they were like to work with. You have a unique career. If I don't do it, someone else will.'

'Let them. I never talk about the past.'

'You're entitled to your privacy,' Justin said. 'We accept that. Neither of us wants to intrude on that.'

'But she does,' Teddy said, looking towards Matty. Matty shook her head. Teddy went on, 'There's no bad secret in my life. I wanted a fresh start. All I did was make a decision to put behind me everything that had happened until then. I was still in my thirties. I'd always wanted to act in films, and I set out to achieve that ambition. It was a rebirth. I came properly alive in 1950. Nobody else is affected by that. No harm was done. Why does my life matter to you, Matty? You two saved me. I'll never forget you. That is what I owe you.'

They heard people moving along the corridor outside the room. There were voices, but whoever it was passed by. One of the people laughed. The door to the adjoining room opened and closed. Justin felt again the transient nature of what he and Matty and Teddy were doing by being made to wait in this lounge, the background anxiety of a pause in travel, the sense of anonymity, the need to solve or understand.

They were neither arriving nor leaving, but waiting for something to happen, a microcosm of the airport experience. Time was passing without regard. It was a time of questions.

He said, more abruptly than he had intended, 'Teddy, what does the name Jeanette Marchand mean to you?'

Teddy was startled, blinked her eyes several times. Justin thought how bloodshot and watery they looked. His own eyes were tired after so long in the air. But Teddy stiffened her poise.

'I know of her, of course,' Teddy said. 'Everyone in my business knows who Jeanette was.'

'She came to Britain in 1949. Did you ever meet her?'

'No, of course not.'

'Of course?'

'She disappeared soon after she arrived. I never had a chance to meet her.'

'Teddy, she landed in London in April 1949, saying she intended to make films with British studios. We know she landed safely, went through the airport. No one has seen her since. Your career began in 1950, when you started making films in British studios. You had a small part as a teacher in a comedy called *Chalkdust and Cheese*, made by Ealing Studios. It was released in 1951, but it was filmed during the summer of 1950.'

'I always said you know your subject well.'

'*Chalkdust and Cheese* is rarely shown these days, but I was able to view a print which was being restored by the BFI. You look almost identical to Jeanette Marchand.'

'Several people said that at the time. I took it as a compliment.'

'So what do you say about it now?'

'What can I say? I can't help the way I used to look back then.'

'In your next film, and all the later ones where I've managed to find copies, you look slightly different. As if trying to disguise yourself.'

'My dear, actors change their appearance all the time.'

'You put on weight for some films, your hair was dyed black, you sometimes wore spectacles. In *Death in the Auvergne* you were disfigured by scar tissue.'

'The life of a film actor—'

'But your physical resemblance to Jeanette was always there.'

'Do I look like her now?'

Matty said, 'Justin . . .?'

'What?'

'It's time to let it go.'

'All right,' Justin said, backing down.

'I've always told you the truth,' Teddy said.

Matty said, 'I asked you several times about your change of name. You always said Theodora Smythe was your real name, and Teddy was your stage name.'

'That is true. By law.'

'So you had it changed. What was your name at birth?'

'Why do you want to know?'

'Because I am a professional biographer and I wish to research your life. I know only one thing for certain about you. You were born in the small town of Leighton Buzzard. There is no trace of you anywhere in the town or the parish, or in the census records, nor of any family with the name Smythe who gave birth to a girl around the time you were born.'

Teddy suddenly smiled, aslant, the trace of irritation.

'Why are you so certain about that?' she said. 'Why does it matter where I was born?'

'I need to know your background, your childhood, your school, the friends you had, who your parents were. Your birthplace is the one of the few facts about you that has never been contested.'

'Facts are slippery, though,' Teddy said. 'Many years ago – you won't believe this, I know, but it is absolutely true. Many years ago, after only a couple of films, I was interviewed by a young man for a fan magazine. It was one of the first interviews I ever gave, and I was inexperienced. He asked me the same question about where I came from, and I thought it was irrelevant and impertinent. I was annoyed. What did it matter to anyone where I was born? I didn't like him. All through my life I have never liked journalists, and it started then. The day before the interview I happened to be on a train that stopped in Leighton Buzzard. I noticed the name, thought it was unusual and amusing, so for a sort of joke I told him that. I discovered later that many journalists don't research properly, but just look through files of cuttings, believe what they find and hand it all on until the next one. What you say once tends to be endlessly repeated. For that reason alone, Leighton Buzzard has been my home town for decades.'

'So what is the truth? Where were you really born? And what is your real name?'

'I changed my name in 1949,' Teddy said. 'I don't want my life researched, by you or by anyone else. I love you, Matty, and I owe you my life from that disaster, but if you persist in this then you must do it on your own.'

'1949 was the year Jeanette Marchand arrived in Britain,' said Justin.

'That was when I started trying to find work as an actor.'

'How did you change your name?' said Matty.

'By law. The law allows me to call myself whatever I choose, and by the same law I need never reveal what my old name was.'

'You were married. What was the name of your husband?'
'Bill.'

'Bill who? Did you change your name to his?'
'No.'

'Bill who?' Matty persisted. 'Presumably William?'

'No – he called himself Bill, and I also called him that.'

'What was his surname?'

'It doesn't matter. We were married only a short time, and

then he was killed in the war. Such a young man.'

'So you say.'

'So I have always said. Or so they say I said. It appears in magazine clippings files. Again and again. Think about that.'

They did.

'Did you have any children?' Matty went on.

'Did Bill and I have any children? No.'

Matty leaned forward intently. 'Did you have children with anyone else?' she said.

For the first time Teddy did not fire back an immediate answer. Then she said, 'No, I have never had children.'

'Before you started acting you must have had a job of some kind. What was it?'

'It doesn't matter. Acting has been my whole life, and it still is. That is the truth.'

'Are you acting now?' said Justin. 'As you are talking to us?'

'No – I'm retired. You know I'm in my eighties. I retired a long time ago. But when you're an actor it never leaves you. That's what I'm saying.'

'Just one last thing. Both Justin and I noticed that at home you have a photograph of a young actor called Roy Tallis. We know that he was Jeanette Marchand's first husband. We also know that when he died he left a young daughter.'

'Yes – you told me his name, Justin. I had no idea who it was until then.'

'Why should you keep a photograph of him?'

'Why shouldn't I?'

'Teddy, it's an incredible coincidence,' Justin said.

'Coincidences happen. Actors grow to like other actors. That's the world we live and work in.'

Justin remembered the personal inscription Matty had drawn in his copy of her book about the director of *Death in the Auvergne*, back when they had only recently met. She disbelieved in coincidence. The circle of connections, double-headed arrows like arms pointing towards each other, a symbol of a loose friendly hug, the names made into a never-ending link. For Justin that day in the old cemetery was the first tentative confession of Matty's love scribbled on the title page of an old book, or the approach of love, or its likelihood. Or its truth. That warm summer's day on the bench beneath the canopy of trees – that was when he and Matty had begun their lives together.

Teddy's demeanour had not changed from the moment they began asking these questions. The frail lady who was so ill at ease in Australia, who smiled nervously for an audience but would not engage with others, who fell out with journalists, who almost drowned there – she had been replaced by the sharp-minded version of Teddy Justin had first encountered. In this airside transit lounge, an anonymous cell of nullity and waiting, she was briefly transformed.

Her hair was now thinner, so was her body, her face was lined, her eyes were set deeper in their sockets, her neck was scrawny, her hands were thin and stringy, the finger joints slightly swollen. She was in her ninth decade. But frail she was not. She gave back what she was given, as good as, better.

Justin said, 'Just one more thing, Teddy. Will you tell me what you remember about August Engel?'

Teddy was sitting erect, saying nothing. She kept her back stiffened, her manner as unyielding as her position. She stared ahead, at neither Matty nor Justin but past them and towards the waiting crowd of passengers. Her silence made it impossible to interpret her reaction: was it stubbornness, a wish to seem strong . . . or was she doubting, trying to remember, thinking hard?

Justin watched her, realizing that this might be the last time he would be able look at her face, perhaps the final moment when it was full and before him, a face now so familiar, a naked and unguarded face, no longer pretty but still beautiful in a fathomless way. It had haunted him for most of his life. Perhaps there would never be another meeting, another chance to identify her. These could be the last few minutes they would ever share.

He was certain now who she really was, her past identity, the one she was hiding. He also realized that the questions he and Matty were throwing at her were intrusive, almost a taunt. A challenge to her past, her story of the past, her pretended lack of interest, or of forgetting herself. Surely she had that right?

Finally, Teddy took a breath, and said, 'How do you know about August Engel?' Her voice sounded less confident, at a higher pitch.

'Do you remember him?'

'A little. Tell me why you ask.' She had clasped her hands together, linking the fingers tightly.

'You know I am obsessed with film,' Justin said. 'I keep notes and check details. I discovered there was a connection between you and August Engel. Do you know what I mean by that?'

'No – not a connection.' She had thought, she had an answer, she was recovering her poise.

'So you do know him?'

'I remember his name,' Teddy said. 'He was with Yorkshire TV? Is that the connection you mean?'

'It's one of them. Engel worked for Yorkshire a few years ago. Back then, you made a television play for children. He directed it.'

'Yes – I think that was the last job I had, before my illness. On the day I didn't know he was the director.'

Justin said, 'Do you mean you didn't know who the director was before that? Or do you mean you knew Engel but that you didn't know he would be there?'

'Why is that different?'

'Did you know him before that day, when he directed you in the play?'

'No!' Her emphasis was so distinct that it was almost a shout. Then she added less assertively, 'No – well, I recognized his name. Of course I knew his name. I was given the role at the last minute, standing in for someone else. I had to learn the lines on the way to the studio. It was only a small part, so that wasn't a problem. At the studio they dressed me for the part, made me up with a face painted like a doll, then we rehearsed and filmed a scene in the afternoon. It was just another job, a normal day's work. One of the other actors later told me the director had made feature films in Germany in the past, and more recently a detective series for British television. I hardly saw him on set. I was only in two scenes. He looked different, and I was hidden by the make-up. I don't think he recognized me.'

'How do you mean he was different? Different from when you knew him before?'

'He had a grey beard and he was wearing glasses. Then,

on the TV show. Not before. He did not work well with actors, and was in the production gallery most of the time. When I looked him up I found a photo of him on a publicity sheet from Yorkshire TV. He looked different in the picture. Younger. No beard.'

'Is that when you knew him? When he was younger?'

'No.' But she said it so faintly.

'Are you sure?'

'Why should I be sure?' She was almost whispering. 'I hardly knew him at all.'

Unexpectedly, she sniffed, and looked around for a tissue. There were still some paper napkins left on the table after the meal and Matty handed her one of them. Teddy blew her nose, then used a corner of the tissue to wipe her eyes.

'I'm really sorry, Teddy,' Justin said.

'Did you love August?' Matty said.

'Yes, a little. I was in such a terrible mess when I met him.' Tears were welling in her eyes. 'I think he loved me very much. He always said so. I couldn't give back to him what I knew he wanted. He was so kind to me. So gentle. I shouldn't have treated him like that.'

After the first group of passengers were called to the boarding gate, Justin, Matty and Teddy followed. They were driven through the terminal, airside in Paris. The battery-powered vehicle had an amber light on a pole that flashed on and off, while emitting a loud electronic beeping noise. Teddy's wheelchair was stacked behind, with their pieces of hand luggage. They rolled past grey walls, signs in French and English, many closed doors, banks of monitors displaying destinations, advertisements, then into an elevator. They descended slowly to the floor below.

Justin reflected that being conducted through a terminal in this semi-official way temporarily removed the feeling of dysfunction. The one mixed blessing allowed to passengers waiting in a terminal, the false and restricted freedom to walk or wander around, was replaced by a sense of purpose, motion, transportation. No options existed. Was this a key to understanding? The solution to the enigma? The elevator halted. The journey resumed. The walls were the same, so were the advertisements.

They headed for Porte 27C, the number printed on the boarding passes the driver had handed to them. Justin recognized the area from his brief walk earlier, but now it was crowded with their fellow passengers. They were late to the gate.

The first passengers were already boarding, a thick line of people moving forward, creating a crush around the checkpoint at the ramp leading to the plane. Everyone was anxious to finish the journey to London. The driver of the transport steered them straight to the checking desk, making other passengers step aside or back.

They dismounted, collected their baggage. Justin unfolded Teddy's wheelchair, and she lowered herself into it. The boarding of other passengers resumed around them.

The vehicle was driven away, still beeping loudly.

Holding his pass Justin stepped forward, but Matty restrained him with a light touch on his arm. He turned back.

From the chair, Teddy said, 'I can't board until I've used the bathroom again. The ones on planes are too cramped for me. I have trouble moving and bending.'

At the back of the gate waiting area there was a lavatory cubicle marked for use of disabled passengers. Justin looked at the steadily moving press of people trying to get on board. He spoke to one of the airport staff checking boarding passes. He indicated Teddy and asked if there was enough time for her to use the bathroom before boarding, but the woman showed no interest, slipping one boarding pass after another under the electronic scanner.

She barely looked up. 'Aucun problème,' she said.

'Would you take her?' Justin said to Matty.

'Yes, but you come too. I want us to stay together.'

Justin took the handles of the chair and wheeled Teddy across the lounge, trying to avoid the other people. He parked it by the door, then pushed the door open. An extractor fan inside started up when he pulled the light switch.

'You needn't wait here,' Teddy said. 'I can manage now. Find your seats on the plane, and I'll ask one of the staff to bring me across.'

'We'll wait for you,' said Justin. 'There's really no hurry. Don't rush.'

'We'll soon be home,' Teddy said.

She smiled then, looking up at Justin: her pale blue eyes, her elegant and beautiful face, the wry grin, mouth slightly aslant.

This woman, now so close, always so distant.

Teddy propelled herself inside, manoeuvring through the door and letting it close on the spring behind her. The lock turned, and a small indicator panel changed from green to red.

They waited.

Matty looked tired, the effect of the long journey showing.

Justin ached for all this to be over, to be back with her at their apartment. No more travels were planned. A period of shared calm lay ahead. He touched his hand against hers, and she briefly rested the side of her face against his.

'Was I wrong to press her like that?' she said quietly.

'I've loved that woman most of my life,' Justin said. 'But I love you more, Matty. Nothing you asked her was wrong.'

The line of boarding passengers was moving on, passing the desk, heading for the ramp. The two members of staff cleared the last group: a family of three, with a child in arms. They went through to the ramp. There was an announcement in French, one of the clerks at the desk speaking into a microphone. The British Airways special flight to London Heathrow from Porte 27C had completed boarding. The gate was about to close.

'Perhaps we should board?' Matty said, looking across at the desk.

'We can wait. They know we're here. We've been allocated seats and the plane won't take off until everyone is on board.'

There was no sound from within the cubicle.

They waited.

Matty leaned gently against him, her hair lightly touching his face and her fingers holding his. Justin felt the fond feelings of familiarity with her, their life permanently together now, a mature and stable love. He knew she must be exhausted and stiff, just as he was. They had been travelling together for more than a day and a half, most of it in suspense, in the limbo of flight. The reward of a long journey was always its end, the return, the stepping back into the reality of life, but for now they were denied that. They remained together, just the two of them, still suspended in the nothingness of travel without end.

They carried on waiting. But then the boarding staff gestured urgently to them. Matty knocked on the bathroom door. Justin noticed that the panel had turned back from red to green. Matty tried the handle of the cubicle door – it was no longer locked. She pried the door open and looked inside. She switched on the light. The extractor fan immediately started up again.

'She's gone,' Matty said, pushing the door wide open.

Justin reached past her to see for himself. 'How the hell—?'

'Someone from the airport must have come for her.'

'We've been standing here the whole time,' Justin said. 'She never came out. That's not possible.'

But one of the staff at the ramp waved again, beckoning them impatiently, so they hurried across the gate area, had their passes scanned then rushed along the landbridge. At last they took their seats in the aircraft.

Next to them was a third reserved seat. It remained vacant.

As the plane took off and started its climb away from the airport, Justin looked down and briefly glimpsed the immense terminal building below, the ground now seen at an angle. Then the wing obstructed his view and the plane flew higher, into the concealing layer of low clouds.

ACKNOWLEDGEMENTS

Thanks are due to Rob Maslen and David Pascoe – to Rob for tipping me off to David Pascoe's book *Airspaces*, and to David for writing it. (Reaction Books, 2001.)

And especially to Nina Allan, this book's secret but invaluable collaborator.

CP